QUESTIONS I WANT TO ASK YOU

QUESTIONS I WANT TO ASK YOU

MICHELLE FALKOFF

An Imprint of HarperCollinsPublishers

HarperTeen is an imprint of HarperCollins Publishers.

Questions I Want to Ask You
Copyright © 2018 by Michelle Falkoff

Library of Congress Cataloging-in-Publication Data

Names: Falkoff, Michelle, author
Title: Questions I want to ask you / Michelle Falkoff.
Description: First edition. | New York : HarperTeen, an imprint of
HarperCollinsPublishers, [2018] | Summary: Pack receives a letter on his
eighteenth birthday from the mother he believed was long dead, and begins
a journey to find her even as he struggles to figure out his future.
Identifiers: LCCN 2017034842 | ISBN 9780062680235 (hardback)
Subjects: | CYAC: Identity—Fiction. | Dating (Social customs)—Fiction. |
Fathers and sons—Fiction. | Single-parent families—Fiction.
Classification: LCC PZ7.1.F35 Que 2018 | DDC [Fic]—dc23 LC record available at
https://lccn.loc.gov/2017034842

Typography by Ellice M. Lee
18 19 20 21 22 PC/LSCH 10 9 8 7 6 5 4 3 2 1
❖
First Edition

FOR MY COUSINS

PART I

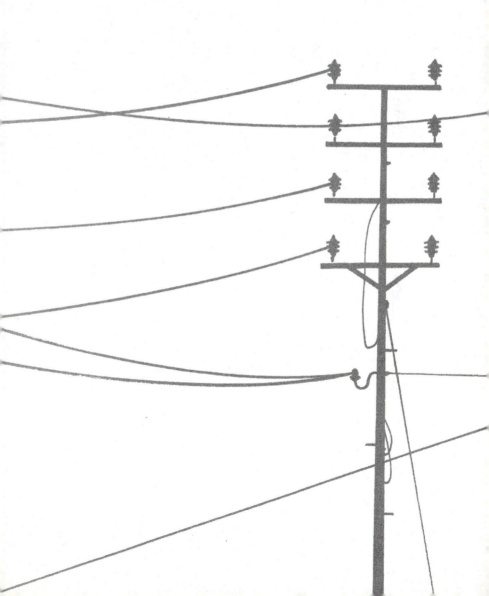

1

The fact that my eighteenth birthday, May 22, also happens to be the last day of school for seniors is a total coincidence, not some sort of miracle. But it feels like one to me.

I have the perfect day all planned out. First up is my usual six thirty a.m. class at Killer CrossFit, despite the temptation to sleep in. The workout of the day will wake me up, and besides, my girlfriend, Maddie, will be there, and seeing her first thing in the morning guarantees a good day. Then school, which isn't normally something I get all excited about, but the last day is always a joke, and besides, it gives me a chance to meet up with my boys and plan our beach time before prom and graduation over the weekend.

The best thing of all is that my dad has to work at the station all night. Which means Maddie and me have the house to ourselves. She told her parents her friend Kelsey is having a sleepover, and for once they bought it. She's coming over to make me dinner, and I can't wait.

Best day ever.

I pick Maddie up on my way to the box. She looks so cute, as always, with her sweet round face and big hazel eyes and her gym clothes. When we first started hanging out, she wore baggy sweats to the gym, but now she has on spandex leggings and a tight tank top with these crazy straps that spider web out from her neck. "I had no idea workout clothes could be so hot," I say as she gets in the car.

Maddie frowns and pulls the tank away from her stomach, but then she lets it go and leans in to kiss me. She tastes like a mixture of coffee and toothpaste, which should be gross but I'm used to it by now. Really, she just tastes like Morning Maddie. Delicious.

"Happy birthday, Pack," she says. "It's going to be a good one, right?"

"It's going to be epic," I agree. "I already picked out a movie for tonight, too. *Zodiac*—it's all about this serial killer who never got caught and the detectives and reporter who searched for him."

She rolls her eyes as I drive. "Please tell me you're kidding. Save all that true crime crap for when you hang out with your dad."

"What? You'll love it, I swear. It has all the actors you like, too—Jake Gyllenhaal, Robert Downey Jr. . . . ." I laugh as she punches me in the arm. "It's my birthday—don't I get to pick?"

"Of course you do, but just remember: choices have consequences. How exactly do you see the rest of the night going, after that movie?" I don't have to look away from the road to picture the expression on her face, and I know exactly what she means. Which is why she's totally right that I'll be watching *Zodiac* with my dad.

"Relax," I say, and pull into the parking lot. "I was just kidding. I got *Nick and Norah's Infinite Playlist*." It's an inspired choice, if I do say so myself. Maddie loves indie music (even if I think it's too whiny) and she loved the book, too. She's been bugging me to watch the movie with her for ages. I knew it would make her happy, and if she's happy, I'm happy.

Maddie bounces up and down in her seat before getting out of the car to give me a hug. "Perfect choice, Pack. Nicely done."

"I aim to please." The day is off to a good start.

It gets even better when I see that Jeff, my favorite trainer, is running the show at the box this morning. He does the best job explaining the proper form for all the exercises and plays the best music—all Kanye and Sia and the Weeknd, a mix of dance and rap—as long as no one complains. Since so many of the people at the gym are older, like my dad and his cop buddies, lots of the trainers pick music just for them:

stadium rock from the seventies, hair bands from the eighties. If I never hear Def Leppard's "Pour Some Sugar on Me" again, I can die happy.

Today's class is small—me and Maddie and some of the younger people—so Jeff can play whatever he wants. Right now he's cranking Missy Elliott's "WTF" and it has me totally amped. I beat my personal record for the clean by five pounds, which I've been trying to do for weeks. Maddie's having a great workout too—she's finally figured out how to do double-unders. Even when the clock buzzes to tell us the WOD is over, she keeps going, the thin black rope swishing under her feet twice for every time she jumps up. She only stops when she's completely out of breath.

"I can't believe I did it!" she yells, throwing her arms around me. We're both tomato-faced, dripping with sweat, but we don't care. Usually Maddie can get self-conscious— she says she feels like a special kind of ugly at the gym, but she's so wrong about that. The look on her face when she does something she didn't think she could do is pretty much my favorite thing. She has that look now, smiling so wide I worry her cheeks will pop from the strain, and pieces of her hair are starting to come out of her ponytail and curl up around her temples. I wish I could stick a mirror in front of her face and make her see what I see. But I know that isn't how it works.

Maddie's changed a lot since the first time I saw her. We both have. She lives on the other side of town from me, and we met in middle school. I thought she was pretty even back then, when her sweet round face was even rounder than it is now. I was a miserable fat kid, teased my whole life, though having a dad who's a cop helped keep the teasing from escalating into bullying. Mostly it was just nicknames. "Padded Paddy" was the first and mildest one, and they only got worse as I got older and kids got more (and less) creative. Patrick the Pastry. Pudding Paddy. Icky Sticky Ricky. Or, my favorite, You Fat Piece of Shit.

I mostly kept to myself, crushing on Maddie from across our homeroom. I was afraid to talk to her, afraid she'd use one of the nicknames and break my thirteen-year-old heart. I still remember her hiding in a corner at Mike Goldschmidt's bar mitzvah party, picking at the front of her dress the same way she picks at her tank top now, and I tried so hard to make myself ask her to dance. But the thought of her saying no scared me even more than the thought of asking her in the first place, so I didn't do it.

I wanted to be someone who could, though. That's what finally made me go talk to Dad about my weight. He always told me not to worry, that the pounds would come off when I hit puberty, but even though I shot up a few inches and sprouted hair all over the place, nothing else changed. I kept growing, and my confidence kept shrinking. I needed something to change. I wanted to go to high school a new person.

Dad said he would do whatever he could to help. We went

through the kitchen and tossed all the take-out menus and the junk food and went shopping for cookbooks so we could learn how to eat better. We tried what felt like a million different kinds of exercise: tae kwon do, boxing, that Couch to 5K podcast with the awful techno music in the background. I hated everything. Martial arts were cool but super boring in the beginning, and fourteen-year-old me wasn't patient enough to ride it out. Boxing was wicked painful, even with all the extra padding. And running just sucked.

When my dad's best friend, Tom O'Connor, a fellow cop he's known since high school, suggested CrossFit, I thought he was kidding. I hadn't made it through the sixty-seconds-jogging-ninety-seconds-walking segment of the Couch to 5K plan; there was no way I'd be able to do even half a minute of whatever they did at his crazy gym. But all my dad's cop friends were super into it, and they convinced him we should give it a shot. "Come to our class," they said. "We'll help you get through it," they said. "You'll love it," they said.

Sure I would.

The first class was like every nightmare I'd ever had come to life. A class full of people watched me fall on my ass every time I tried to do a burpee. But they weren't all as super fit as I was expecting, which helped, and Dad sucked at it too, which also helped. Besides, I wasn't going to quit in front of my dad's friends, who were nothing but encouraging. Everyone was, and the trainers gave me lots of extra attention because I was the youngest person there.

"What do you think, bud?" Dad asked. "Should we try it again? Can you wake up that early tomorrow morning?"

"I guess," I told him. I hated it slightly less than running, anyway.

Going into freshman year I had some solid muscle underneath the padding. It had been a rough couple of years learning what my body was capable of and what it wasn't—I did my first unassisted pull-up, but the two-foot-high box jumps were never going to happen. I fell in love with doing Olympic lifts, and I was starting to feel good about myself. The teasing didn't stop right away—after the kids found out I was doing CrossFit, they started calling me Six-Pack Paddy in a way that was wholly ironic—but the tone was good-natured. Mike Goldschmidt even asked me about the workouts and came with me a couple of times. He didn't stick with it, but we did start hanging out a little. And Six-Pack Paddy morphed into Pack, which wasn't the worst nickname.

Better than You Fat Piece of Shit, anyway.

But I knew things were really starting to change the day Maddie overheard me talking about the box at lunch. She wasn't in my homeroom anymore, but I'd see her walking the halls, and we'd wave and say hi even though we'd never had an actual conversation. We were in the cafeteria; Mike and the guys were eating tacos in blinding yellow shells that even I, as an Irish-American kid just a few generations removed from the potato farms, could recognize as completely not authentic. Sean Kaczynski was giving me shit for bringing my own salad, but I didn't care. He had no idea how much better it tasted than the crap he was eating.

Maddie caught my eye during Sean's rant about how green food was for suckers, and after lunch she caught up with me at the bubbler, where I was rinsing salad dressing out of my Tupperware. "Hey, um, Pack, right?"

The sound of her voice surprised me, and I turned toward her, which somehow made me lean harder on the silver button than I meant to. The water rose up so high it overshot the Tupperware and splashed on Maddie's sweater. "Oh, crap, I'm sorry!" I couldn't believe Maddie was right here talking to me and I'd screwed things up before I even had a chance to say a word.

I was afraid she'd get angry and walk away, but instead she just laughed and shook her arm. Drops of water flew off her sleeve and one landed right in my eye, making me blink. "Now we're even," she said, and the hesitation was gone from her voice. Had she been nervous about coming to find me?

I rubbed my eye, happy to sacrifice a moment or two of being able to see for a chance to talk to Maddie. "What's up?"

"So I was wondering—I mean, I don't want it to sound wrong, but—it's just I don't know if you remember, but we were in the same homeroom—"

"In middle school," I said. I had no idea what she wanted to ask me, but I liked that she'd noticed me then. "I remember."

"And, well—you look—you look different. In a good way, I mean." She was blushing now, and looking down at the linoleum floor. "I knew that wouldn't come out right. I just—"

If I knew where she was going with this, I could help her out, but I had no idea. All I could do was wait.

"What did you do?" she asked. "I mean, how? It must have been so hard."

That wasn't what I was expecting. Everyone at the gym had been really nice about the changes I'd made to my body, but the only acknowledgment I got at school was the new nickname, even if it did come with some grudging respect. "It was," I said. "I worked really hard. Still do. And I changed how I ate. Like, a lot."

"Do you mind telling me where you go, what you do? I don't mean to be nosy. I just need to do something, and I don't have anyone to talk to about it. All my friends are naturally skinny, and my mother—" She stopped, not hesitating this time but clearly not wanting to say anything more.

"Of course I don't mind." I told her about Killer CrossFit, how it started out feeling impossible but turned into something fun, something I loved. She was nodding and into it and I finally gathered up the nerve to just say it. "Do you want to come with me sometime?"

That was the beginning of me and Maddie. We didn't get together right away; first we were just gym buddies, meeting at the six thirty a.m. class, talking a little bit when it was over. She came every day. She was miserable at first; she didn't know how to do anything, and she'd wear these enormous T-shirts and sweatpants and big heavy sneakers that were all wrong, and her shirt would flap around when she tried to do burpees and she'd get all embarrassed. And lifting was a joke—she could barely handle the forty-five-pound bar, let alone put any weights on it, and her form was terrible.

Still, she came. She came to class and did as much as she could, even though it took her forever to finish the timed workouts and even longer to realize that people were sincere in cheering when she made it through. She came for open gym every Sunday, when there was no official daily workout, and worked on her lifting technique. She did extra mobility exercises in addition to the regular WOD even though she was so stiff she could barely squat.

She was amazing. And she didn't even know it. But I did.

After Maddie finishes high-fiving everyone in class in triumph for conquering the double-under, we split up and head to our separate locker rooms to shower. It's a close shave getting to school on time, but we manage it almost every day; it's better than going to the five a.m. class, that's for sure. Besides, we aren't going to get in a whole lot of trouble for being late on the last day of school.

We get ready in record time and meet at my car, a Ford

Explorer Dad got me for my sixteenth birthday, two years ago. The air is spring cool, but we're still red-faced and a little steamy from the workout, so we open our windows and let the wind bring our body temperatures and heart rates back to something resembling normal. Maddie's still pumped and chatters away as we pass the mall, the gas station, and Vincenzo's Sub Shop, a place I used to love before I gave up carbs and adopted the Paleo diet at the recommendation of one of my trainers at the gym. (They have pretty good Greek salads, though. Even without the feta.)

"I've been working on those forever!" Maddie yells over the sound of the wind and the cranked-up radio. Despite the fact that it's my birthday I let her pick out the music, and Lorde shouts about waiting for a green light. "I didn't think it would happen! I feel like I can do anything!"

"You *can* do anything!" I yell back. I park in the Brooksby High student lot and we head toward the front door. "What's the next goal?"

No hesitation. "Pull-ups. Real ones. No bands." The box has these elastic bands you can tie to the pull-up bar, and you put your foot in to get extra help. They're all different colors according to how much help you need. Maddie started with the black band, the thickest one, and she's worked her way through green and blue. Now she's on red; she just needs to master orange and then she's ready to go on her own.

"And the plan?"

Maddie waves at some people as we walk down the hall toward our lockers. She's more social than me, though that's not saying a whole lot; we both spend more time with each other than we do with other people. I chill out with Mike and those guys once in a while, and Maddie has Kelsey and the girls, but it's almost like we have to make ourselves hang with them so we're not spending 100 percent of our time together. I'd be fine if we did, but Dad always makes a big thing about not making all of high school about one person. He likes Maddie a lot; he just worries about me, I guess.

We go to my locker first, which is really *our* locker—hers is on the other side of the building, so she keeps most of her stuff in mine. There's a pink Post-it note stuck on the outside. I pull it off as Maddie rattles off her schedule. "Two more weeks with the red band, then—" She sees me reading and stops. "What is it?"

"I don't know. Just says to stop by the main office when I have a break."

"Have you been misbehaving?" She raises an eyebrow at me, one of her Maddie tricks.

"Me, misbehave? Never." But the note makes me worry. "Maybe I was wrong about not being below a B in one of my classes." If I am wrong, then this isn't my last day of school— seniors have to keep up a B average to skip finals. I'm not a dumbass, but school isn't really my thing, and maybe I cut it too close. But wouldn't one of my teachers have said something?

"Let me know when you find out," she says. "Meet you in the parking lot after school?"

"As always." I drive her home from school every day, too. Not that she doesn't have her own car, but sharing the ride with her is more fun. And her house is usually empty in the afternoons, which means we can sometimes fool around a little before everyone gets home.

One quick kiss and we go our separate ways to class. Maddie's in all the classes for the college-bound kids; I'm in Level 2s and 3s, for kids who just need to get by. I'm not sure yet what I'm doing next fall, but I have some ideas and all summer to figure it out. Often I space out during class and imagine my options—I'm thinking something with fitness, maybe a trainer or a nutritionist or something like that—but today all I can think about is that Post-it. I've never gotten a note like that before; I don't think I've set foot in the principal's office all four years of high school.

The day goes by way too slowly, though because it's the last day, none of my teachers call me out for being such a space cadet in class. At lunch the guys all yammer on about the incredible week we're going to have once the final bell rings—"Good Harbor every day, right, Pack?"—while they stuff french fries into their face holes and drip ketchup on their T-shirts. I can't remember the last time I ate a french fry. I've been making do with baked sweet-potato wedges for years now.

Finally the last bell rings and I bolt out of World History and run to the office. "Slow down, young man," a teacher calls behind me, but I'm already down the stairs and around the corner before I consider reducing speed. I can't wait anymore.

The school secretary sits behind the desk closest to the front of the office. She looks like she's in her twenties but dresses like an old woman, and I don't know enough about fashion to tell whether she's completely unstylish or if it's just some hipster thing. I hand her the pink note. "I'm supposed to come here?"

She wears a chain around her neck with eyeglasses hanging off it, and she lifts them to her face to read the note. Seriously, what's the point of wearing glasses as a necklace and then not even putting them all the way on when you need them? "You're Patrick Walsh?"

I nod.

She opens a drawer in her desk, pulls out an envelope, and hands it to me. "Here you go. But tell whoever sent this not to do it again. This is a high school, not a private delivery service."

This is it? A letter? I can't think of anyone who'd send me a letter. I didn't think people even sent letters anymore. "Um, thanks," I say.

A letter. So strange. I look at the envelope, which has my name and the school address written on it in handwriting I don't recognize, along with PLEASE HOLD UNTIL MAY 22 in all caps on the back. No return address. I start to rip it open but the secretary holds up her hand. "No dilly-dallying in here. You'll miss your bus."

As if any seniors still take the bus. I leave the office, sit on one of the benches near the front door of the building, and open the envelope. There's a single sheet of notebook paper inside, white with pale blue horizontal lines and a pink vertical line at the left margin, like we used to have in grade school. The handwriting is clear and precise, still unfamiliar. *Dear Patrick*, it begins, and I scan down to the signature line to see who it's from. That's when the day starts to get weird.

The signature line reads *Love, Mom*.

For most people, that would be a perfectly normal thing to see. Reasonable, even. But not for me. For me, those words are impossible.

My mother is dead.

2

I read the whole letter this time, slowly, and I decide it has to be some kind of joke. And I'm not about to let a joke ruin a day that so far has been perfect. I shove it in my backpack and meet Maddie in the parking lot. She's leaning on the car, reading something on her phone. Her hair has dried into bumpy waves and she's got this lip gloss on that I like—it looks peachy and tastes that way, too. "So? Was it the grade thing? Do you have to take finals?" She tries to sound casual, but I sense she's worried. We only have a little time before graduation and then we start summer jobs, and we won't have as much time to see each other. Then she leaves for college, but that's a whole other thing.

"It wasn't my grades," I tell her. "Just some issue with my address. No big deal." I'm dying to talk to her about the letter, but it can wait. I drop her at her house so she can go food shopping for tonight, and then I go home to clean.

Dad and I live in a town house complex. It's a mix of multistory units that are pretty nice and smaller, crappier single-story apartments that the complex calls "garden level" but which are basically underground. We live in one of those. The windows are at the top of each room but we only get sunlight for a few hours a day, max, which makes the place kind of depressing. I never noticed how much of a shithole it is until Maddie started coming over, but Dad always says neither of us spends enough time at home for it to matter.

I park in my designated spot and head inside, where the full force of the cleaning task ahead hits me in the face like someone backhanding me with a shovel. *Disaster* is an understatement—I can smell the history of at least three different meals in that kitchen, and I know what awaits me in the bathroom. At least I have the place to myself—Dad's already left for work, which means I can crank the music as loud as I want. I need to keep my brain occupied; otherwise, it's going to wander back to that stupid letter, like it seems to want to.

I start in the bathroom. Maddie's commented more than once on the ever-darkening tile grout, so one of my projects is to impress her by relearning what color it actually is. (Gray, as it turns out. To contrast with the pink fake marble tiles.) Cleaning the grout only highlights that some of the tiles are cracked and badly in need of replacing, but there's nothing I can do about it now. I scrub the stubborn ring around the toilet and get it to fade slightly, but we're out of bleach so it's the best I can do. And the kitchen is even worse than I imagined. Though Dad and I have a deal that he'll wash up if I cook, he interprets that as only including the dishes. The oven, the fridge, the counters, and the floor are all covered in a sticky film, as if someone sprayed the whole kitchen with sugar water and just let it dry. Since I'm the cook in this family, that someone is probably me.

After what feels like days but is really only a couple of hours, the apartment looks respectable. Not great—the living room floor is still covered with stained gray carpeting, and the kitchen fixtures still look like they're about fifty years old. I change my sheets and put in a load of laundry, which makes the house smell like detergent, but it's an improvement over the ghost-of-meals-past aroma I walked into. It will have to do. The cleaning was a good distraction, too, but now that it's over, the letter has migrated its way to the front of my brain. I push it back and wait for Maddie.

She shows up for dinner right on time, wearing a pretty flowered dress, her hair straightened so it looks longer than usual, and with that peachy lip gloss that makes me want to suggest we skip dinner and go straight to my room. But she only allows me a quick peck on the cheek after I open the door; she's loaded down with grocery bags. "We do have food here," I say. "Pots, pans, an oven—all the necessary items."

"You know I like to do things my way." Maddie hands me

one of the bags and we go into the kitchen to unpack them. She went all out—everything is from Whole Foods, which means she must have gone out of town. Brooksby doesn't have any grocery stores that fancy, so if we want to eat the good stuff, we sometimes have to travel. She's bought salmon and brussels sprouts and a whole bunch of strange baking ingredients. I may be the more experienced cook between the two of us, but that's limited to meals. Desserts have been off-limits to me for a while—I've hardly touched one since I went Paleo. I've been afraid that even fake Paleo sweets would just make me want sugar again, and then I'd completely lose control and go back to being Padded Paddy.

"What do you do with *this*?" I hold up a packet of arrowroot powder and wrinkle my nose.

Maddie snatches it away from me. "It's a thickener. For cake. I don't know if you know this, but we're celebrating someone's birthday tonight." She pulls out an even more random assortment of ingredients—tapioca flour, agave syrup, an enormous bag of beets—and sets me to work prepping the beets. This is going to be the most bizarre cake ever. If anything with vegetables in it can really be called a cake. "You've got coconut oil, right?" she asks.

"Yeah, a whole tub of it." I'm not kidding, either. Costco sells enormous vats on the cheap. I've been cooking with coconut oil for two years and we've only just replaced the first tub we bought.

I wash and dice the beets until there's a bowlful of magenta cubes and my hands are stained purple. Maddie stirs together the rest of the cake ingredients and waits for the oven to preheat; she tosses the beets into our sad half-broken blender and purees them until they're a pink pulpy mess. She adds them to the cake batter, pours it all into a square pan, and sticks it in the oven. She sautés the fish and veggies with some fancy Italian bacon and a whole bunch of spices. "This smells great," I say.

"I made the same meal for my parents once," she says, flipping the salmon over. "They were all polite about it, but I could tell my dad wanted to ask where the mashed potatoes were. I think you'll like it, though."

We eat dinner in the tiny dining room instead of sitting on the couch like me and Dad usually do. I even put out cloth napkins and real plates, which feels fancy. The salmon is covered in some sort of spice crust; the brussels sprouts are crispy and taste like bacon, which is always a good thing. Even the cake—a chocolate cake with no frosting—isn't bad, which is saying a lot for Paleo baked goods. And not too sweet, so I don't have to be scared of going down the sugar rabbit hole.

"Thanks so much for dinner," I say, and pull her up for a kiss.

"Dishes first." She smiles, which makes me want to wash

the dishes that much faster. I start collecting our plates and silverware; Maddie tells me to just put them in the sink and she'll take care of them. "It's still your birthday, after all."

"I can think of a better present, though." I raise my eyebrows and try to exude sexiness, but it's clearly not working because she starts cracking up.

"You are such a dude." She goes into the kitchen and turns on the tap.

"I'm *your* dude," I yell, and even over the sound of running water I hear her laughing.

But once Maddie's left the room, my brain runs right back to the letter. It's not that I don't want to tell her; it won't be real until I do, so it's going to happen eventually. I just don't want it to be today. I deserve just one perfect day, don't I?

"What's on your mind, birthday boy?"

I hadn't even heard Maddie come back in from the kitchen. She's standing in front of me, brows all crinkled up. Hiding things from her is pointless—she's always been able to read my mind. I know I won't be able to forget about the letter anyway. "Give me a sec." I go into my room and dig the letter out of my backpack, then bring it into the dining room. It feels like it weighs a thousand pounds. "Read this."

Maddie takes the envelope from me. "What is it?"

I shake my head. She pulls the letter out and I watch her read.

Dear Patrick,

It's hard to know where to start this letter, but the easiest way is to begin by wishing you a happy birthday, assuming you got this when I wanted you to. Perhaps you even received it in the afternoon, right around the time you were born.

The next thing I want to do is apologize. I'm sorry for making so many bad choices when I was young, and for the circumstances that have kept me away from you, for the unnecessary risks I took to make things better that failed so dramatically and that led to me not knowing you, and you not knowing me.

I don't know how much your father has told you about me, though I know he has allowed you to believe that I am dead. I understand why that was easier for him, and if I'm being fair, for you as well. But I've had a lot of time to think about the choices I've made, and it's time to right my wrongs, to make amends, starting with you. I can't take the thought of you not knowing I exist. I would rather you know the truth and hate me; with knowledge comes the possibility of forgiveness, and with forgiveness comes the possibility that someday we may come to know one another.

I wish that were possible now, but this letter will have to do for the moment. Please do not tell your father I've contacted you. I thought getting in touch the old-fashioned way, through this letter, would make it easier for you to

avoid the temptation of showing it to him. Emails are easy
to forward, but this object you hold in your hand is real,
and sharing it has real consequences for me. I hope you can
respect that.

 Someday I hope things will be different; someday I hope
I can tell you the whole story, and perhaps even be a part of
your life. Until then, know that not a day has passed when
I wasn't thinking of you, and when I can be sure it's safe, I
will write again. It's hard for me to picture you as a young
man, despite the photographs I've managed to get my hands
on, from time to time. In my mind and in my heart you are
still the most beautiful baby I've ever seen. Not being there
for you will always be my greatest regret.

 Love,

 Mom

"Holy shit," Maddie says. "Pack." She doesn't have to say anything else.

"I know, right? That's what came to the office before. Sorry I didn't tell you then. I didn't want to think about it today, but now I can't get it out of my head."

"I thought your mother died not that long after you were born." Maddie knows as much as I do about my mother, which is to say, basically nothing. She asked me lots of questions about her when we first started hanging out, but when I couldn't answer any of them, she stopped. These days the topic only comes up when she jokes about how lucky I am that it's just me and Dad because her mom is such a pain in the ass.

"That's what Dad told me," I say. "And I'm still not sure he's wrong."

Her eyes narrow. "You don't think this is real?"

"Why should I? It's not like there's any proof in there. It's got to be some kind of joke."

Maddie's lips tighten. "Who would play that kind of a joke on you? Who would even think that was funny?"

I shrug. How am I supposed to know? "Look, if this letter is real, then Dad's been lying to me my whole life, and I can't imagine him doing that. Can you?"

"Maybe he had reasons for not wanting you to know about her. And maybe she has reasons for not wanting him to know about this letter now. Aren't you curious about her?"

I have to think about that. I never had been before—there's never really been a reason to be—but now? "I guess I'm curious," I say. "But more about why she left, and why it took her eighteen years to get in touch, and why she's being so cryptic about it now. I'm just not sure I need the answers to those questions. I mean, is there any reality where they're going to be good? Are they going to make up for the fact that Dad raised me all by himself? Doesn't that count for anything?"

"I just don't get it," Maddie says. "You spend half your

free time watching unsolved murder shows on Netflix and now you have a real-life mystery on your hands and no interest in figuring it out?"

It's starting to feel like we're fighting, which is exactly the opposite of how I wanted my birthday to go. "You don't understand." I can't explain it, though. She's right that I love mysteries and true crime shows and all that, but they're fascinating because they have nothing to do with me, with my life, which is simple and uncomplicated and moving along just how I want it to. I have Dad; I have Maddie, even if college is looming; I live in a town I plan to stay in for the rest of my life, with a summer job that might lead to a real job that will keep me happy and healthy until I decide what the next thing is. There are no big surprises ahead, and I like it that way. "Can we maybe not talk about it anymore right now? I want to think about happy birthday stuff, not this."

Maddie sits in my lap and puts her head on my shoulder. "Of course, Pack. This is all kind of overwhelming. We can talk any time you want."

I run my hands through her smooth hair, and she leans down to kiss me. "Should we watch the movie?" I whisper in her ear.

"Let's skip it," she whispers back.

Best. Birthday. Ever.

3

Growing up, I never realized that having just one parent was at all unusual. In kindergarten, it took me a while to figure out that the women picking up the other kids after school were their moms and not their next-door neighbors. Dad hired Mrs. Lucas, our neighbor, to watch out for me while he was at work, since he's worked the night shift as long as I can remember. He took me to school every morning when he got off duty, but then he'd go home and pass out until nighttime, when he had to work again. After school, Mrs. Lucas would come pick me up.

One day I came home on a mission. "I told Ms. Silver I didn't have a mommy, but she said everyone has one, even if they're not here anymore," I informed Dad. I climbed into his bed and waited for him to open his eyes; the minute he blinked I pounced. "She said I should ask you."

I was too little then to know how massive that question

was, and how hard it would be for Dad to come up with an answer when he was barely awake. "It's complicated," he said, speaking slower than he usually did. "A lot of the time there's a mommy and a daddy, but sometimes there can be two daddies or two mommies, and sometimes there's just a mommy or a daddy."

"And I just have a daddy!" I yelled. "I knew it!" I started bouncing on the bed, which I wasn't supposed to do, but I couldn't help it.

Dad frowned. "Patrick, calm down. Yes, right now you do just have a daddy, but you did have a mommy. Ms. Silver wasn't wrong about that."

That stopped the bouncing quick. "I do? Where is she?"

"She's gone," Dad said.

"What do you mean?"

"Remember when we went to the pet store, and we got you that little chameleon, Charlie? And you kept it in a plastic box and gave it lettuce?"

I remembered. I kept waiting for Charlie to change colors, so after he ate all the lettuce, I filled the box with colored construction paper and waited for him to turn. Chameleons can't eat paper, though, and I never did bring him any more lettuce. The story did not have a happy ending. "You forgot to feed Mommy?"

Dad laughed. "No, I didn't forget to feed your mommy. But she's gone, just like Charlie, and she isn't coming back.

You can tell Ms. Silver that, if she asks again. And say thanks for me."

I didn't understand that last part then, but I do now. We've only talked about my mother a couple of times since, enough for me to understand that she died after I was born and Dad really, really doesn't like to talk about it.

Which is fine. I don't need a mother. Dad and I get along great, at least most of the time. He's pretty much my best friend, aside from Maddie.

I remind myself of that the next morning as I leave to meet him for breakfast. I'm still not convinced the letter is real, but Maddie's prodding does make me wonder why he's never told me anything about her. If I can get him to talk now, maybe it will convince me the letter is bogus. Worth a shot, anyway.

Dad and I meet at Spiro's, the Greek diner downtown, where we always go. It's set up like a cafeteria, with a line where you order your food from a woman who looks like someone's grandma, complete with dyed black hair showing white roots, and two black moles that I swear get bigger every time I see her. We order the same food every time: I always get the veggie omelet special with no cheese, but Dad isn't nearly as Paleo-committed as I am, so his omelet has like five kinds of dairy in it. We go through the line while the cook works on our eggs, me grabbing black coffee and fruit salad while Dad waits on a grilled bagel. "This is why I'll never go full Neanderthal," he says.

We bring our trays over to a booth, with plastic seats and a plastic table that's supposed to look like wood. Spiro's is hopping, as usual; I don't think I've ever been there during a time it wasn't busy. At lunch it's famous for enormous roast-beef sandwiches on old-fashioned bulkie rolls; at night it serves homemade spanakopita and shepherd's pie with lots of cinnamon. I haven't eaten a meal other than breakfast here in years.

I dig into my fruit salad and Dad bites his dripping-with-butter bagel as we wait for the rest of our food. "Happy birthday, buddy," he says, still chewing. "Sorry we couldn't do something yesterday, but I'm guessing Maddie took care of you."

I'm sure Dad knows she stayed over, but we managed to get out of the house before he came home. He knows we're sleeping together, too; he gave me a million lectures about sex way before anything actually happened. He started with the basics when I was a kid and all squicked out by the details, but then he told me about birth control ("Duh, Dad"), about respecting women ("They're just girls," I said, but he shook his head and told me I should always think of them as women, especially if I was contemplating something as adult as sex), and especially about consent ("You don't know the terrible things I've seen," he said, "and don't think I'll be one of those parents who sticks up for his kid when he's done something as horrible as that"). I took his lectures to heart, and Maddie and I made the decision together to start doing it, when neither of us could wait anymore. That was over a year ago.

"She made me dinner," I say. "It was a good day." Here's my chance to tell him what's on my mind, but I'm having trouble getting started, and then the food comes. We both start eating right away, and I'm grateful to have a little time to come up with the right questions to ask.

By the time we finish our omelets I'm no closer to finding the words, so I just jump in. "Dad, the whole birthday thing—turning eighteen and everything. It got me thinking about my mother. I don't know anything about her, really."

Dad stops mid-bite, holding his fork in the space between his mouth and his plate. He swallows, then says, "You never seemed all that interested in her before."

That's fair. Maddie asked me more questions about my mom than I ever asked my dad. "Well, I am now. How did she die?"

Dad takes another bite of bagel, and I wonder whether he's doing it to buy time. "You sure you want to know? It's not a great story."

"I want to know everything."

"Better start from the beginning, then." He signals to the

waitress for a coffee refill. I wait quietly until Dad pushes his tray forward and then places both hands on the table, as if steeling himself against a possible blow. "Neither of us comes off so good here," he says. "Your mother and me, I mean. There's a reason I haven't told you much. Figured I'd wait until you were older, thought I'd know when the time was right, but you stopped asking, so I thought maybe it didn't matter so much anymore."

"I get it, Dad," I say. "It matters now, though."

He runs his hand over his head, tousling his thinning blond hair. We might be built the same, but we don't look much alike—my hair is dark and thick and curly, though I've clipped it down to almost nothing to keep it from soaking up sweat when I work out; my eyes are dark, too, unlike his, which are almost green. I never thought about the fact that I probably look more like my mother. "Natalie—your mother—we met when we were pretty young. We went to high school at the same time, but she was a year or two ahead of me, and we didn't run with the same crowd, so we didn't really know each other. We met after I graduated from the police academy and came back to Brooksby to join the force. She'd gone to college for a year but got into some kind of trouble and took time off, though at the time I didn't know what kind of trouble. She was trying to get it together and worked at this coffee place near the station. Tom and I used to flirt with her, but she wasn't having it. Then one day I asked her out when Tom wasn't around and she said yes. I was surprised—I didn't think she'd be into dating cops. We're not always the easiest guys to get along with."

I laugh, since that's both completely true and totally wrong. Dad and his friends can be obnoxious and aggressive and competitive and sometimes inappropriate, especially when they don't think I'm listening, but they're also hilarious and hardworking, and being around them always makes me feel safe. Tom especially has come to feel like family—he's the closest thing to a relative I have.

Dad doesn't smile, though. He seems determined to get the story out as quickly as he can. "There's no classy way to tell you this part," he says, turning his head away from me. "We started getting together a lot. Mostly late at night, when my shift was over—I worked second shift then. I had a place downtown—it wasn't much, but she still lived with her parents. I gave her a key and she'd be waiting for me when I got home. We didn't go to dinner or to the movies or even to bars. We just . . ."

"You're saying she was your booty call." I don't get why he thinks this is so shocking. Does he think I made up some fairy tale?

Dad looks relieved. "That's not exactly how I'd put it, but you get the idea. I thought we'd been careful, but one day she told me she was late. We talked about what to do, but for me there was no question. Irish Catholic families take care of their own. Her family was Catholic too—Italian—so I thought it would be obvious to her. But she wasn't so sure she wanted to be a parent, and it wasn't like we were going to get married. I said I'd take care of you and she didn't have to be involved, and she agreed as long as I gave her some money for college—she'd have to quit her job and put off going back for another year. I didn't have any money, but your grandfather was willing to dip into his pension, so that's what we did. He wasn't too happy with me, though, and we've never really gotten past it. But I've always been grateful he put up the money. It's what your grandmother would have wanted."

It kind of sounds like he bought me. I'm not sure how to feel about that. But if he bought me, then my mother sold me, and I'm quite sure how I feel about that. There's just one thing to ask now. "So she didn't die? She just left?"

Dad shakes his head. "I wish that were the end. After you were born and she got the money, she left town. I heard she hadn't used the money for college at all. She'd gotten back into her old habits, and word was she died of a drug overdose. I'm sorry to have to tell you that, kiddo. But that's why I've always been on your ass about staying away from that stuff. And about birth control. I don't want you repeating any of our mistakes."

Now I don't know what to think. It sounds like Dad really

believes my mother is dead. But it also sounds like it's possible she could be alive. I hadn't thought both things could be true at once.

"How you doing there, bud?" Dad asks. "I know it's not a great story, but you can see why I didn't rush to tell you."

"Doing okay," I say. I might even mean it. I understand why it would have been hard to explain the situation to me when I was a kid. Dad's mom died when he was young, so maybe me growing up without a mother doesn't seem so strange to him.

"What if we head home and I give you your birthday present?" he asks. "Or were you going straight from here to the beach?" He knows all about the plan to spend the next few days at Good Harbor; he did the same thing when he was a senior at Brooksby High, way back when.

"I was going home first," I say. "Got to pick up my stuff, change into a bathing suit."

Dad shivers. "Way too cold for that, kiddo. But you're old enough to make your own decisions. I'll meet you at home. Just hang back for a few minutes, let me get things together, okay?"

"No problem." I stay at the table and text Maddie as Dad leaves the restaurant. **Talked to Dad about my mother.**

She texts back immediately. **And? Don't leave me hanging.**

Confusing. Complicated. Fill you in at the beach. Meet you there in an hour or so? Have to get the boys/beer.

She writes back in emoji, alternating hearts with an image of a sun, the beach, an island with a palm tree. It's barely seventy degrees out, but I like the optimism.

By the time I get home Dad's done whatever he needed to do, and he's standing in front of the entryway to the kitchen with a big grin. "Go check it out."

In the kitchen, he's rearranged the counter to make space for a new appliance: a Vitamix blender. I've been wanting one for ages, but they're incredibly expensive, so I've been making do with our crappy blender.

"Dad, thank you so much! You know you didn't have to do this." I run over and give him a hug. We're not big huggers, usually, but this is a special occasion.

"Benefits me as much as you," he says. "As long as I don't have to drink any of those goddamn kale smoothies."

"I'll stick to fruit," I promise.

He yawns. "I'll hold you to it. Time for bed now, though. Have fun at the beach. Don't do anything stupid."

That's pretty much what he tells me every time I go out. "No promises." I always reply the same way, too.

He pauses before his bedroom door. "Glad we talked, son. You know you can ask me whatever you want, right? You can talk to me about anything?"

The questions make me feel weirdly guilty. It makes sense not to show him the letter if it's bogus, but I'm not sure what the right thing to do is if it's real. I still don't know what to believe, so not showing him is the best option. I think. "Yeah, Dad," I say. "I know."

4

For one glorious week after school lets out, Good Harbor Beach belongs to us seniors. There are no lifeguards on duty until Memorial Day so there's no one there to enforce the rules, like not having fire pits or booze. Taking over the beach is a tradition for all regional high schools, and locals know to go to Wingaersheek Beach down the street to avoid us if they want to get near the water. Everyone I know from Brooksby High is there, along with tons of kids from other schools.

Good Harbor is the nicest beach around. The sand is white and soft and clean and flat, which makes it perfect for lying out or playing volleyball. Since today is the first day of our reign, a bunch of guys volunteered to set up the fire pit and the volleyball net. I have a big car, so I've been roped in. After Dad gives me my birthday present, I take a quick shower, put on swim shorts and a T-shirt, throw my towel and sunscreen and wallet in my gym bag, and head out to pick everyone up.

The guys who are coming in my truck are all at Sean Kaczynski's house: Mike Goldschmidt, whose bar mitzvah still looms large in my memories of Maddie, along with Jimmy Murphy and Tony DiPietro. These are the guys I eat lunch with every day, and once in a while I party with them on weekends, though it might be a stretch to call them real friends. They're all outside when I pull up, loaded down with beach chairs and sporting equipment. "We still need to go to Home Depot for the fire-pit stuff," Sean says.

"We need to go to the liquor store, too," Tony says. "You got your fake, Pack?"

He means my ID—I've got the best one out of all of us, and they all think I won't get in trouble if I get caught because of my dad. I'm not sure they're right, but so far we haven't had to test the theory—we found a place in Danvers where the cashier barely glances at my ID at all. I think the short hair makes me look older.

We hit the Home Depot first, stocking up on firewood and lighter fluid, before going to the package store for beer and ice. We empty two cases of Natty Light into coolers and speed down the highway, blasting Kendrick as we go, windows rolled down. I laugh as Mike screams about what's in his DNA and try not to think about what's in mine. I have the whole week off, the weather is sunny and already getting warmer than the reports said it would be, and I'll see Maddie at the beach in a few minutes. For a minute, I put all thoughts of my mother out of my head and instead focus on how happy I am.

It doesn't last long. When we get to the beach, Maddie's wearing cutoffs and a UMass T-shirt. The shirt is a reminder that everything is about to change. She bought it when she officially decided where she was going in the fall. I'd been pulling for her to go to Salem State, the school down the street, so we could stay in Brooksby together. We'd live in an apartment kind of like the one I lived in now, but farther downtown to make it easier for her to commute. She'd study, and I'd work and try to decide what I wanted to be, and once we'd both figured our shit out, we'd get married or something. I don't know. I only know I can't picture being with anyone else, anywhere else.

But we aren't on the same page. We had one of our first and only fights when Maddie showed me her college applications. She wasn't applying to Salem State at all; she was shooting for scholarships at UMass, Holy Cross, and BC. UMass is the farthest away, and when she got a full ride there my dream of us living together in Brooksby ended. She's never said anything about me coming out there with her either, even though I wouldn't want to anyway—I like it where I am. I've never even considered living anywhere else. We haven't talked about what's going to happen when she moves.

Maddie waves me over when she sees me and the guys on the sand with all our stuff. She set up her chair and towel near the crew of girls we hang out with. Kelsey Whelan, Maddie's friend from grade school, is the queen bee; she's going out with Sean, which only makes sense. Lauren Schultz and Brooke Almeida surprised everyone last year by breaking up with their boyfriends and dating each other. They put up with way more crap from people than I ever did when I was teased, but most people have settled down and stopped being assholes by now. They're all nice girls, not part of the super-jock crowd that will show up later, drinking our beers and taking over the volleyball game and never offering anything in return. It's like the jocks extract a price for deigning to hang out with us, even though no one really wants them to.

That's a part of high school I won't miss. But right now it's just me and Maddie and all the people we like. The girls strip down to bikinis and slather themselves with sunscreen, even though the weather isn't quite that warm, and the guys hand them beers from the cooler so they don't have to get up. I guess chivalry isn't completely dead.

Maddie and I don't really drink because of the Paleo stuff, but I don't like beer all that much anyway. I'm happy to let everyone else do the drinking. I know Maddie's brought us big bottles of coconut water so we can stay hydrated and lettuce to wrap our burgers in so we can skip the buns. People think we're weird for how we eat, but we're in it together, and we're both feeling good, which makes it all worth it.

The guys and I set up the fire pit a little ways down the beach and the volleyball net right near where the girls are sitting. I start a one-on-one game with Mike, which turns out to be not my best move—Mike actually knows how to play, and I'm just screwing around, watching as Colin Spencer goes over to sit with Maddie. Colin's also going to UMass, and he's been sniffing around Maddie ever since he found out her plans. I don't want to be a jealous asshole, but Colin is tall and blond and muscular and all the girls think he's hot, and I'm sure he's hitting on Maddie right now. I can't stop watching them.

This doesn't bode well for my volleyball game. I'm not sure whether Mike spikes the ball right on my head before I trip on the seashell or vice versa, but either way I finally manage to take my eyes off Maddie and Colin by face-planting in the sand.

Ouch.

"Pack, for a dude who works out as much as you do, you're the most uncoordinated motherfucker I know," Mike says.

"Duh," Maddie says. "Why do you think he works out instead of playing sports? He has the hand-eye coordination of a blindfolded puppy."

"Thanks," I say, wiping the sand out of my eyes and pretending to sound wounded.

"I compared you to a puppy. That's totally a compliment."

I chase the volleyball down the beach, throw it back to

Mike, then walk back toward Maddie. "I'm out."

"Come here, puppy, I'll take care of you." Maddie goes to pat the beach chair next to her, but Colin's still in it. "You don't mind, do you? We've got all summer to talk about fall."

Colin nods and gets up, but he doesn't look happy about it. I, on the other hand, am thrilled. I collapse into the chair barely seconds after Colin leaves it. "Catch you guys later," he says.

I make a little finger gun as if to say, "Count on it," but Maddie knows I mean something closer to literal. "Be nice," she says as Colin walks away. "He might be my only friend at school this fall."

"Not if you change your mind," I say. "Stay here with me and you won't need friends."

"Everyone needs friends." She looks like she wants to say something else, but instead she frowns.

I kiss her, hoping that will take the frown away. It doesn't hurt that I know Colin is still watching us. She smells like coconut sunscreen and tastes like . . . beer? I pull back and look next to her chair, where a Natty Light is nestled in the sand. "What's that about?" I nod at the can.

She shrugs. "School's over. Maybe we can lighten up on the Paleo thing, hang out with some new people, have a good time. We don't need to be so serious about everything."

I've never considered myself a particularly serious person. And I'm not super into lightening up on the Paleo thing, either. It's been a constant for me for so long I'm not sure how I'd function without it. "You do what you want."

"Oh, don't be mad. Sit with me and tell me how the conversation with your dad went."

"It was fine." I cross my arms over my chest and dig my feet into the sand.

"Don't be like that. The world isn't going to end if I drink one beer, and the thing with your dad is a big deal. Did he tell you everything? Did it help you figure out whether the letter's really from your mom?"

"Yeah, he told me everything," I say. "And no, it didn't help." I tell her what he said, how I can't tell if he really thinks she's dead or if he's lying. Which means I still don't know what to think about that letter. "I mean, he's never lied to me before, so I should assume he isn't lying now, right?"

"That's not quite right," Maddie points out. "He lied to you about your mom dying after you were born."

"She did die after I was born. He just left out a bunch of stuff in between, to keep me from knowing that she was kind of a fucked-up person. Not the same thing."

Maddie gives this little shrug, lips pursed. "Lying by omission is still lying, to me."

"It doesn't mean he's lying now," I say. "I just wish I knew how to tell."

"You have to trust your instincts. What does your gut say?"

I have to think about it. "The story made sense, and his reasons for not telling me earlier made sense, too. The overdose part, though—it was so sad, and yet it sounded like maybe he wasn't sure. Like maybe she could be alive."

Maddie sits up straighter in her chair. "So you believe it now? That the letter really is from her?"

"I don't know. It could be." I wonder why I'm having so much trouble deciding how I feel about it. Maybe I don't want it to be real.

"How can you be so casual about this?" Maddie throws her hands in the air. "You have this opportunity to blow your whole world open, to learn about your mother, who you thought was lost to you forever, to find out if you have even more family when you thought you had no one but your dad—if I were you, I'd be freaking out."

When she puts it like that I get why she finds it—and me—so strange. She's got two parents, a sibling, grandparents, aunts and uncles and cousins who all live within five miles of one another. She has no idea what it's like to have just one parent, to know there's only a single person in all the world you can count on. If I'd always wondered about my mother and her family, maybe things would be different, but I never have. I watch enough TV to know that other people's lives might not look like mine, but the TV people don't look so much happier than me.

How to explain that to Maddie, though? "I like my world

the way it is. I don't want it broken open."

"I know." Again she looks like she's biting back more words, but I can hear the options in the silence. It occurs to me in a way it hasn't before that when she leaves for school she'll really be gone. I've brought up me visiting, talked to her about coming up with a schedule, but we've never gotten it locked down. I thought it was just about logistics, but maybe she's been avoiding the conversation for a reason. If I'm not careful, we'll end up having it now, and I will do anything to avoid that.

"What would you do if you were me?" Better to talk about my mother than our future, I guess.

"Well, if it were me? I'd try to find her, immediately. But if I were you? I'd maybe do some research first before deciding what to do next. I'd look into that overdose."

"How?" I'm not being sarcastic; I don't have the first clue about where to start.

"Research, babe." She smiles. "The internet is your friend. Libraries are your friends. And librarians. There's a big bad world out there—that's what all those term papers you hate so much were trying to teach you."

"Hilarious." She knows how much I hate doing those papers because she's the one who always ends up helping me, even though she says I'm more than capable of doing them myself. She thinks I'm way smarter than I give myself credit for. I'm not convinced, but even if she's right, school has never been my thing. Especially research. "I don't even know her full name. Dad never said it."

"You've got your first assignment, then. Find out her last name."

"I don't think the internet can help with that one," I say. "There are lots of Natalies out there."

"True. But not many grew up here. Besides, there are other places you can look. Where's your birth certificate?"

I have no idea. "Maybe Dad has it? I don't really want to ask him."

Maddie snorted. "You don't have to ask him. You've got that apartment to yourself for like ninety percent of your waking hours. Go get it."

"Like snoop? What if I get caught?"

"Oh, sweetie. Spoken like someone who's never tried to find the Christmas presents before they went under the tree. Is there not one curious bone in your whole body?"

I have an answer for that, but I keep it to myself.

"The fact that you've never gone through his stuff before means you're not likely to get busted now—your dad won't see it coming. Just leave everything the way you found it. The birth certificate's bound to be in the apartment somewhere. Your dad doesn't strike me as a safety-deposit-box kind of guy."

She's got that right. Dad barely believes in banks. He keeps like half his savings in a flour canister in the kitchen.

"So that's where you'd start. The name."

Maddie reaches over to my chair and hugs me. "You'll do it? Really?"

"I'll think about it," I say. I'm not yet convinced it's a good idea, but I like the thought of Maddie and me having a project we can work on together. Maybe we can be so busy looking for my mother that she doesn't have time to talk about college with Colin. It's worth a shot, anyway.

"That'll have to do," she says. She knows she won, even if she doesn't know how selfish my motives are.

The air fills with the smell of charcoal, mixing with the salty ocean air in a way that evokes summer for me. "Want a burger?" I ask.

"Sure, thanks." Maddie reaches into the little cooler she brought and takes out two enormous leaves of lettuce.

"I thought you were branching out. I was going to get you a bun."

"Let's not get too crazy," she says. "Besides, that beer was gross."

5

The idea of going through Dad's stuff makes me a little queasy. He's always made such a big deal out of trust, and as far as I know he's never done anything like that to me. But I thought he'd never lied to me either, and Maddie's whole lying-by-omission thing has me questioning that. I just don't know whether it's enough to justify what I'm about to do. If it keeps Maddie close to me, it might be worth it.

I'm not in the greatest mood after the beach. Maddie went home early, saying she wasn't feeling well but that she didn't need a ride—she had her car. Colin, that sneaky bastard, snagged a lift with her. Can't he wait until they're at UMass together to make his move? I stayed for a while after they left, sulking and thinking about what we'd discussed, like my mother, and also what we hadn't, like our future, as in whether we have one.

Dad's at work, so I don't have to eat dinner with him,

knowing what I have to do. Instead I eat by myself, watching *Cold Case Files* on the couch while I power through a bowl of chicken, quinoa, and roasted veggies. Two hours later, I've watched three episodes and ignored an increasingly frantic series of texts from Maddie asking whether I've found the birth certificate yet. I resist the temptation to write back something snarky about Colin and turn off the TV. No point putting off the search any longer.

Dad's room is a pit, as usual. It smells like unwashed sheets and aftershave, though I've offered to do his laundry with mine whenever he wants. But he doesn't take me up on it all that often, and besides, his room has always smelled this way. There's something comforting about it, so I don't fight him that hard.

Finding anything in the mess is a challenge, though. The floor's covered with workout clothes that double as pajamas—Brooksby Police Department shirts and Adidas track pants, mostly. The closet isn't much better, and it's tiny; I have to plow through more laundry just to see whether he's got any shoe boxes on the floor. Nope. There aren't any shelves higher up, which makes me wonder where Dad really had stored my Christmas presents, back when I was young enough that it mattered for me to believe Santa really brought them.

The only place left to look is under the bed. I sneeze twice from pushing dust bunnies aside so I can peer under it, nearly banging my head on the bed frame in the process. But it's worth it, because that's where Dad keeps his one and only shoe box. I know him well enough to know there's no chance he bought a special container, even for important stuff.

I pull the box out from under the bed, making sure to save some dust bunnies to cover its path, just in case Dad looks for it again before more dirt has a chance to accumulate. The odds aren't good, but you never know. I open it carefully, trying not to leave fingerprints. It's full of papers and photographs.

Maddie was right, of course.

You were right, of course, I text. She deserves the glory.

She must have been waiting with her phone in hand, because it takes her all of 2.5 seconds to write back. **Knew it! So wish I was there.**

The stuff inside the box doesn't seem to be organized in any special way; my dad's graduation certificate from the police academy is on top, followed by a bunch of pictures of sports teams from when he was in high school. I recognize Tom, along with Manny Bettencourt, another of Dad's buddies who goes to the six-thirty class at the box, in one of the baseball team photos. They look incredibly young; Tom even has a full head of bright red hair, not the faded orange fuzz he has left now. They went from one kind of team to another now that they're all cops together.

I wonder whether not being such a team sport kind of guy is why I'm so reluctant to follow in Dad's footsteps. Not that he wants that—he wants me to be the first Walsh to go to college, so he's been pushing for me to sign up for classes at the local community college. But Tom's been on my ass to go to the police academy. He says that between watching me at the gym and listening to Dad and me yammer on about TV mysteries he's sure I'd make a good detective like Dad had wanted to be before he got hurt. I can tell Dad's not completely on board, but he's never shut down the idea either, so I told Tom I'd think about it.

I'm not sure it's for me, though. CrossFit is all about measuring your accomplishments against what you did in the past—that's why personal records, PRs, are so important to track. There's a competitive element, sure; that's why everyone writes their times or their reps on the gym's whiteboard. But I like the fact that, in the end, the only competitor I really care about is my past self.

That said, CrossFitters are the most supportive group of people I can imagine, cheering everyone on during the WODs, no matter how they're doing. In fact, they always cheer hardest for the people who struggle the most, and that meant so much to me back when I was consistently the last person to finish. During those moments, when we're pushing people who are having a hard time so we can help them get through the workout, I feel a brief glimpse of what it must be like to be a member of a team. Would being a cop make me feel that way? I'm not sure yet.

More papers: Dad's birth certificate, high-school diploma. More pictures: still high school, but now fewer sports and more parties. Girls and guys alike with long, lank straight hair, wearing enormous flannel shirts over jeans and hiking boots, as if they were all about to move to Seattle together and live in the woods. I say a silent prayer of thanks that fashion has changed so much. No pictures of me, even from when I was a baby, which seems strange, but maybe all these old photos were taken by other people. And I know Dad's been keeping his photos online for as long as he's had either a digital camera or a good cell phone, which is as long as I can remember. Maybe no one gave him any baby pics, or maybe he wasn't sentimental about keeping them. He's never been a particularly sentimental guy.

Finally, near the bottom of the box, I find my birth certificate. Sure enough, it has my mother's name on it: Natalie Cristina Russo. Dad didn't lie about who she was, at least. I text the name to Maddie, then check the few papers under the birth certificate to make sure there isn't anything else worth seeing; they're just insurance forms. Then something catches the light under the forms, something that isn't paper or a photograph. It's cold when I touch it and at first I'm not even sure what I'm looking at when I take it out of the box. There's a diamond set in gold—a tiny, tiny diamond, barely a chip, even—and I know what it is. An engagement ring.

What would Dad be doing with one of those?

* * *

I'm tempted to ask him the next morning at the gym, but that would mean admitting I went through his stuff, and I'm not about to do that. Besides, Tom and Manny are there, and I don't want to ask in front of his friends. Maddie texted that she's still kind of sick and sleeping in, so it's just me and the guys and Linda—the workout, not the person. All the hardest CrossFit workouts are named after girls. "Women," Dad would remind me. "And don't get any ideas in your head about talking about them the way some of these guys do."

No need to warn me. I find the T-shirts some of the CrossFit guys wear as offensive as Maddie does. She almost quit the gym over it, but luckily the owners of this franchise aren't fans of shirts that say things like "I Smacked Down All These Bitches," with a list of the girl workouts on the back. After Dad complained, they banned members from referring to the workouts that way. Not that it stopped people, but they don't do it as often, and definitely not in front of Maddie or my dad.

The girl workouts are really hard, much harder than the regular WODs. This one, Linda, is informally known as the Three Bars of Death. It's my favorite of the bunch, since it's all lifting and no running, but Maddie likes the cardio workouts better, so she picked a good day to stay home. I can't quite finish the WOD as prescribed, but my numbers are pretty respectable, and I finish in just over half an hour.

"Not bad, little Walsh, not bad," Manny says. He's a beefy dude who almost always comes in first for every workout—he's incredibly strong, and surprisingly fast for someone as big as he is. "You beat your old man, anyway." He punches me in the right bicep.

I can already tell I'm going to be sore from this workout, and the punch doesn't help, but I know enough not to rub my arm in front of him—he's the kind of guy who would call me a wuss for showing that I feel pain. I've never been much of a fan, but Dad and Tom like him, so I try to give him the benefit of the doubt.

"Leave the kid alone," Tom says. "Can't be giving him bruises if we want him getting ready for the entrance exam." He's talking about the physical fitness test I'd have to take to get into the police academy. It's pretty intense. Tom gave me a printout of it a while back, along with a list of extra workouts he suggested I do to get ready. I thanked him and put it away; I haven't looked at it since. But I didn't throw it out. I'm still not sure why.

Dad groans. "Don't you start. I got enough on my plate trying to get him to do something besides staying in this gym forever now that school's out."

We all start the cooldown together, walking a couple of laps around the box, doing some stretching, then rolling out. I learned the hard way how important cooldowns are after the first time I did the Linda workout—I left right after instead of stretching and was so stiff the next day I looked like the Tin Man from *The Wizard of Oz*.

Manny starts singing in a screechy rock band voice about school being out for summer and playing air guitar. People have no idea how goofy some cops can be when they're not at work.

"You realize that song's like a hundred years old, right?" I ask.

"That song never goes out of style." Manny arches his back over the foam roller and groans. "We brought boom boxes to the beach when school let out and blasted it every day. You guys still have barbecues at Good Harbor?"

"Heading there later today. I was there yesterday, too. We've let go of the boom boxes, though. They have these things called smartphones now? And Bluetooth speakers? Fit right in your pocket."

"Yeah, wiseass, I know all about you kids and your fancy technology. Maddie going with you? Nice girl, that one. You got good taste, like your pops."

Tom nods his approval but doesn't say anything. I remember Dad saying that Tom knew my mother too, at least a little bit. I wonder if he'd tell me what she was like, if I asked him. I'd have to do it when Dad wasn't around, though.

"Maddie's sick today."

"Beach is always better with a girl," Manny says. "You remember those days, right, Joey? After graduation, you and the hot chick you were so into, the Italian one—dark hair, nice rack, always with that lipstick. What was her name?"

Tom frowns, and Dad glares at Manny. "Angela," he says.

"What happened to her?" Manny says it casually, but something in his voice sounds odd.

Dad moves his roller to the back of his head. "High school ended. That was that."

"Is that right." Manny makes it a statement more than a question. I wonder why the weirdness. Maybe he'd been into Dad's girl. Or maybe he was just kind of a dick.

"I keep forgetting you all went to high school together," I say, hoping to break the tension. I don't say it's because Manny looks so much older than my dad, his leathery skin appearing almost cracked in places.

"Yeah, we've been running with the same crowd for years," Tom says. "Baseball, football, then the police academy."

"Some of the guys went to college first, but not the three of us," Manny says. "We weren't college material." He says it as if he's joking, but the undertone in his voice is knife sharp. I'd hate to have been the person who told him he wasn't college material.

"We've got street smarts," Dad says, and that seems to lighten things up.

We finish rolling out and go to the locker room. It was easy not to think about all the questions from the night before while we were busy with the workout, but now the list starts running through my head. What was Dad doing with that ring? Was it for my mother? Did he ever give it to her? Had he lied about their relationship? Like, a real lie, this time? I hate the feeling of doubting him.

It's early enough that Maddie's probably still sleeping, and I don't want to go to the beach yet. I keep thinking about Manny bringing up Dad's old girlfriend and how annoyed Dad got, and it gives me an idea. I hit Spiro's for some breakfast and then go to the last place I ever thought I'd want to be during my first week of freedom: Brooksby High. School might be out for seniors, but it's still open for everyone else, and the library is full of old yearbooks. I can look up pictures of my mother, and after maybe I can use the computers to see if I can find out anything else on the internet. Then I'll have something to tell Maddie when she's feeling better.

Most of the spots in the senior lot are empty, and home-room's already started, so the halls are quiet. There's almost no one in the library, either, which is good. I don't feel like explaining to underclassmen what I'm doing there, and I don't want anyone thinking I didn't make the grades to get out of finals. I may not be a brain, but I'm not stupid, and only the most boneheaded seniors are still stuck in the building.

The old yearbooks are stacked up in a dusty corner. I dig through them until I find the two for the years right before my dad graduated; I'm not sure exactly what class my mother was in. The yearbooks are heavy, covered in leather and embossed with a silver eagle, the school mascot. The leather feels almost padded; it dimples when I press on it.

I flip right to the alphabetical photos of graduating seniors, searching for Natalie Russo. There's no one with that name from the year before Dad graduated, and the only Russo from two years before is someone named Regina. She does have dark hair like me, but Dad didn't mention Natalie having a sister. Which doesn't mean much—he didn't tell me anything about her family, really—but it's weird not to find Natalie. I go back and get two more yearbooks, going further back in time, but still nothing. How could it be that Dad told me the truth about her name and yet I can't find her in the yearbooks?

I guess the answer would be obvious to most people, but for me it's a shock to open the yearbook from Dad's class and find Natalie Russo's picture right there, between Nathan Rosenberg and Janine Sanderson. It's an even bigger shock to see the deep red lipstick Manny described, the lipstick Dad said belonged to some girl named Angela.

What's going on here?

Natalie—my mother—is dark haired and pretty, exactly as Manny described her, and I put my face up close to the photo so I can take in the details. Do we have the same eyes, nose, hair? The coloring's the same, for sure. Now I realize why I look nothing like my dad: because I look exactly like my mom.

It hits me that I've just uncovered the first official Dad lie: he said Natalie graduated a year or two ahead of him, and yet she was in his class. It's not the biggest lie in and of itself, but it has big implications: if she's the girl he brought to the beach after graduation, then he knew her in high school. Went out with her in high school, even. That's lie number two.

Just to check, I look through all the other pictures to see if there's somehow a girl named Angela with dark hair and red lips, but there's only one Angela: Angela Capicelli, a cute blond-haired girl with bright pink lipstick. Definitely not the girl they talked about at the gym. A third lie.

Now I have to wonder how much of the story he told me is true. I'm tempted to text Maddie about it, but then it will be real, and I'm not quite ready for that. I put the yearbooks back and go to a computer carrel, and then I type the name Natalie Russo into the browser to see what I can find. There's like 11 million entries, so that's not going to be helpful. I type in her name plus my dad's, but Joseph Walsh is even more common, and using his nickname, Joe, is even worse—it's the same as some old rocker from the seventies. So annoying how people always assume the internet has all the answers, but that's completely untrue when there's this much information to choose from. I get bored real quick scrolling through websites and decide to get out of there.

I'm not satisfied, though. Apparently I've flipped some sort of curiosity switch in myself, and turning it off isn't easy. I go back to my truck and sit in the parking lot for a while, listening to Chance the Rapper, reading and rereading my mother's letter. It was so easy to dismiss at first, and even doing some research didn't feel like such a big deal when I was doing it mostly to satisfy Maddie. But now that I'm having doubts about Dad, I'm starting to have questions about my mother, too. Why did she write to me now? Why doesn't she want Dad to know? Why doesn't she want to meet me? What's the point of any of this anyway?

I don't have any answers yet. But now I want them.

6

Maddie's not at the box the next morning, and she's not answering my texts, either, which isn't like her. I'm dying to tell her what I found, so after the workout I go straight to her house. She lives on the other side of town from me, where all the houses are new and kind of look the same. Her neighborhood is best known for having been home to a serial killer a few years back, but everyone seems to have agreed that the only way to get people to forget about that is really aggressive landscaping.

Her house is no different. Split-level, vinyl siding, two-car garage, unnaturally green lawn. Her car, a used Honda Civic, sits in the driveway, but I breathe a sigh of relief to see her parents' cars aren't there. Not that I don't like them—they're nice enough people, it's just that they're not too crazy about me. Besides, I want to be alone with Maddie.

Unfortunately, I forgot that she might not be by herself—

there's still the possibility of yet another car in the garage, which I remember only after I ring the bell and Maddie's older sister opens the door. Ashley was two years ahead of us at school and lives at home while she goes to Middlesex Community College. The plan is for her to transfer after she gets her associate's degree, but I think the whole Brower family knows that's never going to happen. Ashley takes afternoon classes and bartends at night, and she likes the party life. I'd lay money on her dropping out of school and picking up more bar shifts over transferring any day. I know she's the reason Maddie's so worried about me staying in Brooksby—she doesn't want me turning out like her sister. I keep telling her there's no chance of it. "We have nothing in common. You know that."

"Still. You don't know what will happen if you leave Brooksby and try someplace new, but you have a pretty good idea of what it will be like if you stay."

"Exactly." She doesn't get it, and I haven't yet managed to explain it in a way that will make her understand.

Ashley looks pretty wrecked after what I assume is a typical night of working at Local Heroes and then doing the late-night thing. She has wavy brown hair and hazel eyes, just like Maddie, but where Maddie keeps hers just long enough so she can pull it into a ponytail when she works out, Ashley's hair falls halfway down her back, chopped into a bunch of layers that are either artfully styled to look messy or are really a tangled disaster. Last night's makeup is smudged around her eyes, and she's still in what I guess are her pajamas: a ripped-up crop top and pilled leggings.

"She's still in bed," Ashley informs me, without even saying hello. "She's sick. Not sure she's going to want to see you, or anyone else."

"Glad to hear you're doing well," I say, though sarcasm is lost on her. "It's nice to see you too. Can you let Maddie know I'm here?"

Ashley makes that awful *uch* sound that only girls seem to know how to make, complete with an exaggerated eye roll. But she goes upstairs to Maddie's room, and after a minute Ashley yells for me to come up. That already isn't a great sign—Maddie usually yells for me herself.

I walk up the stairs and down the hall to Maddie's room. All the floors are covered in thick, plush beige carpeting, new and squishy and pristine. Maddie's mom goes on a decorating binge every couple of years. Since that's her job, she always says her home has to be a proper showcase.

Maddie insists on keeping control of her own room, which is why she's covered the carpet with a polka-dotted throw rug and the walls with both fake and real motivational posters. The real ones are mostly Nike and Adidas ads ripped from magazines, but the fake ones are hilarious—she found a website that converts calendar slogans to be more realistic and ordered posters. My favorites are "Mistakes: Sometimes the purpose of your life is to serve as a warning to others" and "Procrastination: Hard work often pays off over time, but laziness always pays off now." They always make me laugh.

As soon as I see Maddie, I know I won't be doing a lot of laughing today. She's still in bed, buried under mounds of blankets and her quilted orange comforter so only her face sticks out. Her eyes are bloodshot and puffy and her hair is matted to her forehead. "I wasn't expecting company," she says, her voice raw and scratchy. "Don't even think about kissing me—I haven't brushed my teeth in like two days."

I sit on the edge of the bed, move her hair off her forehead, and drop a kiss there. "How's that?"

"Nice gesture, but I don't want to breathe on you. Go sit at the end of the bed."

I'd rather stay, but I get it. "Everyone missed you at the beach yesterday. Are you feeling any better? I didn't hear from you and when you didn't come to the gym I started to get worried."

"I'm on the mend. Just extremely dehydrated and super tired."

"I'm glad," I say. "I thought maybe you'd run off with Colin." The minute the words come out of my mouth I wish I could reach into the air and catch them.

"So you're not here to see if I'm feeling better," she says. "You're here to check up on me."

"That's not what I meant," I say. This would be more convincing if I had thought to bring something, like soup. I'm such an idiot. "I was worried about you. It was just a bad joke is all."

Maddie pushes aside the covers and props herself up to a sitting position, leaning on her pillows. "Pack, I'm going to lay it out for you one time. Colin is not into me. I am not into Colin. Colin and I are both going to the same school next fall, and neither of us has ever left Brooksby in any meaningful way. We are terrified, so we are trying to help each other. I'm sorry that's making you all insecure, but you have to get over it." She sounds really mad. I want to fix it.

"I get it. I'm sorry. I really did come by to see how you are, and to tell you I found more than the birth certificate." I fill her in on everything—the ring, the conversation between Dad and Tom and Manny at the gym, the yearbooks. "There's more to the story than what Dad told me, and now I want to know what he left out."

The angry look leaves her face, replaced by a little smirk. "That feeling you're having? It's called curiosity."

"Funny," I say. That's exactly what I thought yesterday, though. "I'm not sure I like it. I really wanted to believe that Dad wasn't lying to me. But now . . ."

"So what's the plan?"

"The plan?"

"What are you going to do next? You've confirmed the name, you know something's weird because of the ring and the yearbook. Are you going to research the overdose next? Or do something to try and find her? You have to take initiative here. Obviously your dad isn't going to clear things up, so it's on you. This is your life. Act."

Now she's back to sounding mad. I don't get why everything I say and do is making her so angry. I'm just being myself, same as always. I have to prove her wrong. "I am going to act. I just haven't decided how yet."

"Well, maybe you should come back when you figure it out," she says.

Ouch. "Kind of harsh, don't you think?"

"Look, Pack, I don't want to fight. I'm just really tired. Can we talk later?"

"Of course." I get up to kiss her forehead again before I go, but she's already closed her eyes.

It's not like Maddie and I never fight. We have little arguments all the time—about where to go when we go out, what movies to watch when we stay in, that sort of thing. She's always trying to get me to do new stuff, like go into Boston to visit museums, or do nature walks around the North Shore, boring things like that. Sometimes our fights are bigger, about why Maddie lets her mom get to her, or why I'm not more into school, or how Maddie doesn't exactly get my relationship with Dad. But the fights are always about specific, isolated things.

Something different is happening now. Bigger. This isn't about Colin, or my mom. It's about a lot of things we're not saying.

I don't know what to do about it, but being at the beach without Maddie isn't helping. Everyone can tell I'm in a bad mood—I snap at the girls when they ask where Maddie is and have to apologize, and avoiding everyone by going in the water is a stupid move, given that the ocean is way too cold to swim in. There's no one here I want to talk to about why I'm upset; I only want to talk to Maddie, who clearly doesn't want to talk to me.

It's not long before I give up and go home. I have to turn on the heat in my truck to get the bluish tint off my lips, and I left before the grilling started, so I'm starving. It's not good for me to wait so long to eat—I haven't had anything since I grabbed a smoothie at the gym, and when I'm this hungry the temptation to make bad choices kicks in. I dig around in the fridge to see what we have to cook, but I've been spending all my time at the beach and not at the grocery store, so we've got nothing left but some sad, wilted lettuce and a packet of precooked chicken strips. I put together a pathetic-looking salad and sit at the counter, eating and worrying about whether I've screwed things up with Maddie for real.

I've just finished the salad when Dad staggers out of bed.

"Thought you'd still be gone," he says. "What you got there?"

"A sad excuse for a salad," I tell him. "I'll go grocery shopping tonight, I promise."

He looks at me closely. "Something wrong, bud?"

How does he always know? I do kind of want to tell him about the fight with Maddie, but I'm still trying to sort out how I feel about him lying to me. I don't come to Dad with Maddie problems very often, but he's always helpful when I have questions or need advice. I have to be careful about the details, that's all. "Things kind of suck right now."

"Problems with Maddie?" It's like he's psychic or something. My face must show surprise, because he laughs. "You're a pretty easygoing guy, Pack. If something's wrong, it only makes sense it would have to do with Maddie."

"It's not anything specific," I say. It's not like I can describe our conversation. "It's just—she's leaving for college in the fall, and we haven't really talked about what's going to happen, and I thought—but now I'm not sure—"

"You thought you'd stay together and everything would be the same, just long distance." Dad goes over to the coffeemaker and gets a pot started. "I hate to tell you, kid, but even if that was the plan, things are going to change. There's no stopping progress."

"How is it progress if we're not going to be together anymore? That doesn't feel like progress to me."

"I just mean both of your lives are about to change a lot,

no matter what you want to happen. She's moving to a new place, and she's going to make new friends and start thinking about what she wants the rest of her life to look like. You might be staying here for now, but that doesn't mean you shouldn't be thinking about those things too."

"Why can't we change together?" I'm still not buying the whole progress thing. "Lots of people meet in high school and spend the rest of their lives together."

Dad sighs. "Some people do, sure. But more people think that's how it's going to happen and then they turn out to be wrong. Thinking that way can hold you back. The world's a complicated place, and you're both still young. You don't have to plan your whole future now. Remember, this is all a lot scarier for Maddie than it is for you. You're going to have some consistency for a while—you'll still be living here, and working at the gym, and all that is familiar. The only real change will be not having Maddie around."

I'm tempted to point out that I also won't have school, but that will only remind him to bug me about signing up for classes.

"But for her," he continues, "she's starting a whole new life, and she has to think about more than just how that will affect you."

I think about what Maddie said about Colin, how they talk about how nervous they are about college, how they're trying to help each other out. Hearing Dad say basically the same thing makes me feel like a jerk. "You're right," I say. "I've been kind of selfish."

"Ah, I bet it's not as bad as you think." He pours himself a mug of coffee and waves the pot at me, but I shake my head. "Maddie knows you pretty well. Probably better than you think. Still, if you feel like you need to make it up to her, make sure you've got all your ducks in a row for tomorrow night."

Of course. It isn't like I forgot, but I'd put it out of my mind. Tomorrow night is prom.

I thank Dad for helping me clear my head, and then I go to my room to run through my list of things to do in the morning. I have to give the truck a bath, pick up my tux and Maddie's corsage, and confirm the motel reservation—I don't have enough money for both a limo *and* a motel, and I know which one is more important.

Dad leaves for work, and I spend the rest of the night watching TV and checking my phone to see if Maddie's texted me. Are we fighting for real? I type and delete what feels like a million messages, ranging from **What's going on?** to **You're not breaking up with me, are you?** to **I'm going to miss you so much when you're gone I don't know what to do**, finally landing on **We still on for prom?**

I wait all night for a response but nothing comes in until the next morning.

Of course we're on. I'll see you tonight.

7

I'm sure every guy thinks his girlfriend is the hottest girl in the world on prom night, but they're all wrong, because none of them is going to the prom with Maddie. I'm waiting at the bottom of the stairs at her house with her parents, and after standing awkwardly with them for what felt like hours but was probably maybe ten minutes, max, Maddie has finally emerged from her room. I don't even know how to describe her dress—it's strapless and shimmery and fitted all down her body until it flares out in a little skirt right at her feet. The material is turquoise and green and iridescent and looks like scales, and she's put matching streaks in her hair and made her makeup all turquoise and green too. Even her lips are blue, but in a way that's more like the sea and less like drowning. The dress shows off her body in a way I can tell makes her feel good, nipping in her waist and making her look like a super-sexy mermaid.

I feel like I'm going to pass out.

Her dad looks pretty close to passing out, too, as she walks down the stairs and does a little twirl when she reaches the bottom. Her parents are extremely conservative, which is kind of ironic given what a hot mess her sister is. "You going to put on a sweater or something, sweetie?" he asks.

Her mother purses her lips. "I thought we agreed on the black dress. The one with the high neck."

I almost start laughing, but I'm worried someone will punch me, and I don't want it to be Maddie's dad. Or her mom, for that matter. "Maddie, you look beyond amazing," I say, hoping it will be enough to neutralize the damage I know her parents have already caused.

Maddie flexes her biceps. "It seemed like a good time to show off all the hard work."

Her mother shakes her head. "I don't know how you found a strapless bra with that figure of yours." It's clear she doesn't mean it as a compliment.

"Oh, it's a very elaborate combo of electrical tape and Spanx," Maddie says cheerfully. I recognize the tone; it's the one she takes when she's decided nothing her mother says is going to bother her. It's like she puts up an invisible shield, and the subtle insults and digs just bounce right off. Kind of like Wonder Woman, who Maddie resembles right now.

Maddie ignores her parents and comes right for me. "You ready to get out of here?"

I hold up the corsage I picked out with a lot of help from the florist. It's a bunch of white flowers on a stretchy band that she can wear as a bracelet. Like one of Wonder Woman's golden cuffs. I don't know what kind of flowers they are, but they smell good. I'm glad I didn't get one I have to pin on her, because I wouldn't want anything to hide any part of that dress.

Maddie holds up the corsage and sniffs before putting it on. "Mmmm, freesia."

How do girls know this stuff? I hand her the matching boutonniere and ask her dad to take a picture of us with my phone while she pins it on me. I'd have thought her parents would be snapping pictures all over the place—Dad would have if he could have been here, and he made me promise to take a million and send them to him—but Maddie's parents just stand there looking all cranky. Her dad agrees to take the photo, though, and he takes a couple of other pictures too.

"Thanks a lot, Mr. Brower," I say. "I'll bring Maddie home after the senior brunch."

He frowns, and for a second I worry Maddie didn't actually get permission for all the prom stuff: the after-party, the motel, the brunch tomorrow morning. But he's just frowning because that's what he does, and he halfheartedly waves good-bye as I walk Maddie out to my truck.

"Have a good time," her mother says. "Make sure to pull up the dress if the bustline starts to droop."

Maddie rolls her eyes. "Such a Mom thing to say," she mutters as I open the passenger door.

"I hope her being an asshole isn't getting to you. You really do look incredible, you know." I'm already in my seat and buckled in before Maddie gets the rest of her dress stuffed into the front seat. Way to be a gentleman, Pack—it only occurs to me after the fact that she could have used some help. Especially since I'm not even sure whether she's still mad at me. I did take her backpack and put it in the backseat with mine. That's something, right?

We're quiet on our way over to the prom, though it's not necessarily a bad silence—I can't really tell. Sometimes being quiet with her feels more like real closeness than having an actual conversation with someone else.

Prom is at a hotel two towns over from ours. It used to be at a country club the next town over, but a couple of years ago some junior got wasted and puked everywhere, and the school was invited to never come back. It's a bummer, too— the country club is really pretty, with a wide-open main room and dance floor surrounded by a moat and flowers, with golf greens beyond that. (It's where Mike Goldschmidt had his bar mitzvah party, so I still remember it well.) Now we're stuck at a Hilton. At least it has a parking lot.

I take Maddie's arm as we walk toward the entrance. "I might need you to prop me up tonight," she says. "These shoes are a bitch to walk in." I look down but can't really see what she's talking about, since her dress goes all the way to the floor. She sticks out one dyed-teal strappy sandal with scarily tall sharp heels.

True to her word, Maddie stays on my arm as we enter the reception hall. The hotel isn't exactly new, so the hall is all frosted green glass and chrome and angles. Not super festive, even with the decorations the prom committee brought. We don't have themes like other schools, so there are some disco balls in random places and glitter everywhere, but that's about it.

I can't understand how the whole party doesn't stop to take a deep breath when Maddie walks in. She looks so gorgeous, and so unusual compared to the other girls, who mostly wear long, slim dresses in black and blue. They look grown-up and sophisticated, sure, but they all look the same.

Prom itself is kind of lame. The music is too loud to hear anyone talk, and it feels like we're all just killing time until the after-party, when everyone can let loose. Maddie and I slow-dance a couple of times, but mostly I sit by myself at a table, avoiding the sugary punch, while Maddie and Kelsey and everyone run around talking about how great everyone looks and wondering about who's going to be on the prom court. We stay until the announcement, mostly just to see if anyone we know will make it on there. Brooke ends up getting named to the court, and some jocks end up being king and queen, no shock there. We clap for

Brooke, and then it's time to move on.

The after-party is at the Clam Shack, a restaurant owned by one of the senior kids' parents, which means not only can we get it for free after-hours, but no one's checking to see what's inside. Some of the cooler parents collect keys at the door, figuring everyone knows drinking is going to happen somewhere, and this way they can keep an eye on us. The cops stay away too, opting instead for five times the number of speed traps in case anyone manages to drive drunk anyway. Thankfully I'm not in charge of booze tonight, though someone clearly is—there are coolers full of beer and hard lemonade all over the place, in between all the game tables: pool, foosball, air hockey.

I'm driving, so even if I wanted a drink there's no chance I'd have one, but I wasn't expecting Maddie to drink either. She grabs a hard lemonade as soon as we walk in, though, and glares at me when I glance over at her. "It's prom night," she says. "Lighten up."

There's nothing that makes me want to lighten up less than someone telling me to lighten up. Maybe she's still mad at me. I decide to give her a little space, just in case, and wander off to play Ping-Pong with Mike. I haven't magically developed hand-eye coordination, but Mike hasn't magically gotten less wasted—he was pounding a flask in the bathroom at prom—so we're pretty evenly matched. The game keeps me from checking on Maddie, though after missing the ball a bunch of times because I'm craning my neck to find her, Mike's had enough. "Get out of here, Pack," he says. "You're not even trying."

"You're right." I hand off the paddle and head over to where Maddie teeters in her high heels, talking to Colin. I'm surprised she hasn't taken off her shoes already, but apparently she isn't feeling much pain. Maybe she's had more to drink than I realize. I get to her just as she's about to tip over; she falls into my arms like we're in some sort of romantic comedy. Except it doesn't feel all that romantic to me.

"Oh, Pack," she says. "Always there to rescue me. As if I need rescuing."

"You're the strongest girl I know," I say. "Of course you don't need rescuing."

"Don't speak too soon. I might need to be saved from these shoes." She smiles, and I know we're okay.

"You can go barefoot," I say. "I won't judge."

"Me neither," says Colin.

Ugh, I forgot he was even here. I have to remind myself that I resolved not to be such a dick about the two of them.

Maddie wrinkles her nose. "Have you seen the floor here? Besides . . ." She leans over and whispers in my ear. "Didn't you get us a room? I need to get out of this dress, not just the shoes."

My face turns bright red even as I realize she might just be saying the dress is uncomfortable, not that she's desperate to get naked with me. "Message received." I pick Maddie up and sling her over my shoulder, caveman-style. "Sorry, bro," I tell Colin. "Got to go ravish my girl." It's not nice, but I can't help myself.

Maddie laughs as I move through the room as fast as I can. "I could have managed," she says as I deposit her next to the car.

"It would have taken way longer. Besides, you can't just say stuff about taking off your dress and not expect things to move fast."

"Very funny," she calls out as I walk over to the middle of the parking lot, where someone's mom is sitting in a lawn chair reading a backlit e-book. She doesn't look up until I'm right in front of her.

"How much did you have to drink?" she asks.

"Nothing. What do you need me to do?"

She peers at me closely. "You're Joe Walsh's kid?"

I nod.

"Your dad would kill you if he caught you driving drunk," she says. "That ought to do it. Which keys are yours?"

"Killer CrossFit tag," I say, and she hands them over.

I come back to the car and open Maddie's door. She doesn't stuff the dress in right away this time; instead, she sticks her legs out the door where I'm standing. "Help. Please. I can't bend in this thing."

I laugh until I actually get the little clasps unhooked on

the teeny fasteners of her sandals, at which point I see the deep grooves in her skin from where the ribbony straps cut into her. "No wonder you were done walking. That looks painful."

"I'm good as long as nothing's bleeding," she says. "But remind me never to wear high heels again, ever."

I won't forget the look of her feet anytime soon. Being a girl seems really hard. "On it," I say.

The motel isn't far from the after-party, and it's known for being lax about renting to teenagers on prom night, so we won't be the only high school couple there. I'm all excited about what's going to happen when we get in there until it hits me that I don't know how much Maddie's had to drink. Dad never stopped the consent education, well past the point he knew I understood. He'd text me links to random articles and leave pamphlets around the house. I'd been so nervous the first time with Maddie that I'd asked permission for every single thing we did, until it became part of what made it all exciting. "Can I kiss you here?" *Yes.* "Can I touch you here?" *Yes.* "Do you want me to—?" *Yes, yes, yes.* It's part of our secret language now.

But there's nothing less appealing than the idea of being with Maddie if she's not all the way into it, so I have to make sure she's sober first. She doesn't seem all that drunk on the drive; she chatters away about how cute all the other girls looked, how she's always thought prom was overrated but how she'd had more fun than she thought. Did we even go to the same prom? Maybe I just don't know how to tell if she's wasted; maybe she sounds fine and just says weird shit.

I park the car right in front of our room—I picked up the key this morning—and ask Maddie whether she wants me to grab her sneakers or carry her into the room.

"I'll make a run for it," she says. "The concrete doesn't look nearly as gross as the Clam Shack floor."

She's not kidding about the run—she picks up the skirt of her dress and darts over to the room as fast as I've seen her run in any of our workouts. I get our backpacks out of the backseat and meet her at the door. I've barely got it closed behind me when Maddie pulls me to her by my cummerbund (turquoise, to go with the dress). "Can I kiss you?" she asks.

"Isn't that usually my line?" I say. "But as long as you're asking . . ." I lean in, and she kisses me in a way that makes me think getting this motel room is the most genius idea I've ever had.

"Can I—?"

"Hold on a sec. Let's see where we actually are." I turn on the light and then think maybe I shouldn't have bothered. The room is kind of sad, really. Peeling gold wallpaper, matted and stained greenish carpet, matching greenish comforter that was once embroidered with flowers but now just has threads popping out all over the place. But the bed is queen-size and it's ours for the night.

"It's better than the backseat of your car," Maddie says. "Now come on, help me out here." She turns around so I can unzip her dress.

I stand behind her and kiss the smooth white skin of her neck before tugging the zipper down. If this were a movie she'd be naked underneath, and I could just keep kissing all the way down. But she wasn't kidding about the Spanx and the electrical tape—she's all bound up under the dress, and I have no idea how to set her free.

"Don't look," she says. "It's scary under there. You have my bag?"

I hand her the backpack and she takes it into the bathroom. I hear the scratchy sound of her ripping the electrical tape, followed by a squeal. After a minute she comes out in a long T-shirt. I'm still in my whole tuxedo. "Guess it's time to ditch this," I say, and take off the jacket.

Maddie undoes my tie and throws it across the room. Then she reaches down and unhooks the cummerbund. "This is kind of like taking off a girl's bra."

"Not as much to look forward to, though."

"Speak for yourself." She throws the cummerbund near where the tie landed, then starts unbuttoning my shirt. This is new. I know Maddie likes the things we do together, especially since I convinced her to teach me what worked with her, but she's not usually the aggressor. I'm into it, but I'm not sure where it's coming from.

I help her take off my shirt. Then she reaches for the button on my pants and says, "Can I take these off?"

This seems like a good time to hit the pause button. "Everything's okay, right?"

Maddie frowns. "Why wouldn't it be?"

I'm not sure how to say what I'm feeling, and I don't want to say something that will offend her. "I want this to be a perfect night for us, so I just want to make sure you're happy, that this is what you want. You're not, like, drunk or anything, right?"

"I'm not drunk," she says. "I didn't even finish that first hard lemonade. It was worse than the beer."

Then she does something totally unexpected. She pulls off her T-shirt and stands in front of me completely naked, something she almost never does. She, like me, has some silvery stretch marks from where her body's changed over the years. The Spanx left stripy marks on her torso and legs, just like the sandals had on her feet. Her skin is creamy and her ass is dimpled and she's real, she's beautiful, right in front of me, and all I want to do is grab her. But I'm not sure what the rules are tonight. Usually I'd ask first, but it seems like she wants to be in charge, so I wait.

"Is this enough?" she asks. "To show you everything's okay?"

"You have to say it," I tell her. "You have to say everything."

"I want this," she says, and goes back to taking off my pants. "I want you, I want this night together, I want it all. And I want to be in charge. Can I be in charge?"

I laugh as she navigates the difficult project of removing my pants now that there's an impediment. Not to mention that I'm sitting down and she's still standing up. I reach out my hands to help, but she pushes me back on the bed and finishes pulling off my pant legs. Then she sits on my thighs, takes my hands, and holds them over my head. "Well?"

I love this reversal of what we normally do, with her asking permission instead of me. I'll still know what she wants, which is the most important thing. "You're in charge," I say.

"You'll do whatever I say?"

"Anything you want."

"Arms stay where they are," she says, and I comply. She kisses my lips, then my neck, then starts moving down, and though she keeps giving me orders, or asking for what she wants, I pretty much lose the power of speech.

8

Maddie and I don't make it to the senior brunch, a decision I can't imagine ever regretting. Something about that shift in our dynamic, with Maddie taking charge, makes me feel like everything's changed. I'm not nearly as worried about the fall, which makes the prospect of graduation far more sweet than bitter.

My friends all decided that we would wear bathing suits under our gowns, and though Dad's not super impressed, he doesn't stop me. "Step one in learning to be a real adult is making your own choices, even when they're stupid," he says when he sees my hairy legs sticking out from under the hem of my gown. I nod and smile and put on my cap, where we painted our graduation year in glitter nail polish. Being with Dad is still a little awkward for me—I don't know what to think about what I found in the box, but I'm not about to ruin my own graduation day worrying about it. Especially not after last night with Maddie.

Dad has the last laugh when we get to Brooksby High and realize that at some point on the ride over, the weather has completely changed. The day started out sunny and beautiful and warm, but now the wind is whipping so hard, chairs are toppling over, and the temperature's dropped twenty degrees as the sky grows dark. "Might get ugly out there," he says. "Better grab a seat near the aisle in case you need to run."

Dad knows full well the seniors are seated alphabetically and that I'm in the middle of a row of Wallaces and Welches. "The cap will protect me," I say as Dad chooses a seat conspicuously next to the exit. He saves the seat next to him for Tom, his plus-one—we all got four tickets so people could bring their parents and siblings or grandparents or whoever, but I just have Dad. I'd always assumed my only other living relative is his father, my grandfather, and they don't get along, so I don't see him much. I wasn't about to invite him to graduation, that's for sure. It made more sense to invite Tom. He was super flattered and got the day off work and everything.

Maddie's nowhere near me, since her last name is all the way up in the Bs, but we find each other quickly before we have to take our seats. As the sky begins to clear and the temperature creeps back up, I discover I'm happier than I expected to be on a day I'd otherwise been dreading. Graduation seems like the end of something, but now I wonder if maybe it's just the beginning. Last night felt like the beginning of a new stage for Maddie and me, and I'm into it.

The valedictorian, a brainy guy who also was head of the track team, gives a boring speech about hurtling toward the future, and the crowd gets restless and starts sending beach balls around. Lauren is salutatorian, and thankfully her speech is sharp and funny and personal. She talks about how lucky she was to find herself in high school, how that gave her the confidence to try new things and go on new adventures, like leaving Brooksby to go to school in Colorado. She ends with a joke about things that are legal in Colorado that aren't in Massachusetts, which I'm sure the school would never have allowed her to say if they knew what she was planning, but I'm still stuck on all the stuff about finding herself, about the adventures. She sounds like a next-level version of Maddie, whose idea of leaving starts with smaller steps. It makes me wonder whether I'm the only person who doesn't have those kinds of dreams. I know that's not true—lots of kids are staying close to home—but I'm starting to see that the interesting people want more than what they have here. Does wanting to stay mean I'm boring?

I've got a little too much time to think about it during the endless diploma conga line, but finally my name is called and I'm able to shut off my brain for a while. Next up is the afternoon of barbecues. The first one is Maddie's, a family event in her backyard. Dad's met her parents before, and I was impressed that he never seemed annoyed at how they talked down to him once they learned he was a cop. I don't know what makes Maddie's mom think interior design is so much higher up the evolutionary food chain than protecting people, but whatever. Dad's a better man than I am. If I were him I'd never want to see them again, but he has no problem going over there for the party. He even wears a shirt with a collar and offers to man the grill when Maddie's dad struggles with the charcoal, though what that really means is getting it lit and then leaving me there with the marinated chicken and Fenway Franks while he tracks down the good beer.

The afternoon goes way better than I hoped. By the time I finish grilling, Dad's bonded with Maddie's father over their mutual love for the Sox and the Patriots, and they're laughing like old friends. Maddie's mom doesn't even look annoyed. It's easy to picture years of weekends like this, maybe even with little kids running around that look like me and Maddie (more like Maddie, if there's any justice in the world). Even Maddie isn't letting her mom get on her nerves, though the only food is meat, vegetables, and fruit. "I get the message," Maddie whispers to me, "but just because she wants to 'help me keep up the good work,' as she puts it, doesn't mean she has to make everyone else suffer." She chews on a celery stick so loudly it almost seems like she's trying to hurt the celery.

"Don't worry," I whisper back, "the next party will definitely have cake."

"*You're* going to eat cake?" she asks, in mock surprise.

I shrug. I'm not planning on having any, but I want her to know I listened when she said we should loosen up.

She laughs, then checks her phone to see what time it is. "Okay, then. Let the countdown to cake begin. It's six o'clock. We wind this party down in T-minus-sixty minutes." She even sets an alarm.

We spend the hour entertaining Maddie's various relatives. I can't believe how many cousins she has, and they all seem to know each other so well, telling stories about games they played together when they were little. For the first time I wonder whether I have any family besides my mother. Is Regina Russo from the yearbook my aunt? Does she have a husband, kids? Do I have grandparents I've never even met? It's weird that the only people I consider family (besides Dad) aren't even related to me—Tom and his wife and their three kids are here too. Which is perfect—they'll keep Dad company when it's time for me and Maddie to go.

Once the clock strikes seven, Maddie and I keep our promise and move on to the next party, at Lauren's house. I'm right about the cake, an enormous vanilla full-sheet monstrosity from Market Basket, with frosting flowers in our school colors. Maddie scarfs down a small piece while I look around for something I can eat. The food table is covered with pizza and potato chips and soda, so I'll be going hungry for a while. Good thing I filled up on chicken and fruit salad at Maddie's house.

"The cake was totally worth it," Maddie says. "One little piece won't kill you."

"That would be the gateway drug for one bigger piece, which would lead to two bigger pieces, and then it wouldn't really matter if I had some chips and a little Pepsi, and then tomorrow I'll still be having sugar cravings, and since I was so bad the day before, I might as well enjoy being off Paleo for a while, and then it won't be worth going back until next Monday, because new habits are always better when you start on Monday, but maybe next Monday it will be someone's birthday, and there'll be cake, and . . ."

"Okay, okay, I get it." Maddie holds up her hands. "God forbid you do one different thing. Everything could change. And that would be so horrible." Her voice is light, but somehow we've landed back on the topic of how terrible it is that I want things to stay the same.

"Kind of harsh, don't you think?"

"Sorry," she says, but I hear a silent "not sorry," too. "I'm going to go say hi to Lauren and her mom and thank them for the party. I'll let you know if I see a vegetable tray anywhere."

I wander around the party alone, trying and failing to distract myself from thinking about what's going on with us. I've gone from worrying we were breaking up to thinking we were better than ever, but now I'm back to worrying. I know I shouldn't overanalyze her comments over a piece of cake, but

I know Maddie better than I know anyone, and something is definitely wrong.

As night falls, the party changes; Lauren's parents go out and the rest of the parents leave, and the boys bring over a keg and set it up on the porch. Graduation day is over, and graduation night means the start of a summer of freedom.

But I haven't seen Maddie for a while, so I decide to check and see if she's still mad at me. I weave my way through the growing crowd looking for her. She's not in the kitchen, which is filling up with people trying to get to the keg on the back porch. She's not in the living room, where a game of I Never is underway. I finally find her downstairs in the rec room, where a bunch of guys are watching baseball. She's wedged on the couch between them, which doesn't make sense until I see Colin. He just won't give up.

Maddie jumps to her feet when she sees me. "You found me! I thought I lost you there."

She makes it sound like she's been looking for me, but she seemed pretty comfortable on that couch. "I'll always find you," I say. Colin rolls his eyes. "You got a problem with that?"

"Nah, man, no problem here." He holds up his hands like he thinks I'm about to hit him.

"Pack, let's take a walk." Maddie grabs my hand and pulls me away from the couch. She is definitely not happy.

"Anything for you, babe," I say, making sure Colin can hear.

"Outside." She digs her nails into my palm. I am definitely in trouble.

Though lots of kids are hanging out on the porch, the party hasn't yet spilled into the rest of the backyard, which is small but fenced in so Lauren's dog can run around outside. The dog is tiny and yappy and gets very excited when it sees Maddie and me coming, so we throw around some tennis balls that we find lying in the grass until we've exhausted the dog and the tennis balls are covered in its drool. The three of us collapse on the ground, the dog putting its head in Maddie's lap. I'm not a dog person, but it's pretty cute.

The dog keeps Maddie from yelling at me right away, too, which is a plus. She rubs its head until it practically purrs like a cat, and then turns to me. "What is wrong with you?"

I expected her to sound angry, but instead she sounds resigned, which is way scarier. "What do you mean?"

"Don't play dumb, Pack." She stops petting the dog and looks me right in the eyes. "I've told you a million times there's nothing going on with Colin, and yet you're still a nightmare around him. You don't know him, so you have no reason not to like him unless you think he's some sort of threat to you. And for you to believe that means you don't trust me."

"Of course I trust you. I just don't trust him." The dog runs away, like it knows things are about to get ugly.

"And you think you're somehow going to save me from him? Like I need your help? Or do you think I'll be so overwhelmed by your protectiveness that I'll just decide to blow off college and stay here with you?" She makes little air quotes around the word "protectiveness" and I know I'm in even bigger trouble than I thought. If there's one thing Maddie hates, it's when I—or anyone else—tries to help her with a problem she can solve herself.

"It's not like that," I say.

"It's not? Why don't you tell me what it is like, then?"

"It's not about Colin. I just thought things were different now. That we were going to be okay. And then I saw you with him, and it made me feel like I was wrong."

"What do you mean, different? Than when?" She looks genuinely confused.

"Last night. After prom. Things were . . . different. It felt like something changed, and I thought maybe I didn't need to be nervous about the fall."

"Last night was amazing," Maddie says. "But I'm not sure I get what you mean by different. I'm still going to college this fall. That's not changing."

"I get it. You're going to college, and I'm not. But why are you acting like you're getting on a spaceship and colonizing Mars? You're moving two hours away."

Maddie runs her hands through her hair and looks off to the side. "It's so strange how the things you like most about someone can also be the things that create the biggest problems," she says, not making eye contact with me. "You're a very literal guy, Pack. I bet you've calculated the mileage between here and Amherst and mapped out the best routes depending on traffic."

I totally have. "Is that such a bad thing?"

"Of course not. I love that about you. I've never had to worry about what you were thinking, or whether you were being honest with me. I've always trusted you."

"Past tense much?" She isn't exactly making me feel better.

Now she turns to face me, and I see that resignation again. It's still worse than anger. "You're right that I'm only going to be two hours away. But I'm not a literal thinker like you are. Two hours isn't much in terms of time, but it's not just about the two hours. It's about me not living in my parents' house anymore. Me taking care of myself, making my own choices about where I want to be and what I want to do. Picking classes, thinking about my future, thinking about whether two hours is a good test run for four hours, or six, or even more than that. Two hours is the first step on my way out, Pack. I'm not coming back here. And you never want to leave."

I can't do anything but look at her for a solid minute. This is new to me. I assumed she'd go to college but then come back, that my challenge was just trying to make it work until she returned. Whatever she wants to do with her life she can do in Boston, and Brooksby is a great commuter town. In truth, I have our lives mapped out already, as surely as I have figured out the fastest route to UMass from my driveway. We have something real, I know it, so I don't see the point of having to go out in the world to find something else when what we need is right at home. But Maddie clearly doesn't feel the same way. "Ever?"

"Most likely," she says.

"So you're going to college, I'm staying here, and we spend the summer pretending it doesn't matter? Do you even want me to visit when you leave?"

She pauses, and I feel sick. "Pack, we have time to talk about this."

"You mean during our epic last summer together? Maybe we shouldn't bother." I say it as sharply as I can, hoping it's the verbal equivalent of a slap.

It's not. For a second Maddie looks relieved, I think. "Is that what you want?"

"Of course it's not what I want." My voice is getting louder, but I try not to yell. "I want you. I've never wanted anyone but you. I want our one last great summer and I want it to be so amazing you change your mind about college and stay here with me forever. Why is that such a horrible thing?"

"It's not horrible. It's flattering and it's lovely and in some ways it's also my nightmare."

Now I'm the one who got slapped. She's way better at this than me.

"I'm so, so sorry to have to say it like this but you haven't been hearing me." Maddie puts her hand on my knee, and her touch feels good even as I pull my leg away. "All I want is to leave here, and all you want is to stay. It's not that I don't see a future for us—it's hard to imagine a future without you. But I can't imagine that future here, and you won't imagine it anywhere else. So we only have one choice to make, really: do we enjoy the summer together or not?"

I shouldn't feel so blindsided. It's not like she hasn't been hinting at this for ages. But I never believed she really meant it, and even if she did, I thought she'd change her mind. Or I could help her change it. If that's not going to happen, what's the point of spending the summer together if it will only make us more miserable at the end? She doesn't want me to come visit; she wants to leave and start over like Brooksby doesn't exist, and I'm part of Brooksby.

Fuck that.

"Not," I say.

"What?"

"You asked if we should enjoy the summer together or not. I vote not. You can plan your new exciting life without me distracting you, and I'll—" I have no idea what I'll do. "I'll work more hours at the gym and figure out what I want to do with my life, which will have nothing to do with you."

"Pack—"

I'm not done. "You'll promise not to go to the morning

class and I won't go to the one at noon. You're working nights anyway, so it won't be hard. Are we good now?" I stand up and wipe the grass off my shorts. The little dog comes running back across the lawn at the sight of movement, collar tags clicking. Not what I want to deal with right now.

"Come on, sit back down." Maddie pats the space next to her. The dog takes that as a cue and replaces me in the dented grass. "We need to talk about this."

"No we don't," I say. "You've known all along this was coming; it was just a question of when. Well, since you got to decide the big stuff, I'll be the one to decide this part. I don't want a summer of pretending with you, and I don't think there's anything left to say."

"Nice, Pack. Way to respect the last few years." Maddie's voice shakes a little, and I don't know whether she's reached my level of anger or whether she's crying.

I don't care.

I turn around and walk away.

9

My plan is to spend the whole day after graduation in bed. It's not like I have anything else to do. I don't start work until next week, I don't feel like going to the gym, and everyone who isn't starting their summer jobs today is too hungover to go to the beach. Nothing matters now that there's no more Maddie.

"What do you mean, you broke up with Maddie?" Dad asks. He's trying to get me out of bed now that noon has rolled around, even though he should be sleeping—he has to work tonight. But he has that sixth sense for when something's up with me, so here he is. It makes me feel guilty, but then I remember the diamond ring in the shoe box and the lies (or at least half-truths) he's been telling me, and I decide I don't care. I try hiding under the covers so I won't have to talk, but that rarely works and it doesn't work now; he yanks them off and frowns when he sees I'm wearing yesterday's clothes.

"Preemptive strike," I say. "She was going to dump me at the end of the summer, before college, so I beat her to it." I pull the comforter back over me and turn to face the wall, hoping he'll just go away.

No such luck. Dad rolls me and the comforter off the bed. He hasn't used that move since grade school. "Get your ass in the shower, then come have breakfast. Brunch. Whatever. You'll tell me everything then."

It's not a request. I untangle myself from the blankets and go into the bathroom. I turn the heat of the shower up so high my skin turns bright red, but it feels good. By the time I towel off and throw on shorts and a T-shirt, Dad's finished cooking. Breakfast is the only meal he's really mastered, and it's kind of nice having him take care of everything.

Dad doesn't even pretend he's really interested in the food, though. "Tell me what happened," he says as soon as we sit down on the couch.

I'm surprised to find myself hungry, so I've already started crunching away on a slice of bacon. Extra crispy, just like I like it. "I told you," I say, still chewing, "she was going to break up with me, so I broke up with her first."

"Did she tell you that?"

"She didn't have to. She's going to college, and I'm some loser who's going to stay home and live with my dad—no offense."

"None taken," Dad says with a smirk. "Making some

assumptions there, though, aren't you?"

Now he's making me nervous. "Wait, can I not stay here? I thought—"

"Not the assumption I was talking about. Don't worry, bud, as long as I've got a place to live, you do too. You know that. But unless you haven't been telling me everything, you haven't exactly settled on your future plans, have you?"

He's right I haven't been telling him everything, but he's wrong about the topic. "To say I haven't settled on my future plans is a serious understatement."

"Well, who knows what could happen between now and the fall? You've got that job at the gym, and you know I'm hoping you'll take some classes and consider college."

Eye roll. "Consider, yes. That's all I said I'd do."

"Enough for me. And enough for you to stop thinking of yourself as a loser without a plan. You're just in between plans right now. And I think you know that already." He still hasn't eaten anything, which tells me he's taking this more seriously than I realized. It's hard to stay annoyed at him when he's trying so hard to help.

"Yeah, I guess."

"So if I know that, and you know that, don't you think Maddie knows that too?"

I shrug. "I don't know what she knows."

"Don't get all stubborn with me," he says. "Just trying to make you see reason here is all. Why did you ruin your last summer with Maddie when you didn't have to?"

How am I supposed to answer that? He's making me sound so stupid. "It was ruined already. I thought we were going to stay together when she left. I thought I'd go see her every weekend and it would be almost the same as now. It's not like we saw each other so much during the week anyway. I didn't think everything had to change. But she did. And she was going to wait until the fall to tell me so I could have one last clueless summer before she told me what an idiot I was, but I figured it out early and it wrecked everything. So I just beat her to the punch. I guess I'm not an idiot after all." Except I am, of course. Maybe I'd be better off with a fun, clueless summer. It would be better than how I feel right now.

Dad and I sit quietly for a while. He starts eating his food, but I push mine away. I'm not hungry anymore. The weight of what I did hits me hard, and it makes me feel kind of nauseated. Yeah, it would have sucked to get left behind when Maddie went to college, but she'd find a way to make it sound okay. We wouldn't have gotten into the kind of fight I started, we wouldn't leave mad at each other, and our whole relationship wouldn't be retroactively ruined.

I blew it.

"You're not dumb," Dad says. "Don't know where you got that idea, but you're a whole lot smarter than you think.

Always have been. Why do you think I ride you so hard about going to school?

Funny, he sounds just like Maddie. "I don't know about that."

"Come on, I'll test you," Dad says. "See if you can figure this one out." He turns on the TV and pulls up Netflix. Which means he's going to dig up some suspense thriller movie he's already watched and see how long it takes me to determine who did it. Pretty much the perfect way to spend a crappy afternoon. The guilt kicks back in at the thought of him basically pulling an all-nighter to take care of me, but Dad's stubborn, and I know nothing I can say will change his mind. I lean all the way back and settle in.

Dad leaves for work, and I'm alone in the apartment. That's not unusual; I'm alone in the apartment all the time. But now I feel alone in a completely different way. Dad's been his usual helpful dad self, and I put aside all the questions and doubts and let him take care of me, like he did when I was little. But when he left, they all came rushing back, along with the constant gutted feeling of remembering that Maddie's gone too. It's like I keep forgetting and have to relive the breakup over and over again. When I figure out the bad guy in the movie I immediately go to text Maddie that Dad couldn't stump me, and I'm halfway through typing before I remember I don't get to text her anymore, and our fight replays in my head. In the empty apartment I keep thinking about my mother, and the lying, and I want to talk to Maddie about it, but all I can hear is her voice reminding me how afraid of change I am. I stare at my phone wondering if I should call her, apologize, tell her I want our summer back, but the anger of her leaving outweighs the loneliness and I put the phone down again.

I'm alone in the apartment, and now I'm alone in the world, too.

But in a weird way, the anger helps. I'm still mad at Maddie for wanting to leave, for being right about me not wanting things to change. I'm angry at Dad for whatever lies he told me, even if he thinks he's being helpful. And I'm angry with my mother, for sending me that letter and making me question everything about my stupid life. How could she not leave me a way to get in touch? Why does she want some inroad back into my life when she'd been fine leaving me and never looking back?

The more I think about everything, the angrier I get. But I'm not an angry person by nature, and I can't live like this. There has to be something I can do to make myself feel better. I'm not ready to talk to Maddie or Dad about what I'm really feeling, and I can't talk to my mother because I don't know where she is. Though maybe that can change.

I go to the desktop computer I share with Dad and pick up where I left off at the school library. It was just a few days ago, but it feels like months. I go through the archives of the *Brooksby Gazette*, looking for an obituary for Natalie Russo, to see if there's some chance Dad was telling the truth, that she really is dead, that I was right about the letter being some kind of fake. I'm not shocked that I don't find anything. Maybe I've convinced myself the letter is real. Or maybe I just want it to be.

Then I run the search for her name again. There are still a gazillion results, but I narrow the search as many ways as I can. I look for her name and Dad's; her name plus Brooksby; all the social media sites I've ever heard of and a few that are new to me. She's nowhere to be found.

I'm not sure what to do next until I remember Regina Russo, who may or may not be related to her. I type her name into Google, hoping I'll get lucky—it seems like a less common name than Natalie. Of course, I'm totally wrong about that, and Google spits back like eight million sites for me to check. Whole lot of nope there.

I try searching for Natalie and Regina together, but still nothing. It's not until I get on Facebook that I have any luck. There are still lots of people named Regina Russo, and even more if you use it as a middle or maiden name. How am I supposed to figure out which is the right one? Then I scroll through the names that pop up, and I see one with a photo that might be an older version of the girl I saw in the yearbook. Her full name is Regina Russo Lombardi, so if it's her, she's married. I click on her picture to look at the page, but it's locked down. I keep staring to see if there's any way I can be sure, but it's like the image gets less and less distinct the more I look at it. I try clicking on her friends list to see if there's some Brooksby connection I can find, but that's blocked too. Literally the only thing I can see is that photo.

I have to go at it another way. Since Regina went to high school just a couple of years ahead of Dad, it's possible some of his friends might be connected to her. Just for kicks I check Dad's page first, but he's hardly friends with anyone, let alone anyone with the last name Russo. He mostly uses it to keep track of the pictures he takes on his phone. I look for Manny, but he's not on there—he probably spends all his time on dating sites, given how he talks at the gym. I know Tom's on it, though—we always joke about how Facebook is for old people. I barely check my own page myself.

Tom isn't friends with anyone named Regina Russo either, but he's a member of a reunion page for their class at Brooksby High, which gives me the idea to check whether Regina Russo's class has a page, too. That's when I hit pay dirt: there's a page, and Regina Russo Lombardi is on it. Confirmation.

More than that: I have a relative. I think. She's got to be at least a cousin, but more likely, she's my aunt.

Having her full name gives me something to search, so I click over to Google and look her up. This time finding information is much easier. She lives in a town just outside of New Haven, Connecticut; I even find an address. I search as hard as I can for a phone number, but no one has land lines anymore, and cell phones are nearly impossible to track down. Email would be useful, but I strike out there, too. The address and Facebook page are all I have.

Now I have to decide what to do next. As far as I can see, I have three choices: I can go old-school like my mother and send a letter, I can send a Facebook friend request, or I can jump in the car and show up at Regina Russo Lombardi's door.

A letter could take months; it could get lost in the mail or thrown out. A Facebook request is too easy to ignore, and if Regina Russo Lombardi is like me, she never checks her page anyway. I know what I want to do.

But showing up at a stranger's house with no plan is not a good idea. It's impulsive and reckless and risky, and if Maddie's right about anything, it's that impulsive and reckless and risky are not exactly my trademarks.

Maybe that's the problem. Maybe it's time to be brave. To prove Maddie's wrong about me. If I leave tomorrow morning I won't have to face another day alone in the apartment, and I can avoid dealing with Dad for a while, too. I've got nothing to do before I start work except sit around and be miserable, and that's not a great option.

The more I think about it, the more it feels like the right

thing to do. I can show Maddie that I really can change, and then we'll have something to talk about when I get back. I can get some answers, and then Dad and I can have an honest conversation about my mother for once. And, most important, I can confirm that this letter is real, that I actually have a mother out there somewhere. I still don't know whether I want to find her, but I don't have to decide that now. I worry a little about leaving without talking to Dad, but I can leave him a note telling him I'm doing a beach road trip with some of the guys before work starts. It might not keep him from freaking out, but it should buy me time. Besides, it's only a white lie; it's not any worse than what he's been telling me. He'll get over it, like I'm trying to.

That settles it. In the morning, I'll put in one good, hard workout, and then I'll get in my car and drive away.

PART II

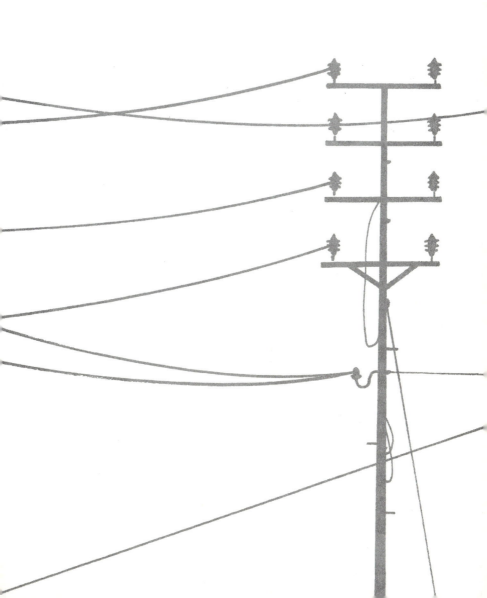

10

I've never been this far from home before. Sure, I've driven into Boston a few times, and I've gone to some nearby towns to take Maddie shopping or to the movies, but as best as I can remember, I've never traveled more than an hour from Brooksby. The only times I've even been out of state are to go get booze in New Hampshire once in a while, where it's cheaper. The lie I left in the note to my dad—that I'm going to the beach in Maine for a few days—would have taken me farther away than I've ever been. With Dad's work schedule we never really took any vacations, and to be honest, I've never cared much about seeing the world outside where I lived. The news makes it seem like bad things can happen anywhere—girls get murdered on island vacations, tourists get blown up in terrorist attacks, families get wiped out in car accidents on the Autobahn. I'm safer at home.

At first, I don't think much about any of this. The early

part of the trip is on familiar highway, Route 128 to the Mass Pike, and even when I move farther away from Boston, all I notice is that there are more trees. Otherwise? Dullsville. I make it to Hartford before I have to dig out some almonds and beef jerky to keep from getting too hungry—I was so eager to get on the road that I just had a smoothie after the workout instead of a real breakfast. I stop at a gas station to fill up the tank and eat my snacks outside, leaning on the car. The day is perfect—sunny, warm, blue skies, no clouds. I could be at the beach, accidentally-on-purpose nailing Colin in the nose with an errant volleyball spike. Except hardly anyone will be at the beach today; almost everyone's started their summer jobs.

No looking back, though. I get in the car and crank Nas, but my nerves are starting to twitch. It's not just leaving Brooksby; the reality of my decision is kicking in. I'm about to show up on the doorstep of someone I've never met, someone I haven't called, someone who may be part of a family I never knew I had and that I'm not sure I want. Who wouldn't be nervous about that?

My racing thoughts carry me all the way to New Haven. I exit the highway and enter a part of town that looks more like a suburb than a city, and a nicer suburb than Brooksby at that. I made good time—the trip only took a few hours, even with the stop—so it's not even noon yet when my GPS leads me through the back streets to my final destination: a big white house with one car in the driveway, a lawn that someone obviously cares about, with a sign for some political candidate I've never heard of.

This is it. I check my phone one more time to make sure I have the right address. It feels like I've already been gone for days, and for a minute I'm tempted to turn around and go home. I can apologize to Maddie, pretend I never got the letter, and, for one last summer, ignore the fact that my world is changing. What's the point of all this, anyway? But I'm here, so I steel myself and walk up to the front door, hesitating only briefly before ringing the bell.

Then I wait for a while, long enough that I'm almost convinced no one's home despite the car in the driveway. Just as I'm about to turn around, the door opens. It's not Regina Russo who opens it, though; it's a boy, about my age, about my height. He has shaggy dark brown hair, a lot like what mine looked like before I buzzed it down. Dark brown eyes, like mine. He's dressed for working out, in a faded gray T-shirt, track pants, and regular sneakers.

We could be brothers.

"Whatever you're selling, we're not interested," he says. He doesn't sound mean or anything, but he's definitely hoping to get me off his front steps as soon as possible.

"Um," I say, wishing I'd prepared some sort of script, wishing I'd even considered the possibility that someone other than the woman who I'm increasingly certain is my aunt would open the door. "Is your mom here?"

"She's at work." The boy stares at me, waiting for an explanation, which makes total sense. Except I have no idea what that explanation might be.

"I'm Patrick. Pack," I say. Maybe he knows about me, even if I didn't know about him.

He keeps staring. Nope.

"I think I'm your cousin."

He draws back his head in surprise. "You think? Why?" Clearly he's a pretty chill guy; he still doesn't sound rude. Just curious.

"It's kind of a long story." I'm not sure what to say, really. "Can you tell me when your mom will be back?"

He thinks for a moment, trying to decide whether to give his mother's schedule to a complete stranger, most likely. "Give me a sec, okay?"

"Sure." What else can I do?

The boy goes back in the house, leaving the door cracked open behind him but not in a way that makes me feel like I can follow. It doesn't take him long to come back, his phone pressed to his ear. He's already started the call, and I can hear the tinny sound of ringing through the speakers. What if she doesn't pick up? What will I do then?

Then there's the muffled sound of a woman's voice, though I can't tell what she's saying. "Hey, Ma," the boy says. "There's someone here who says he's my cousin. His name is—" He glances at me. He's already forgotten.

"Patrick," I say.

"Patrick . . ."

"Walsh."

"Last name's Walsh," he says. I wait for more mumbling, but there's silence on the other end of the line. I'm not sure what to make of that.

"Natalie's son," I say.

"He says Natalie's his mother," he says. "Who's Natalie?"

So he doesn't know who Natalie is. Which means either Regina Lombardi hasn't told him about her, or I've got the wrong person.

Finally I hear the mumbling again. "Uh-huh," the boy says. "Yup. Got it." He ends the call and opens the door wider. "Come in. She says to stay here. She can't get away from work yet, but she doesn't want you to leave."

Holy shit. I did it. I've found the right person. I can barely believe it.

As soon as I step into the house it's clear my aunt and her family have a lot more money than we do. It isn't that everything is so fancy, or even that the house is particularly big; it's just obvious that the people who live here care about their space in a way I'm not used to. It's not like Maddie's house, all polished and decorated to serve as an advertisement for her mom's business; there's a warmth I feel right away, in the open spaces, the big kitchen with copper pots and pans hanging from a rack suspended from the ceiling, the living room with lots of squishy couches and a geometric-patterned rug and colorful throw pillows.

My cousin, who still hasn't introduced himself, leads me to a little table in the kitchen, where he gestures toward a chair. I sit down as he opens the fridge. "Soda?" he asks, taking out a Coke for himself.

Weird how someone who obviously works out—he's in better shape than me, despite my efforts—would pour liquid sugar into a body he takes care of. None of my business, though. "Water would be great."

He gets out a glass and holds it against the dispenser in front of the fridge. Our fridge doesn't have one of those, and even though the water in Brooksby isn't the greatest, we never bothered with a filter. I bet the water here doesn't even need a filter, even if the fridge already has one. Either way, it tastes so much better than what I'm used to, it's almost like an entirely different drink.

The almonds and beef jerky made me even thirstier than I realized, and I drain the whole glass before my cousin even sits down. "Another?" he asks, but I shake my head. It feels like we're delaying the inevitable, even if I don't know what the inevitable is.

"So," he says, after he sits down across from me. "Cousins, huh?"

"I guess." I don't know what I'm supposed to say. Are there

even things someone is supposed to say, in a situation like this? "I didn't know about you until recently. I didn't know about anything. Still don't, really."

"Well, obviously I know even less than you. Like I don't even know who you're related to. I thought I knew everyone in this family, and god knows there are a lot of us."

"There are?" Who's this "us" he's referring to?

"Sure. There's me and Mia—that's my sister—and Nonna and Poppa, and Dad's family—he's got three brothers and I have like a million cousins on that side. But you're not on that side, right? Do you know any of my mom's family?"

"I don't even know you," I say. "You haven't told me your name yet."

"Right," he says. "I'm Matteo, but everyone in my family calls me Matt. Or Matty."

Matty. It sounds exactly like Maddie, how he says it, and I can't help myself—I start laughing. Not just giggling laughing either, but full-on, hiccuping laughing. I bend over, trying to keep from choking, and will myself to make the laughing stop, but I can't.

"Dude, are you okay? It's not that weird a name. No weirder than Pack, anyway." I hear him stand up and walk around the table, like he thinks he's going to have to do the Heimlich or something.

Finally I catch my breath. "I'm fine. Sorry about that. It's just—my girlfriend's name is Maddie. Or was. I mean, she's still Maddie, she's just not my girlfriend anymore."

"Oh," Matt says. "Sorry." I can tell he doesn't understand why it's all so funny, and honestly, I don't either. Maybe it's just all too much. He walks back around the table and sits down again.

"No worries," I say. "Yeah, I'm on your mom's side, and I don't know anyone."

"Are you like a second cousin or something? Who are you related to?"

He really doesn't know who Natalie is. "First cousin. Your mother's sister is my mom. Apparently."

He stares at me for a minute, lips pressed together, trying not to show how surprised he is. I get it—he doesn't know me, and he has no idea what to say now.

"She never told you about her," I say.

"Nope." He sounds pissed off, which I totally understand. To find out his mother has a sister she never told him about is pretty crazy.

"I didn't know about her either, until like a week ago. I thought she was dead, and then I got this letter." I didn't plan to say that, but I figure maybe it will make him feel better to know he's not the only person who's been lied to.

He keeps looking at me, and I wonder whether he's seeing the same things in my face that I see in his. "I don't know what to think about all this," he says. "But, like, why are you here? Why find us and not this Natalie person?"

"I don't know where my mom is," I say. "She didn't tell me. I'm trying to track her down, and I found your mom. I thought maybe she would know." I'm not feeling so sure about that now, though.

"She probably wouldn't tell you even if she did," he says, and he doesn't try to hide the bitterness in his voice. Me coming here is definitely going to start some trouble. I don't know if there's anything I can do to stop it, but changing the subject might help.

"You said you have a sister? Mia?"

"Yeah," he says, and some warmth comes back into his voice. His relationship with Mia must not be anything like Maddie's with her sister. "She's five years younger than me. She's at some theater camp or some other artsy bullshit. She's kind of a pain in the ass." He smiles, and I'm glad I got him out of the bad place, at least for now.

"How old are you?" I ask.

"Seventeen. Going into junior year. You?"

"Just turned eighteen. Just graduated, too."

"So this isn't some discover-your-roots college essay prep or anything like that."

I shake my head. "No college for me."

He raises his eyebrows. "Really? What are you going to do now?"

I'm probably going to have to answer that question a million times. "Don't know yet. Still figuring things out. For now, I'm just trying to find my mother."

"So we're, like, the first step in a treasure hunt. A Tomb Raider kind of thing. You play?"

I'm not super into video games, which I assume is what he's referring to. "Not really. Not much of a gamer." I hope he doesn't think I'm weird. I don't want my first new family member not to like me.

Instead of frowning, his face lights up. "So you're, like, a noob!" He jumps out of his chair. "Come on, we're going downstairs."

Anything to avoid talking about my lack of future plans. I follow him as he opens a door off the kitchen that I thought might lead to a bathroom, but instead it hides a staircase. We go down into the basement, which is clearly the kid zone in this house. The ceiling is low, the walls are wood paneled, and the couch looks like a couple of La-Z-Boy chairs connected together with some extra seats in the middle. I hope the legs pop out like my couch at home.

The centerpiece, though, is the TV. It's one of the most massive I've ever seen. It covers almost the entire wall. "How big is that thing?" I ask, feeling almost reverent.

"Sixty-five inches," Matt says, with some pride. "You won't believe the graphics, either. Here, let me show you." He gets out a remote that's the size of a computer and starts hitting a bunch of buttons, and the room explodes in sound and color. There must be speakers everywhere, because I feel like the noise is coming from all around me. Matt's loaded up some sort of game demo, and the graphics are so realistic it's like being in a war zone. "Crazy, isn't it?"

It's actually kind of terrifying, but I'm not about to tell him that. "Totally," I agree.

"Want me to teach you how to play?"

"Sure, why not? But do you have a game that isn't so . . ." I watch as someone's head blows up on the screen, the sound of pieces of skull and brain hitting the ground all too easy to identify.

"Gross?" He grins and hits a few more buttons, and the chaos onscreen is replaced with a still-realistic, super-hot girl. "Better?"

"Much." Turns out this is Tomb Raider. Playing with Matt is more fun than I expected; he shows me what to do and we act as a team, killing zombie-people in increasingly violent ways, though nothing as bad as that scene from the demo. We play for a long time, mostly in silence other than yelling out when exciting things happen. Hanging out with him is surprisingly comfortable even though we're not talking; I wonder whether this is a family thing or whether this is how all guys I know feel when they play video games together. I've been invited to their houses to play before, but I always begged off, preferring to hang with Maddie or my dad.

But there's something about being on this imaginary quest that's helping me get to know Matt, even without talking. He's aggressive even within the game, willing to take all sorts of risks even if it means having to start over. He's always conscious that nothing we're doing is real, so there's no harm in players dying or doing crazy stunts just to see if they're possible.

I, on the other hand, am as cautious as ever, even in a world that's entirely imaginary. I can't help but try and keep our characters safe; when the game opens up possibilities to travel off the obvious path, I always question them. It's hard for me to say okay, and it makes me think about everything Maddie said about me. I've come all this way, so I have to try.

We've been playing for at least two hours when Matt's phone dings, and he pauses the game to look at it. "Crap, I totally forgot. I have to get Mia at camp. Sneaky little thing programmed an alarm into my phone, though it's probably good she did or I'd have left her there. Want to come with me, or do you want to stay here and keep playing?"

I can't believe Matt's willing to leave me alone in the house after knowing me for all of three hours, but just because he's willing doesn't make it a good idea. Although maybe he wants time alone with Mia, to warn her about me? "I'll come with you, if that's okay."

"Good." I can tell that's what he hoped I'd say. "Just be warned, though, Mia's kind of her own thing. She's a chatterbox, and nosy as hell. She's going to have a lot of questions."

Her and me both.

11

Turns out the car in the driveway is Matt's, a used Camry with some mileage on it but otherwise in good shape, if you don't count the fact that its seats are covered with dirty gym clothes and baseball equipment. I try to be subtle about opening the window, since the car smells about what you'd expect a car to be filled with that stuff to smell like, but Matt looks over and laughs. "Yeah, I haven't driven anyone around except Mia since my last breakup. I guess it's getting kind of rank in here. Mia complains all the time, but I just ignore her."

Apparently Matt's not a gym rat, just a jock. He already seems like less of a dick than the jocks at my school, so that's a plus. And now we have something in common. Funny he didn't mention it before. "You just had a breakup too? Sucks, doesn't it?"

He pulls out of the driveway so fast the tires squeal. I

didn't think grown-up type sedans could do that. "Ah, no big deal. Better to go into senior year free and clear, don't you think?"

"I wouldn't really know," I admit. "I was with my girl-friend for most of high school."

Matt's driving really fast given that we're on side streets, but he seems to be in good control of the car, so I try not to worry. I've rarely been a passenger in anyone else's car since I got my license, except occasionally Dad's, and he always says it's important for cops to model proper behavior. Which means the speed limit, always. Still, even Matt seems surprised to find himself swerving around a corner to make the highway onramp. "You sound bummed," he says. "Must have been a rough one."

"The roughest," I say, but I don't elaborate. We may have bonded over the video game, but we're not exactly buddies yet.

Matt gets off the highway almost as soon as he's gotten on it, and not long after he turns into the parking lot of an elementary school. "I thought you said Mia was twelve. Is she not in middle school yet?"

"She is. But they're using the auditorium here for camp. Pain in the ass, if you ask me, since I'm the one who has to cart her around until my baseball camp starts."

That explains why he doesn't have a job, like most kids I know. Or maybe it's just because they have money. We wait for a short time until the front door of the school opens and a whole bunch of middle-school kids stream out, each one goofier-looking than the next. I've never seen so many kids with multicolored hair before. This is definitely the drama crowd.

A girl with long black hair and a big royal blue streak down the front runs up to the car, opening the passenger door before Matt can signal for her to get in the back. "There's a person here," she says, looking over at Matt. He nods, and she opens the back door and gets in.

I turn to watch her shoving aside his baseball stuff and wrinkling her nose at the smell. "Hi, Mia," I say.

"This person knows my name," she says to Matt, then turns to me. "Who are you?"

Matt was right about Mia—she's very direct. "My name's Pack," I say. "I'm your cousin."

"No you aren't," she says. "I know all my cousins already. Who are you really?"

"Mia, don't be rude," Matt says as we leave the parking lot. "Pack will explain everything when we get home. And you can think about how you're going to explain that blue streak to Mom. She's going to lose her mind when she sees it."

"That's technically impossible," Mia says. "Besides, it's not permanent. Mr. McMillan brought colored hairspray to camp. Lots of colors. Everyone tried it."

That explains the multicolored heads. I'd been wondering

whether parents in Connecticut were way more lax about hair dye than parents in Brooksby.

"So you chose blue. Shocker."

"It's not shocking at all. Blue is my favorite color. Blue is one of only three primary colors, and without it we wouldn't have green or purple or aqua or lavender or—"

"We get it, Mia," Matt says as I try to keep from cracking up. "Pack doesn't know you yet, so we're going to keep things simple for him, okay?"

Mia's like a pint-sized encyclopedia, but she doesn't seem to get sarcasm. Matt called her annoying, but he sounds awfully gentle even as he's basically telling her to stop talking. Their relationship is already interesting to me, especially given the contrast with Maddie and her sister, whose sibling dynamic is the only one I've seen up close.

I watch Mia in the backseat. She's bouncing up and down a little, but not in an anxious way. At Matt's reminder to keep things simple, she nods her head like she's heard it before. "Simple. Yes. Absolutely."

I already like her, though I can't explain why. "How was camp?" I ask. "Are you going to be in a play?"

Mia considers my question, head tilted even as she continues that slight bouncing. "I like camp. There are other kids like me there. It's just for fun. I don't want to be in plays. Plays are long and you have to sit still the whole time. I like books better."

"Don't you have to sit still while you're reading?" It's maybe too early in our new relationship to tease her, but she's pretty funny.

Matt snorts. "You haven't seen Mia read. It's a contact sport. She paces and doesn't look where she's going."

"Active movement is healthy," Mia says.

Back at the house, the sight of my truck on the curb gives me an odd sense of comfort. I check my phone; it's only four, so we probably have some time before Regina gets home. I follow Matt and Mia into the living room, and me and Matt sit on the sofa while Mia takes the love seat. She doesn't hesitate before jumping right in. "How can you be my cousin, when I know all my aunts and uncles and cousins already?"

"Let him sit, will you?" Matt says.

"Nah, I'm good," I say. I like how straightforward she is. "Mia, I only just found out about you guys too. Your mom is going to explain everything to us when she gets home." I hope she is, anyway.

Mia contemplates this, head tilted, eyes closed. Then she opens them. "This is all very strange. But I can wait until Mom gets home."

"And having a new cousin is exciting, right?" Matt says. I'm glad to hear it; it wasn't clear how he felt about me just showing up like this. I'm not sure whether he means it or if he's trying to coax Mia on board. "It's like a surprise."

"I suppose," Mia says, but she doesn't sound convinced.

"Okay, surprise cousin, tell me your life."

"Tell you what?"

"Your life. Tell me your whole life." She sounds genuinely interested.

I glance at Matt to see how he's reacting to all this. He has a little grin, and I realize he doesn't actually think she's a pain in the ass at all. The two of them get along really well. He's not about to stop the interrogation, either.

"Fine, but only if you tell me yours," I say. "Both of you."

Matt shrugs, and Mia starts bouncing again. "Yes! We can do that! Now go."

How am I supposed to sum up my whole life? I like the question, though. There's a comprehensiveness to it, a desire to really know things about me, rather than the more generic questions, like "Where are you from?" or "What are your plans for next year?" I decide to give it a try, to be as honest as I can.

"Okay, here goes," I say. "My life, by Patrick Anthony Walsh. Except I go by Pack. Born eighteen years ago, plus about a week. I live in Brooksby, Massachusetts, just graduated from high school, not sure what I'm going to do with my life yet. My dad's a cop and he wants me to go to college, but I'm thinking about becoming a personal trainer or a nutritionist. Something to do with health. I was a fat kid and I didn't feel good about myself, and I want to help people feel better about themselves, no matter how they look." I'm surprised to hear myself say that part out loud, but there it is. I push on. "Up until a few days ago I had a girlfriend named Maddie, who was also pretty much my only friend. Until I turned eighteen, I thought my mother was dead and that my dad was basically my only family. Is that enough life for you?"

Mia claps her hands, still bouncing. No wonder she's so skinny—that girl has energy to burn. "Very efficient! I'm not sure that's everything, but it's a good start. You next." She points at Matt.

"This was your idea," he protests, but he's resigned. "Let's see: Matteo Andreas Lombardi, but Matty or Matt is better, though I get why Pack is probably not going to start calling me Matty anytime soon. Seventeen, heading into summer of senior year, shooting for a baseball scholarship so I can help pay for college, currently serving as Mia's chauffeur until baseball camp starts, single for the summer and ready to party. That's all I've got."

"Matty is kind of boring," Mia says. "It's okay, though. He's a good person. That's more important."

"I'm sure he's not boring," I say. "If he is, then I am too."

"Maybe," she says, but it's somehow not insulting coming from her. "He's leaving things out too, but that's okay. Matty says we don't have to share everything with everyone all the time."

"You have to share some things, though," I point out. "It's your turn."

She nods. "Correct. It is my turn. I'm Mia Nicole Lombardi. I don't have a nickname because my name is too short and it would be confusing if people called me something like Mi. Then they'd sound silly." The thought of it clearly entertains her, though. "I'm twelve years old and I'm in middle school. I like school because I like learning, but I don't like school sometimes because the other kids aren't always so nice. I'm going to drama camp this summer so I can learn to get along better with other people. It's only been a few days but so far I think it's working. I don't know if you noticed, but I like to say what I think. All the time."

"I noticed," I say, stifling a laugh, because I can see it's a big deal for her to tell me this. "I think it's terrific."

"You do?" She sounds surprised.

"I do. I'm excited you're my cousin. I like the idea of being part of your family." I mean it, too. Meeting Matt and Mia is like getting a birthday present I didn't even know I wanted.

"Okay, then," she says. "I'm going to go upstairs and think about things for a while. Matt, let me know when Mom and Dad get home."

"Will do," he says.

Mia runs upstairs. Matt waits until she's out of earshot, then says, "That was huge."

"What was?"

"She likes you. She doesn't like a lot of people. She can be kind of a lot, and not everyone reacts to that very well."

"I don't know why," I say. "I like her."

Matt looks closely at me, trying to figure out whether I really mean it. I don't know what my face is telling him, but he leans back, satisfied. "That's good. I have a feeling things are about to get kind of complicated around here, and it's better not to have any more drama than we need to, you know?"

Oh, I know.

"I have to admit, I'm pretty pissed at Mom for keeping this a secret. Can't promise there won't be some yelling."

"I understand," I say. "I've been trying to hold back on the yelling myself."

Before I can say more, I hear the sound of a car pulling into the driveway, and I try to prepare myself for what's next.

My aunt is home.

12

Matt gets up and goes over to the window. I follow him, trying not to stand too close like some sort of creeper. He pulls
the curtain aside and I see two people get out of an SUV.
"Mom and Dad are home," he says.

I haven't even contemplated the fact that I have an uncle,
too. "They share one car?"

Matt nods. "They both work downtown, and they decided
they'd see more of each other if they carpooled. My car used
to be Mom's, but they figured they didn't need it. It's only
been a few months, so we'll see how it goes."

I'm impressed Matt managed to make that car so very
much his own in such a short time, down to the smell of his
baseball gear. I've been kind of religious about keeping my
truck spotless, but that's just how I like it.

I watch my aunt and uncle walk up the driveway. I'm not
sure what I was expecting them to look like in person—I only

had a hint of what my aunt looks like now from her Facebook picture. She looks basically the same—a lot like Matt and Mia, with the same thick, dark hair and strong nose. She isn't pretty, exactly, but she's a person you want to look at more. I wonder whether she looks like my mother now. She does kind of look like me. And my uncle may as well be related—he's also dark haired and dark eyed, and not very tall. Where my aunt has laugh lines around her eyes, he has frown lines by his mouth. I hope it's not a sign of his personality.

I have no idea what will happen when they open the door, but I'm about to find out. My uncle comes in first, holding two big bags with Asian lettering. Apparently they got Chinese takeout. My aunt walks in behind him, keys in hand. So she does the driving. I don't know whether to walk up to them or stay where I am, which is all but hiding behind Matt. "Mia!" he yells. "The parents are home! With food!"

I wait as Mia comes running down the stairs. She practically slams into my aunt, who neatly dodges her, puts her keys down on a side table, and drops her purse on top of them. Then she turns to me and opens her arms. "Patrick," she says warmly.

I'm stiff for a second, but then I step forward. She pulls me into a tight hug that lasts longer than I thought hugs were supposed to. But then again, Dad and I aren't big huggers, and hugs with Maddie are usually a stepping-stone to something else, so what do I know? And it feels nice. Comforting, even, though my aunt can't know how much comforting I need after the breakup.

"Pack," Mia says. "That's what he said we should call him."

"Pack, then," she says. "I see you've met the kids already. That's good." She grabs her husband's hand and tugs him toward me. "This is your uncle Mike. And you can call me Aunt Reggie." It's my first official confirmation that I was right about her being my aunt. "We're so happy to have you here. Are you hungry?"

I'm not, though given that I've barely eaten since breakfast, I should be. Everyone else seems pretty eager to eat, though, so I nod. "I'm glad to be here."

"We have a lot to talk about, but dinner first. Do you like Chinese food?" She walks into the kitchen and starts pulling white cartons and aluminum trays out of the bags my uncle left on the table.

"Sure." I haven't actually eaten Chinese food in years that I didn't make myself. I use liquid aminos instead of soy sauce, since soy is a legume and therefore not part of the Paleo plan. And the Chinese food I ate as a kid was mostly appetizers—spareribs, Peking ravioli, fried chicken fingers dipped in bright pink sweet-and-sour sauce. We called it Boston Chinese, as if to highlight how not-authentic it was. If the soy wasn't enough to get me to stop eating it, the sugar and flour and grease were.

What my aunt and uncle brought home looks healthier, though. Lots of colorful vegetables, chicken, tofu, and brown rice. I can skip the tofu and the rice and keep the sauce minimal and it won't kill me, I figure. Better that than to have their first impression of me be of how strange my eating habits are. Besides, Maddie was on me to be more flexible. If only she could see me now.

We all load up plates with food and then sit at the big dining table that separates the open kitchen from the living room. Dad and I usually sit in front of the TV when we eat together, on our big leather couch, so this kind of family dinner is unusual for me. I feel both out of place and totally welcome at the same time. It's not a bad feeling; it's just confusing, like everything else these days.

Despite the fact that we're all sitting together, dinner is a more chaotic affair than I'm used to. Mia talks nonstop, and Aunt Reggie and Uncle Mike are so busy trying to keep up, they don't seem to notice that Matt barely says a word. I don't know whether this is normal or a function of how angry he is, though from what he said I thought the yelling would start right away. Apparently he needs a little time to process before he launches into whatever fit of rage he has in mind.

I can tell Aunt Reggie wants to ask me as many questions as I want to ask her, but it's also clear she doesn't see dinner as the appropriate setting. Instead, when Mia finally exhausts her list of stories about camp, she and Uncle Mike start in with stories of their own, about work. Uncle Mike works in a bank as a loan officer, and he's got lots of funny anecdotes about people who come in to request loans for seriously bizarre things—one woman wants to get plastic surgery so she can work as an impersonator for a famous movie star; another man wants to start his own casino so he can make back all the money he lost gambling. As I watch him talk, I see that the lines around his mouth aren't from frowning at all. I've never heard anyone laugh so hard at his own jokes.

Aunt Reggie works at a different bank as a teller, which explains why they're able to align their schedules so easily. She doesn't say much about the people who come to her window; her stories are all about coworkers. Apparently banks are as full of drama as high schools. "You know they fired Teresa, right? I must have told you all that. It's why we've been so busy. Anyway, they finally replaced her, and guess who they hired?" She looks around the table as if the answer should have been obvious. "Cynthia Rourke. You know her son Dylan, don't you, Matty?"

She says it all casual, but Matt instantly loses his sulk for a minute before he remembers he's still mad. He slumps back down in his chair. "Yeah, I know him." Then he pretends not to look interested while he waits for Aunt Reggie to say more.

There's a long pause, and it's so strange—it's like I can hear a whole conversation in the silence, though I'm not sure I understand it. Aunt Reggie knows Matt's pissed off, but she's not going to take it on directly. Instead, she's going to draw him out by talking about someone he knows, and based on the combination of sulk-loss and face-reddening, there's something significant about him. I just don't know what it is.

"She mentioned that you and Dylan had some classes together this year. Is that right, honey?"

"Trig," Matt grunts.

"He's going to be around all summer. Extra training for the track team, apparently. Dylan told her the track they're running on is right near the field where your baseball practices are held. Isn't that interesting?"

"He told his mother that?" Matt's sitting back up in his chair now.

"I guess it just came up in conversation," Aunt Reggie says. "Maybe you'll run into him one of these days. It sounds like he might enjoy that."

The way they're talking reminds me of the kind of shit we used to give Sean before he got together with Kelsey. But Dylan's not a girl . . . and I'm an idiot, I realize. Matt's gay.

Clearly Matt's crush on Dylan is old news to the family. I look around the table, where Mia has made a perfect circle of rice around the outside rim of her plate and divided her food into neat categories. Uncle Mike is hiding a smile, and I'm glad to know that they all seem to accept Matt for who he is. When Brooke and Lauren came out they had a really hard time; I hope it wasn't like that for Matt.

"I could text him," Matt says, pretending to sound all grudging. He's not fooling anyone, except maybe Mia.

Aunt Reggie nods, as if to indicate she's accomplished her mission, and then she turns to me. "Pack, I can't tell you how happy I am that you've started getting to know the kids. I have so many questions for you. Maybe after dinner we can—"

She doesn't get the rest of the sentence out, because Matt is on it. She's only delayed the inevitable. "We spent the whole afternoon hanging out," he says. "You can do the get-to-know-you stuff without us. How about you explain why we didn't know we had another cousin? Or that you have a sister?"

Aunt Reggie frowns. Uncle Mike starts to say something, but she shushes him. "No, hon, it's okay. Matty's right. We do have some explaining to do."

"This ought to be good," Matt mutters, and this time Uncle Mike doesn't hold back.

"You asked the question, so now you'll let your mother talk, and you'll listen. Respectfully." I guess some of those lines are frown lines after all.

"Fine," Matt says. "Whatever."

Aunt Reggie turns to me. "Pack, you have to understand, this is a very complicated situation. We have a lot to discuss, if you don't have to run off—we have a guest room and we'd love to have you stay."

"Stay!" Mia shouts.

This is all the encouragement I need. I don't love the idea of driving home in the dark, and I looked up some inexpensive motels in the area, but it's cheaper to stay here. And more fun.

"I'm so pleased." Aunt Reggie looks at Matt and Mia. "Kids, I'm sorry we didn't tell you about Pack and his mom. We didn't mean to lie, but we thought it would be confusing for you. To be honest, it's quite confusing for me as well. Now, I know you want to know everything right away, but I'm going to need a little time to think about how best to explain all this and it seems only fair that I talk to Pack first."

Matt's about to interrupt, and I don't think whatever he's about to say will make his parents happy, so I jump in first. "I don't mind if everyone hears. We all want to know the same things."

"That may well be true, and I appreciate your openness, Pack, but not all parts of the story are necessarily appropriate for everyone." She's clearly talking about Mia, who's more than smart enough to figure that out.

"You're not going to say I'm too young, are you? You know I hate when you say that. I'm old enough to get married in some countries."

"Well, you'd need an appropriate suitor first, and parental consent," Aunt Reggie says. "And besides, the fact that you're old enough to do something doesn't mean it's a good idea. Do you remember when I let you read whatever books you wanted when you were little, and you gave yourself night-mares with that book about the pets that came back to life after they died? Was it a good idea for me to let you do that?"

"Yes it was, because I learned to set limits even when I read above my age level." Mia crosses her arms over her chest, secure in the knowledge she's scored a solid point.

Aunt Reggie groans. "I don't know why I ever try to argue with you. Mia, you're going to have to let me sleep on it. I will tell you as much as I deem appropriate, but it might not be the same time I talk to Pack. Can you give me that time to think?" She asks in a way that indicates she'll really listen to the answer, like if Mia says no she'll come up with some-thing else. But Mia nods reluctantly; they've obviously had conversations like this before. "Now, I do want a few minutes alone with Pack. Mike, how about you take the kids out for ice cream, once they're done with the dishes, and I can show him around?"

He nods as Mia squeals and Matt scowls. It's very clear who's in charge in this house. I wonder whether it would have been like that in my house, had my mother been around.

Aunt Reggie gets up and gestures to me to follow her upstairs, giving me a little house tour as we go. "You've already seen the kitchen and the living room, and appar-ently you spent half the day in the basement. Such a shame on a beautiful day like this. The master bedroom and bath are on the main floor as well. Up here is kid territory, which means I can't vouch for how any of it looks or smells. I don't go upstairs unless I have to." She says it with a laugh, but I'm not sure she's kidding.

I become convinced she's serious when we peek into Matt's room, which is basically a replica of his car, with sports equipment and workout clothes all over the place. It smells like the car, too, with an overlay of body spray. Mia's room is much more orderly, all spotless and primary colors and right angles. Even the books on her shelf are organized by color, giving it a kind of rainbow effect.

My aunt leads me down the hall to a small room with light-colored walls, a double bed with a navy comforter, a plaid armchair in the corner, and a simple wooden dresser. It's small and neat and perfect. "This is your room, Pack. For as long as you want it. We're so happy to have you here. I know I keep saying that, but it's true."

"I'm happy too," I say. And I mean it, but some other feelings besides happiness are starting to creep in. Along with more questions, like if she's so glad to see me, why didn't she seek me out earlier? Why did she wait for me to find her?

Aunt Reggie looks at me intently. "Are you sure? Is everything okay?"

I'm not used to someone watching me so closely, especially not someone who can so easily tell how other people are feeling. I want a good start with her; I don't want to ask all the hard questions so soon. Especially not before she's told me everything I want to know about my mother. "I'm fine," I say. "I just broke up with my girlfriend a couple of days ago, and I guess I'm still kind of dealing with that."

"Oh, honey," she says, and wraps me in another hug. Two hugs in one day—it must be some kind of record for me. "I'm so sorry. Breakups are just terrible, aren't they?"

I nod into her shoulder. I feel guilty using Maddie as an excuse to avoid talking about what's really bothering me, but it's not like I've somehow gotten over the breakup, either. Just mentioning it brings everything back, that wave of guilt and anger mixed with a strange humiliation, like getting goaded into dumping Maddie is some kind of embarrassing personal failure. It's hard to explain, even to myself. But being here does make me feel better, even if it's only as a distraction.

Aunt Reggie lets me go and pats my arm a couple of times. "I know it seems like the pain and sadness of this will last forever, but I promise those feelings will fade. They won't disappear for a long time, but someday you'll be able to look back on the time you spent together and remember the good things, and think about what you both learned from one another, and the bad feelings won't be the ones that dominate. It may take a while, but you'll get there."

"I hope so." I want to believe her, but she doesn't know me and Maddie.

"When did it happen?" she asks.

"This weekend." It feels like minutes but also years, in a weird way.

"Is that what made you decide to come?"

It kind of is, but not necessarily in the way Aunt Reggie might think. There's an easier way to explain it. "Partly. But really it's because I got this letter. From my mother."

Aunt Reggie's head draws back in shock. "She wrote to you? That's surprising."

"Well, it was definitely surprising to me. I didn't even know she was alive. It's all been really confusing."

"I can imagine," she says. "How about we go downstairs and I make us some tea—do you drink tea?—and you can tell me all about you. I know I said we'd talk about your mother, but I do need to get my thoughts together, so perhaps we could do that tomorrow. Tonight I'd like to get to know you a little better. Does that sound okay?"

As much as I want to know the story, I respect that it makes sense for her to want some time. She's been so cool about the fact that I just showed up here out of nowhere; the least I can do is give her one night. "Sounds good to me," I say, and follow her back downstairs.

13

I stay up with Aunt Reggie until well after midnight, which, for someone who's usually up before six, is practically like pulling an all-nighter. It helps that she makes us black tea—it has way more caffeine in it than I realized, so I start feeling a little buzzy.

But really I'm able to stay awake because Aunt Reggie is so easy to talk to. She's curious about me and wants to hear everything I'm willing to tell her; I see where Mia got her whole tell-me-your-life thing. She knows how to ask the right questions, and I find myself blabbing away about everything—the breakup, my lack of plans, how Dad wants me to go to college but I'm not sure. I can tell she's being careful to skirt topics that might lead to my mother, like how she doesn't ask too much about Dad other than to follow up on things I said. We spend most of the time talking about Maddie, anyway. Even though I'm here to learn about my mother, Maddie's still basically the only thing on my mind.

I want to know more about Aunt Reggie, too, but she's good at deflecting questions away from herself. Instead, she tells me more about my cousins. Matt left out more than just his interest in guys; he doesn't really need a baseball scholarship to go to college. Aunt Reggie wants him to go to Yale, but he thinks that's too close to home. "He must be really smart," I say. Even I've heard of Yale.

"He is," she says. "They both are, in their own ways."

I tell her how much I like Mia, and how glad I am that she likes me. "She's a special girl," Aunt Reggie says. "Making friends has been one of her challenges—not everyone can see what makes her so wonderful. I'm glad you can."

It doesn't seem that hard to me, but then again, the world is full of judgmental assholes. Not that I say that to my aunt. I'm not used to watching my language except at school, but I don't want her thinking I'm some kind of degenerate.

We finally call it a night when Aunt Reggie catches my eyelids drooping—I've practically fallen asleep sitting up. "It's been a long day for you, hasn't it?" she asks, and I know she's referring to more than just how long I've been awake. "We'll plan on talking tomorrow night. You okay to hang out with Matt tomorrow? Mia will be at camp again."

"No problem," I say.

As tired as I am, I have a hard time falling asleep. I can count on one hand the number of nights I've spent not in my own bed, and it feels so strange being in someone else's house. Not to mention that I'm still not used to ending the night without talking to Maddie, or texting her. I haven't checked in with Dad, either, though I don't know that he'd expect me to, if I were really where I said I'd be. My brain keeps bouncing between Maddie and Dad and what I might learn about my mother tomorrow until all my thoughts blur together and I finally conk out.

I wake up to the sun shining through the curtains. It's just before six, when I usually get up, so I guess my body doesn't care that I've barely slept. I open the guest-room door as quietly as I can and tiptoe down the hall to see if anyone else is up. Unsurprisingly, I'm alone.

I decide my best plan is to get in a workout, so I slip out the front door, get in the truck, and check my phone for a public park. There's one not too far away, and the park's empty when I get there, with a running track, which is perfect. I spread a mat on a patch of grass inside the track so I can do some rounds of push-ups, sit-ups, and squats before getting in a run. I push myself hard, something I usually find difficult without other people cheering me on, but I need the energy today. Even the running, which I usually hate, is helpful; I go faster than usual so I can clear my head, which is still spinning from all the different thoughts swirling around. I run until my lungs ache and I can practically feel the lactic acid building up in my legs, and I don't slow down until I can't breathe. I jog for a while then walk to cool down, and by the time I'm done it's nearly seven, so my aunt and uncle are probably up, even if the cousins are sleeping in.

If I were a better person, I'd probably go find some bagels or doughnuts or something, but I don't have a ton of money on me and I've been away from that stuff for so long I probably wouldn't know what to order. Besides, maybe everyone is still sleeping and they won't even realize I've been gone.

It becomes obvious how untrue this is when I open the front door. Everyone's awake and in the living room, talking at the same time, but their voices aren't loud enough to drown out the sound of my aunt. Sobbing.

"What happened?" I ask. Has someone died? Am I going to miss meeting a family member by just one day? That seems too unfair to be real.

Aunt Reggie runs over to me and grabs me so hard I think she'll knock the breath right out of me. "You're here!" She's still crying, but she doesn't let me go.

I feel bad—I probably stink after that workout, but she doesn't seem to care. "Of course I'm here. I just went to get a run in. Is everything okay?"

"She's crying because she thought you left," Mia informs me as Aunt Reggie sniffles into my shoulder. "She thought you were mad she didn't tell you about your mom yesterday and that you left and were never coming back."

Now I feel worse than bad. I squeeze Aunt Reggie a little

tighter and then let go, hoping she'll take the hint that I kind of need to be done with the hug now. She gets it and pulls back, wiping her eyes. "You must think I'm so ridiculous," she says. "But after you finding us, the thought of losing you again was just too much."

It doesn't quite make sense to me, especially given that I'd been wondering about how she never reached out to me in the first place. But maybe that's all part of the story. "I'm sorry," I say. "I'm not used to anyone noticing me coming and going—Dad usually works out with me, or else he's sleeping or at work when I get up. It didn't occur to me anyone would notice I was gone. I didn't mean to cause trouble."

"Don't worry about it," Uncle Mike says. "Your aunt's just a little sensitive right now. I'm sure you understand."

I mean, I don't exactly, but whatever. "Sure." Now that I'm not being smothered in the hug, I notice that Uncle Mike and Aunt Reggie are all dressed for work, but Matt and Mia are still in pajamas. Matt just has on a ratty T-shirt and shorts, but Mia has a matching outfit with rainbows and unicorns on it, which seems fitting.

"I promise I'm not usually like this," Aunt Reggie says. She's calmer now, if a little sniffly.

"It's true," Matt says. "I don't think I've ever seen her cry before."

"We're not big criers around here," Mia says. "Dad's the only one who cries a lot."

Now Aunt Reggie is smiling. I can't tell whether Mia ratted out Uncle Mike to make Aunt Reggie happy or if it's just a coincidence, but I'm inclined to think she did it on purpose. She's a smart one, that Mia. And a lot like her mom.

"I do get a little emotional," Uncle Mike admits.

"Yeah, at the really important stuff," Matt says. "Like TV commercials."

"And pretty much all family events," Mia adds.

"What can I say? Family is important to me." Uncle Mike seems unfazed by how hard his kids are selling him out.

"Don't forget movies," Aunt Reggie says. "I can hardly take him anywhere. And if *Beaches* or *Terms of Endearment* ever comes on TV, just forget it."

"Gone too far," Uncle Mike says.

"And *Steel Magnolias*," she says.

Everyone's laughing now. I've stumbled into a long-running family joke. I'm not sure whether to feel left out or included.

"What about you, Pack?" Mia asks. "Do you get weepy at sad things?"

I shake my head. Dad and I are both pretty stoic. But then again, nothing that bad has happened to me. Even the breakup with Maddie makes me more angry than sad, though I suppose the sadness will kick in eventually. "I can't remember the last time I cried. Maybe when I was little?" I had a neighbor who was into bike stunts and taught me to power skid by braking into a pile of dirt and then swinging the bike around. The first time I tried it I skinned my knees pretty bad, and with all that dirt, it stung something awful. I'm sure I sobbed like a baby then.

"Well, then, you're like us," Mia says.

With that, warmth washes over me. I'm one of them. I like it.

"Reggie, we should get going," Uncle Mike says. "If we leave any later, traffic will be a nightmare."

Aunt Reggie touches my arm, as if to confirm I'm still there. "You go on without me. I'm going to call in. I'm sure Pack's anxious to talk about his mother, and I'm obviously a nervous wreck. I'd be useless at work anyway."

Uncle Mike doesn't seem too surprised at this. He nods, gives her a kiss, and heads out the door.

"Can I stay home from camp, too?" Mia asks. "Please?"

"I don't think that's such a good idea," Aunt Reggie says. "Matt got up just to take you, and you know how much he loves to sleep in. If it turns out to be for nothing, who knows what he'd do?" She keeps her voice light, but there's an undercurrent of nervousness there. Maybe Mia's someone who throws fits when she's angry. Maybe Matt's not the only one who yells.

Mia grits her teeth. Something's about to happen, and I don't want it to. I don't want to lose that warm feeling. "I promise I'll tell you everything when you get home," I say, and try to silently telegraph to Aunt Reggie that I'll edit out whatever Mia shouldn't hear. "I won't keep secrets from you."

"You promise?" Mia looks uncertain, but it sounds like she's willing to give me the benefit of the doubt, even if I haven't earned it yet.

"I swear." I hold up my right hand and hover my left hand in front of me as if placed on an invisible Bible.

It takes a second for Mia to give the okay, but Aunt Reggie's sigh of relief is audible. "Wonderful. Now that that's settled, I'm going to change out of my work clothes into something more comfortable. Mia, you go get ready for camp. Matt, please tell me you're not going to drive her there in whatever it is you've got on right now. Pack, there's a pot of coffee brewing in the kitchen, and I didn't know what you liked for breakfast so I left out all the cereal. There are hard-boiled eggs in the fridge, or I can make you some oatmeal once I've changed. Whatever you like."

"Eggs and coffee are perfect." I say. Thank god there's more than just cereal.

They all go off to their rooms to change, and I go into the kitchen to get some food and decompress from what just happened. So much emotion—Aunt Reggie went from crying about me being gone to laughing about Uncle Mike and his movie sobbing in the space of what, five minutes? It's not what I'm used to, that's for sure.

Neither is the coffee. I don't know what kind of fancy

stuff they drink in this house, but it's about a thousand times better than the Maxwell House we brew at home, and at least a hundred times better than the Starbucks I splurge on every once in a while. I'm not usually crazy about hard-boiled eggs, but I'm starving after that run and I'm on my third one when Aunt Reggie comes back into the kitchen, dressed in jeans and a pink shirt. She pours herself a cup of coffee and sits down with me.

"Egg fan, are you?" She points to the pile of shells on the paper towel in front of me.

"Am I eating too many?" I suppose it's too late to stop, but still.

She laughs. "Eat as many as you want. We go through three cartons a week around here."

Mia and Matt come running down the stairs, Mia in jeans and a rainbow unicorn shirt that isn't pajamas, Matt in a version of the workout clothes I saw him in yesterday. "You hitting the gym on the way back?" Aunt Reggie asks.

Matt looks over at me, then back at her. "Oh, so I'm not going to be part of this conversation either? Great. Come on, Mia." He blows out the door so fast I don't have time to say anything. Mia just shrugs and follows him.

"That went well," Aunt Reggie says after they're both gone. "He's pretty upset with me. I suppose I can understand that. We've talked a lot about honesty in this family, and now he sees me as a hypocrite. Which is somewhat true."

I want to tell her it isn't, to say something to make her feel better, but what do I know? "We're big on honesty too, me and my dad. But he didn't tell me about my mother. He even let me think she was dead up until recently. I was mad too."

"How long did it take you to get over it?"

"I'm not sure I have," I admit. "That's one of the reasons I came here. I was so frustrated with him. I wanted to know the truth. Can you—will you—?" I'm not even sure what to ask.

"I'll tell you what I know, and I'll be as honest as I can," she says. "But I don't know the whole story, and I don't know what your dad's told you, so I don't know if we see things the same way."

"I get that. I just don't think he told me the truth. But I didn't think the letter was real either, at first, so I guess I don't really trust my own judgment right now."

She nods. "I know that feeling. Do you think it would be possible for me to read the letter? That might give me a good place to start."

"Sure." I've still got my backpack with me from working out—I haven't even gone upstairs to change, myself—and I get it out of the front pocket and hand it to her.

Aunt Reggie takes the letter out of the envelope carefully, as if it's something she could break. I like that—she knows how important it is to me, and that matters to her. I watch her read and remember how I watched Maddie read, too. There's no shock on Aunt Reggie's face like there had been on Maddie's, though, no real surprise. She purses her lips a little, but that's about it. When she's done, she folds up the piece of paper and puts it back in the envelope as delicately as she took it out, then hands it back to me.

"Natalie put a lot of time into that," she says. "She never used to care so much about words."

That's not what I expected her to say, but then again, I didn't expect anything in particular.

"When did you get this?"

"On my birthday, about a week ago. She sent it to school so Dad wouldn't see it. That's the part I don't understand." I pause. "No, that's not right. There are like a million parts I don't understand."

"I'll see what I can do to help," Aunt Reggie says. "Now that I've seen the letter, I'm guessing you came here hoping I could tell you where your mother is, and I don't want to leave you in suspense. I don't have the answer to that question, Pack. I don't know where she is. I haven't seen her in over fifteen years."

"Most of my life."

She nods. "Not just me, either. That's how long it's been since anyone in this family has seen her, or talked to her. As far as we were concerned, she may as well have died back then, just like your father led you to believe. Your mother— she had a lot of problems, and we tried for a long time to help her, but at a certain point she went too far, and we had to let her go. It was hard, but we didn't really have a choice." She looks down. "This is so hard to talk about. It's been years since I tried. I hope you'll bear with me."

I'll do whatever it takes to get the whole story. "What did she do, though? What could be so bad her whole family would cut her off?"

Aunt Reggie looks back up, right into my eyes, and then she says something I couldn't possibly have predicted. "She kidnapped you."

14

"She did what?" I ask. I can't have heard her right.

"She took you away from your father and tried to leave the country. She got caught before she could leave, and—" Aunt Reggie stops herself. "Let me back up. Maybe this wasn't the best place to start."

I feel like she's just dropped a bomb on me, but that doesn't mean it was a bad place to start. It does mean Dad's done a whole lot more lying than I thought.

"This is going to be harder than I imagined." Aunt Reggie stands up and starts pacing around the kitchen. "It helps me to walk while I think." Another thing I bet she has in common with Mia.

I want to say it's fine, that I understand, but I need her to keep talking and I don't know what to say to make that happen. "Please. It doesn't have to be in order. I just need to know whatever you can tell me."

Aunt Reggie stops pacing long enough to pour us both more coffee. As if lacking energy is really the problem. Then she sits back down and drums her fingers on the table until I want to put my hand over hers to make it stop. She takes a deep breath and starts over. "Your mom—Natalie—we never really got along. She was a tough kid, always getting into trouble, and she was still young when she got into drugs. She'd been going out with a boy who played hockey—everyone thought the Bruins were going to draft him—but he got injured, and the doctors prescribed OxyContin. Long story short, he developed a problem and got Natalie into it too, and it didn't take long for them to switch from Oxy to heroin."

That makes sense. Oxy is crazy expensive, and Tom's told me all about how bad the problem in Brooksby used to be before he took over as Brooksby's unofficial drug czar.

"Her boyfriend didn't make it—he died of an overdose not long after it became clear his hockey career was over. They wrote an article about him in *Sports Illustrated*, using his story to talk about drug problems among athletes. His death really scared Natalie, enough for her to quit. At least for a while."

So far, nothing she's telling me contradicts anything Dad said. I'm getting details now, but the stories line up. I wait to hear where the shift will happen, where his lies begin.

"She started seeing your father during junior year, when she'd been off the drugs for a while. They got serious fast, and by senior year they had it all planned out: your dad would follow in his father's footsteps and go to the police academy, while Natalie would go to Holy Cross—she'd gotten a full scholarship. She was always smart, and once she was done with the drugs, she could concentrate on school. After college, they'd get married. My parents weren't thrilled about her marrying someone who wasn't Italian, but at least he was Catholic, so they were on board."

"So they were, like, together?" I ask. "For real?" I've uncovered the first big Dad lie—my mother wasn't just some hookup—and now I have an explanation for the ring.

"Very much so," Aunt Reggie says. "They were head over heels for each other. We all thought it was crazy for them to be so sure about their future, especially with Natalie going off to school, but they insisted they knew what they were doing. At first everything seemed to be going according to plan, but the summer between your mom's freshman and sophomore years of college, she got pregnant. It wasn't as scandalous as it could have been, though the family might have handled things a little better if they'd gotten married as soon as they found out. Your dad wanted to, but Natalie wanted a big fancy wedding like I'd recently had, and she refused to have one while she was pregnant. She said we'd all have to wait. She did agree to baptize you, so my parents calmed down a little."

I wait for her to continue, but she gets up from the table

again and leaves the room. I'm not sure whether to follow her, but I don't have to think long before she comes back, holding a photo album. How retro. She places it on the table between us and starts flipping through it, stopping first on a page where my very young father is wearing a suit and standing next to the girl from the yearbook photo, who's wearing a red dress to go with that dark red lipstick. "Prom," Aunt Reggie says. "Or maybe one of those other dances. Who can remember, these days?"

They're both smiling so wide it looks like it hurts. "I've never seen a picture of her before," I say. It's not true, but she doesn't know I've seen the yearbook photo, and she doesn't need to. Yearbook photos aren't the truth. They don't say anything about who you really are. Mine is almost unrecognizable to me, and my mother's has that same overly posed quality. This photo is real. This is her young and happy and in love. My dad, too. Honestly, they look kind of like me and Maddie. What could have changed so radically that Dad would pretend it never happened?

My aunt turns the page to photos of a baptism. I groan. "I'm guessing the kid in the white frilly dress is me?" It's embarrassing, really, but that's not the strangest part. It's the fact of the baptism itself. Sure, we're Catholic; I went to CCD with all the other kids, but only until First Communion. We never go to church, but there's Dad, holding me next to my mother as a priest flicks water on my head.

There are a ton of photos, both at the church and the after-party, or whatever you call the party that follows a baptism. Aunt Reggie points out all the friends and family members who are there; it's the first time I've ever seen a photo of my grandparents. My grandmother—Nonna, as Matt calls her—is elegant, dark haired like her daughters, wearing a navy suit with little crystals around the collar. My grandfather is pretty much her height, which is adorable, and they're looking at me with so much love in their eyes it's hard to imagine they'd ever have let me go.

"Your grandparents are very eager to meet you," Aunt Reggie says. "I don't know how long you can stay, but I called my mother as soon as I heard you were here, and she'd like to have a dinner for you. We usually all get together Sunday afternoon."

"I don't think I can stay that long," I say. "I start work Monday morning."

"Where are you working?"

"At the gym." I can tell she wants to know more, but I really want to get back to the story.

She gets it, because she doesn't press me further. "I'll talk to her about moving it up. I'm sure she won't mind. I think she started cooking as soon as I hung up the phone. She's a wonderful cook—she makes old-school Italian food, recipes that have been in my family for years. Sound good?"

Italian food? Like, pasta? I briefly contemplate making up a gluten allergy, but I don't want to lie. And I don't want to be rude and not eat homemade food. "I kind of don't really eat carbs, and some other stuff," I admit.

"Oh, half of us are off carbs these days, so we've cut way back on the pasta. She makes lots of protein too, so we'll figure something out." She closes the photo album. "But you want to know the rest, I'm sure. This is where it gets confusing, so I'll do my best, but I don't know all the details."

"Whatever you can tell me," I say, relieved to be off the topic of food.

"Okay. So after you were born, things were good for a while. Your mother loved being home, taking care of you—I don't know if she even planned to go back to college at all. The family was closer than we'd been in years. I was already living here, and I'd recently had Matty, but he was a good baby, and it was an easy drive to come home and see her. Then one day your father called and said Natalie wasn't at home and asked if I'd heard from her. He'd come home from work and the two of you were gone, and some of your things were missing, including Max."

"Max?"

"Your stuffed monkey? You wouldn't go anywhere without it. You loved when I read *Where the Wild Things Are* to you, and you'd started calling your Curious George monkey Max."

Funny that even as a kid I shied away from curious things. "How old was I?"

"Maybe two? Barely, even. I thought maybe she'd just taken you for a drive, but then he said there was a suitcase missing too, and some of her clothes. She'd left him, and he had no idea why."

I've found another Dad lie—he said she died soon after I was born, but even if he really did think she passed away, we'd had years together first. As a family. "Did you know why?" I ask.

She shakes her head. "I didn't have a clue. They seemed so happy. Your mom had even started planning the big wedding she wanted; she decided to wait until you were old enough to be ring bearer, since she thought having you walk down the aisle would be so cute. To this day, I have no idea what prompted her to leave."

"How long was I gone?"

"That's the thing," she says. "I suppose it helped that your dad was on the force, because as soon as he figured out she was really gone, he told his boss and they caught her almost immediately, at the airport. She was getting ready to leave the country. She had passports for the two of you, and tickets to Italy—she'd tracked down some family we still have there. But there were also drugs in her suitcase. A lot of them. I don't know whether she was back to using herself, or whether she was going to sell them, but the drugs changed everything. She was arrested for kidnapping and intent to distribute, and they could have brought in the Feds because she planned to leave the United States, but before they could do it she agreed to plead guilty."

"I don't understand," I say. I'm not even sure which part I'm referring to.

"We don't either," she says. "But she refused to explain, or even to talk to us about it. Nonna and Poppa wanted to get her a lawyer, but she said she didn't want one. She had a public defender negotiate the deal, and while I don't know all the details, I know she ended up in prison way out in western Mass, and she refused to see us. She turned you over to your dad. Nonna and Poppa wanted to sue for custody, but the lawyer told them they'd lose."

"Why would she take me away from my dad only to give me back and never see me again?" I ask.

"We've been trying to figure that out for years. The only explanation we could come up with was that she was using again and the drugs were affecting her thought process. We tried talking to your dad—we thought we had a good enough relationship with him—but he wouldn't see any of us. He even took out a restraining order against us, which meant we couldn't see you, either."

"He did what?" That doesn't sound like him at all. Though

it does explain why the family never reached out to me. If the choice was between me and not going to jail, it wasn't really a choice at all.

"He thought we'd helped her," Aunt Reggie says. "I admit I hated him for that for a long time, but eventually I came to understand. He was terrified of losing you, and he knew Nonna and Poppa were thinking about the custody suit. Nonna's never forgiven him, but I have."

This isn't the story I wanted to hear. We've traveled so far from what Dad told me it's like we're on a different planet now. So many things seem wrong, not least of which is what I'm learning about Dad, both the lying and the fact that he's the one who's kept me from the family for so long. The only thing that makes me feel better is how all Dad's actions sound like they were meant to protect me. But that only makes me feel worse, because it convinces me that Aunt Reggie's story is true.

"We thought maybe someday your mother would explain, but we never heard from her, even after her prison term ended. We still don't know where she is, and I have to be honest—now that we have you, I don't care if we ever hear from her again. It's hard to believe someone I'm related to, someone I grew up with, could do something so awful as to take a child away from his family, and I can't let that go."

We've come full circle. I came here to find my mother, and the first thing Aunt Reggie told me was that she didn't know where she was. Now that she's told me everything, I know that not only is she not going to be able to help me, she wouldn't want to. I can't blame her.

I'm not sure I want to find her myself. Not anymore.

15

Aunt Reggie leaves it to me to decide what I want her to tell Matt and Mia. I say I need some time to think and go outside, promising I'll come back. I wish I hadn't worked out already; as much as I hate running, sometimes it helps to clear my head. I went too hard this morning, though, and I'm too sore to do anything but walk. But walking's better than driving.

The sky is overcast now, but it's still nice out, with a breeze blowing and the smell of flowers in the air. Maddie would probably recognize the scent, but I have no clue. I wonder what Maddie would think of Aunt Reggie's story, what she'd tell me if I explained all the different things I'm feeling. As I walk, I pretend she's here, and in my head I tell her everything. How I'm mad now that I know how much Dad lied, even though he did it for me; how angry I am that I've missed out on this family for so long; how I'm no longer sure looking for my mother is such a good idea.

I want to talk to Maddie so bad it's all I can do not to get out my phone and call her. But if I do that, I have to apologize and hope she'll forgive me and we'll be back in the same place we were when I left. If she even agrees to talk to me in the first place. Nothing will be different, and everything will be terrible. I can't go back to her until I can tell her something new about me, about who I am. Something she didn't know. Something that will make her see me differently. All I have now are new facts, and that's not the same thing.

If calling's not an option, at least I can try to imagine what she'd say, if we were still us and I could still ask for help. She probably wouldn't be quite as forgiving of Dad as I'm inclined to be, though maybe she'd think now's the time to tell him about the letter. She'd probably be as excited as I am about this new family; I bet she'd like Mia, too. Would she still think I should try to find my mother? I have no idea.

I know I have to stop thinking about Maddie and figure out how I feel about all of this myself, but it's so hard. I miss her so much, and even though my aunt's story answers a lot of my questions, it raises so many more I don't even know what to do.

I haven't kept track of where I'm going, and all of a sudden it's clear that I'm lost. I try to recall which houses I passed, how many turns I've taken, but nothing stands out. There are lots of houses that look like my aunt's, big and white with two stories, but there are others, too—some made almost entirely out of brick, some that are only one story but longer, lots painted blue and gray, all nicer than what I'm used to seeing in Brooksby, except maybe some of the houses in Maddie's neighborhood.

All my thoughts keep coming back to her.

I'm just about to get out my phone and map my way back to the Lombardis' when a car rolls up next to me. Matt. "Mom said you were wandering around the neighborhood," he says. "Come hang out with me and my friends. We're going to get some food."

Food? I have no sense of how much time has passed. I look at my phone and see that it's past noon. "Sure," I say, though I'm not necessarily in the mood to meet more people. Still, it's better than going back to the house to do more thinking. My head can't take it.

I get in the front seat, and Matt takes off before I've fastened my seat belt. He drives like someone who hasn't had a car very long, or who doesn't have a cop for a dad who swears none of his friends will let me off if I get pulled over. "So, you talked to my mom," he says, trying to sound casual and completely failing.

"Yeah, it's all kind of nuts." I glance over to see him watching me instead of driving. He wants to know what's up, and though I said I'd wait for Mia, I decide to give him the short version. "Basically my mom kidnapped me and got busted with a bunch of drugs. She was in prison for a while and no one knows where she is. Sounds like they don't want to know, either."

Thank god we're deep in the suburbs with no one around, because Matt swerves so hard I think he's going to hit a car in someone's driveway. He gets it together enough to say, "That's seriously fucked up," then starts driving slower, which is a relief.

"You don't have to tell me."

"Did Mom tell you why she never told us about her? Or you?"

I don't want to tell him that he and Mia weren't exactly the focus of our conversation. "We didn't get too far into it. She said she'd talk to you guys later on."

He frowns—my answer isn't what he hoped to hear, though I can't imagine what I could say that would help. "We'll see. So are you, like, okay with all this? Do you still want to find her?"

"I don't know," I say. "I mean, I figured the story wouldn't be good, whatever it was. I need to think about it." What I don't say, but what I'm starting to realize, is that I feel kind of bad for my mom. Not that stealing me and running off with a bunch of drugs should inspire a pity party, but something must have made her run, right? Aunt Reggie made it sound like she and my dad were happy, and then she'd just taken off—there must have been a reason, and instead of finding out what it was, everyone gave up on her. Dad was even willing to believe she was dead. It's possible I don't need someone like her in my life, but she reached out, and there's still so much I want to know.

Matt pulls onto the highway, and we travel a few exits before getting off in downtown New Haven. He parks near a pizza place with a huge line in front, and my stomach turns over—how am I supposed to explain that I don't eat pizza? Not to mention the smell coming out of the place is amazing and I kind of want some.

Two guys wave at us from the front of the line, and Matt waves back as we walk up to join them. I thought he'd hang out with jocks who look like him, but these guys definitely aren't jocks. One is a white guy, basketball-player tall and the skinniest dude I've ever seen, with no muscle tone at all and a light-brown ponytail. The other is black, about my height, with glasses and a Yankees T-shirt, something I can't let go undiscussed as a proper Red Sox fan.

Matt introduces me as his cousin; the tall guy is Devon and the short guy is Parker, which both sound like rich-kid names to me. "Nice to meet you," I say. "But isn't Connecticut still part of New England? How am I supposed to eat lunch with someone wearing that?" I gesture at Parker's shirt and hope he knows I'm just messing around.

"Pack's from Massachusetts," Matt explains. "He hasn't learned how to behave outside the Boston area."

"That's true," I admit.

"No worries," Parker says. "I'm not a huge fan. It's just a T-shirt."

Just a T-shirt? If anyone I knew heard someone talk about baseball that way, it's more than possible the day would end in a fight. I pretend to understand. "Are they not your team?" I ask.

"Nah, I'm just not that into sports," he says.

"He's all about politics," Devon says. "I'm surprised he's not wearing some fancy model United Nations swag."

"Is that a thing?" I ask, and they all start laughing. What? No one I know is into that stuff. It could have been real.

The line moves slowly, but the guys are easy to talk to, and I get to know them a little as we wait for a table. Devon wasn't kidding about Parker and politics—apparently he's Student Council president and planning to apply early to Georgetown to study political science so he can run for office one day. I was right that Devon isn't a jock either; he's about to leave for some pre-pre-med summer camp.

"You mean you're going to school in the summer?" I ask. "Voluntarily?"

"It's not as bad as it sounds," Devon says. "It's on a college campus. There'll be classes and stuff, but also sessions on what colleges to apply for so I have the best shot at getting into a good med school. There will also be girls, and not a whole lot of supervision." Devon is clearly at least as excited about the girls-and-no-supervision part as he is about the med-school-prep part.

We finally get our table, and I scan the menu for something, anything other than pizza. The guys don't need to look—they grab a waiter quick and ask for an extra-large clam pizza, which sounds beyond disgusting. "I'll have a green salad, no cheese," I say.

The table falls silent.

"Matt, did you not tell Pack where we are?" Parker asks. "This is Pepe's Pizza. It's famous. The clam pizza is even more famous. There are no options when you eat here. No *salads*." He says the word like I ordered garbage dressed with poison. He'll make a great politician, I think, visiting all those local joints that serve weird food, like loose-meat sandwiches and fried Twinkies.

"Yeah, I'm sure putting clams on pizza is totally normal," I say. "But I'm good with salad." Please let it go, I think. I wish I had an easy way to change the subject, and I'm tempted to bring up that guy Aunt Reggie mentioned and tease Matt about it, but I don't know whether he's out to his friends, or whether that's something they joke about.

Devon shakes his head. "You have so much to learn, young Jedi. But fear you must not. Teach you we will."

Oh, lord, they're into Star Wars. The guys eat their disgusting-looking clam pizza and I eat my sad, mediocre salad and wish I'd asked for chicken on it. They start talking about people at school, and I watch how they talk to one another, how comfortable they are. They've clearly known each other a long time, but they know more than just the facts. Me and the guys I hang with have the basics down, like whose parents are divorced and who drinks in the bathroom at school and thinks no one knows. But we don't know each other like these guys do—they know each other's whole lives, as Mia would say. They make some casual reference to Matt's ex, so I know they talk about that part of his life too.

On the surface, they don't seem all that alike. I'd thought Matt was a typical jock, and Devon is a science nerd, while Parker's one of the good kids—I bet he doesn't party at all so no one has dirt on him when he runs for office. But as they talk, I can see the connections. Like how Devon's not the only Star Wars fan—they make me watch the trailer for the new movie on Parker's phone and obsessively break down everything they know about the movie from those few minutes of video. I've never really gotten into science fiction, though Dad made me watch all the original Star Wars movies way back.

And I've read Matt all wrong. He might play baseball, but he's not a jock. Not the way I think about jocks, anyway. I like his friends, and I like what the fact that they're his friends says about him. What does hanging out with Mike and Sean and those guys say about me? Are they really my friends at all?

The more I think about it, the clearer it becomes that they aren't. Maddie's my only real friend, the only person who knows me the way Devon and Parker obviously know Matt. And that's my own fault, really. The guys tried to include me in stuff, but I wasn't that into spending time with anyone but Maddie. And even if I had been, I can't picture talking to them the way Matt and his friends talk. The fact that they're not all that alike is part of what makes them all so interesting, both to me and, it seems, to each other. Maybe that's why Matt's not nearly as devastated by his breakup as I am about mine—he's got people to help him through it, not just his parents.

Maybe I need friends.

I keep listening quietly. There's not much for me to add when they're mostly talking about their other friends, who I don't know; the conversation soon turns to college, which is when things get a little awkward. When Matt tells Parker I graduated, he asks where I'm going to school in the fall.

"He's not," Matt jumps in. "Can you believe it?"

It's like he told them I'm from another country, or even another planet, though with their Star Wars obsession they'd probably be less surprised if I turned out to be an alien. "It's no big deal," I say. "Lots of people I know aren't going to college." Which is true. Maddie is, sure, and Colin, yuck, but most of the guys aren't.

"I don't know anyone who's not going to college," Devon

says. "My parents would kill me if I even suggested it."

"Mine too," Parker says. "You know what my parents are like. They need me to be ten times as good as everyone else or else they panic."

I can't imagine having two parents, let alone two who put that kind of pressure on me. I bet Parker's pressure is way more intense than Devon's, too, though I know I can't begin to know what his life is like. "Aunt Reggie and Uncle Mike seem pretty laid-back," I say. "Do they ride you hard about college?"

Matt looks puzzled. "I wouldn't describe it like that. But there's never been any question I was going. Getting out of New Haven is the only thing anyone talks about, and college has always been the way out."

"Why would you want to leave?" I ask. "You're all so smart, and Yale is like right down the street. Isn't it one of the best schools in the country?"

"Yale's a great school, but it's practically in my backyard," Devon says. "My parents would come by the dorm just to say hi. And what if I was—" He thrusts his hips back and forth under the table.

"You're such a pig, Devon," Parker says. "No wonder you can't get laid anywhere within a fifty-mile radius of New Haven. Hope band camp treats you better."

"It's science camp, not band camp," Devon protests, totally missing the joke.

"Make sure he leaves the pie at home," I say, and Parker high-fives me. It makes me feel like part of the group. I didn't know how much I'd been missing, though what does it say that all these people I like feel the same way about getting out of New Haven that Maddie does about getting away from Brooksby? Have I been wrong about thinking it would be better for her to stay?

What else have I been wrong about?

16

After lunch, Matt and I go pick Mia up at drama camp and then head back to the house. Aunt Reggie's in the living room, looking through the photo album she showed me that morning. She glances up from it when we come in. "Pack, if you can stay a little longer, my parents would love to have us all over for dinner Thursday night."

That means I could drive home Friday, which would give me the weekend to get ready for work. Plenty of time. And I can't miss a chance to meet the grandparents I only just found out I have.

"Stay!" Mia yells. "Nonna and Poppa make great dinners."

"That would be terrific," I say.

"Wonderful. I'll let them know. And don't worry—there will be plenty that you can eat."

Matt gives me the side-eye, and I know he's thinking

about the pizza. But he doesn't say anything. Instead, he sits on the love seat across from Aunt Reggie. "We're all here now," he says. "Anything you want to talk to us about?"

Aunt Reggie sighs and puts the photo album to the side. "Come sit, Mia." She pats the space on the couch next to her. "Pack, you too."

I sit on her other side and settle in to listen to her explain the situation to Matt and Mia. She tells basically the same story she told me, minus some details about my parents' history and minus most of the stuff about drugs. I've already told Matt a little about that, so I hope he understands that she's editing for Mia's benefit. He seems to; he doesn't interrupt, at least.

It's probably for the best she skipped the drugs, because the kidnapping is already a lot for Mia to handle. "What do you mean, she took Pack? She didn't tell his dad?"

Aunt Reggie shakes her head.

"She can't just do that," Mia says. "That's not right."

"No, it's not," Aunt Reggie says. "Do you understand why we don't talk about her now?"

"No," Mia says. "She's your sister. Even if she did a bad thing, you're supposed to make up. Isn't that what you always tell me and Matty?"

Aunt Reggie looks down at the coffee table, where she's placed the photo album. "You're right," she says quietly. "That is what we tell you two. And we mean it. We expect you kids to work to get along, even if it's sometimes hard. But Mia, sometimes people do things that are so bad it's hard to forgive them, even if they're family. I know that's a difficult thing, and that's why we've never talked about it."

It's starting to make sense to me, too. Mia, smart as she is, seems to understand rules better than exceptions. Matt gets it, though; I watch his face soften as he listens to Aunt Reggie, and I know there isn't going to be any yelling.

"I think you're wrong," Mia says. "I think she's your sister and you should find her and talk to her and make everything better. I bet that's what Pack wants, too."

Leave me out of it, I want to say, but that won't help, and I want to be someone who helps. "I get why your mom doesn't want to talk to my mom," I say. "I'm not sure I want to either."

"How can you not want to talk to her?" Mia asks. "I can't even imagine not having a mom. I know some people who don't have dads, or whose dads don't live with them, like Susie and Peter and . . ." She runs down a list of all the kids she knows whose parents are divorced or whose dads are otherwise gone, but apparently she's never met anyone who doesn't have a mom.

Her question does bring me back to my own: Do I want to meet my mother? Getting to know the Lombardis has definitely made me excited about the idea of meeting more family; I'm super into meeting my grandparents, for sure. My mother's a different story. First she didn't exist, then the letter arrived and I started to think I might want to know her. My dad's story made her sound awful; my aunt's story somehow made her sound even worse. But even though Dad's story is basically made up, while Aunt Reggie's is real, there are still so many questions that only my mother can answer.

Maybe I should meet her. She's my mother, after all.

Thankfully, I don't have to make any decisions right away, except for whether it's time to call my dad. He's left a couple of messages that I've ignored so far, but I don't want to have to lie to him on the phone. Instead, I send a text. **Beach is great. Staying a little longer than I thought. See you over the weekend.** I hope that will be enough to keep him at bay.

The next day I do my morning workouts, hang out with Matt and his friends during the day and Mia in the afternoon, and sit around with the family over dinner and movies we watch on the big TV downstairs. It's comfortable being around them, almost like I've known them for much longer than a couple of days.

To get ready for the Thursday night dinner I shower and make myself as presentable as I can (which isn't all that presentable, given that I only have a backpack full of stuff and it's mostly workout clothes) so we can go to my grandparents' house. It feels weird to even think it—"my grandparents," as if they're something I've always had.

When I come downstairs in my cleanest track pants and

T-shirt, Aunt Reggie gives me an up-and-down look and shakes her head. "Sorry, Pack, but I can't have you meeting your grandparents for the first time looking like that."

I turn to see Matt already downstairs, wearing pressed khaki pants and a button-down shirt. "Oh. Um, I didn't really bring anything else."

"You and Matty are about the same size. I'll find you something of his." She goes upstairs, and I'm not sure whether to follow her, so I hang with Matt.

"Is that okay? Me wearing your stuff?"

He laughs. "These aren't exactly my most treasured possessions. Besides, as much as I hate to admit it, she's right— Nonna and Poppa have a real thing about people dressing for dinner. No need to get you in trouble with them before they have a chance to get to know you."

"They sound kind of scary," I say as Aunt Reggie comes back down, holding a pile of pants in one arm and a pile of shirts in the other. She dumps everything on the couch.

"Pick one of each. Anything will do." She looks down at my sneakers. "What size shoe?"

"Ten," I say.

"That won't work," Matt says. "Unless he stuffs socks in mine."

"The sneakers aren't the worst," she says. "Better pick some black pants, though."

I'm wearing my usual Inov-8s, lightweight black sneakers

with a little bit of white and red. They're not as big as regular sneakers, but they won't pass for dress shoes, either. I hope my grandparents won't automatically hate me. I find a pair of pants that look like they'll be long enough to cover the tops of the sneakers and choose a striped shirt that looks almost like Matt's.

I run upstairs to change, then come back down so Aunt Reggie can evaluate me. Oddly enough, I'm almost looking forward to it. The only person who ever notices what I'm wearing is Maddie. I wonder what she's doing right now. Probably working at the restaurant where she waitresses—the night shift is busy, especially over the summer.

"Not bad," Aunt Reggie says. She glances over at Matt, and then at Uncle Mike, who came down while I was getting dressed. He's wearing olive pants and a striped shirt. The three of us basically look the same. We definitely look related.

Mia thumps downstairs in a denim skirt and a sweater and shirt that are the same color purple, hands clenched into fists at her sides. Uh-oh. "I don't see why they get to wear pants and I don't."

"Because you're young and your grandparents are old and it's much easier for you to do what makes them happy than it is to try and change them," Aunt Reggie says. "Besides, you look adorable. And I'm wearing a dress, so we're in the same boat."

Even I know the word "adorable" isn't going to help matters any. And Aunt Reggie looks so comfortable and happy in her dress that there's no way they're sharing a boat. "You look really nice, Mia," I say. "If Matt had a skirt, I'd wear one with you."

Her eyes widen. "You don't mean that."

"Probably not," I agree. "But it's funny to think about, right?"

She giggles. Uncle Mike watches our exchange with a smile. "We should get going, kids."

We all pile into their SUV. Mia sits between me and Matt in the back, and I listen as they fight about who gets to plug in their phone and play music. Finally, I say, "If you guys can't choose, I will," and grab the jack to plug in my phone. That's how we end up listening to Chance the Rapper all the way to my grandparents' house. I play the song about his grandma, which would have been even more fitting if it were Sunday, the day they usually have dinner. It's still nice, all of us together, listening to something they'd never have heard if it wasn't for me.

My grandparents live on the edge of New Haven proper, where the houses are a little older and smaller and the cars aren't quite as nice. It kind of reminds me of Brooksby. I hang back as everyone goes inside, waiting a minute before I meet these new people. The house is warm and smells incredible, all tomato sauce and garlic, and the scent only gets stronger as Aunt Reggie hustles me into the kitchen.

I recognize my grandparents from the baptism pictures Aunt Reggie showed me—they're older, obviously, but my grandmother still has dark hair like her daughters (dyed now, I imagine), and she's still slim and elegant, dressed in a beautiful suit under an apron covered in tomato sauce. My grandfather has a little less hair than he had in the picture, and he stoops a bit so he's even shorter than my grandmother; he's standing next to her chopping vegetables, and they look like a team.

"Pack, these are your grandparents," Aunt Reggie says, after she's kissed them both.

"Nonna and Poppa," my grandmother—Nonna—says. She quickly takes off the apron and places her hands on either side of my face. "Patrick. You're all grown up." She kisses each cheek and then hugs me. Big huggers, this family. But it's kind of nice. "It's wonderful to have you here, just wonderful. You don't know how long I've waited for this day. We've missed you so much."

I don't know what to say to that; it's not like I've missed them, since I didn't know they existed. Although logically I should have—it's not like I hatched out of thin air. Thankfully, I'm saved from having to reply by Poppa, who puts down the big knife he's using to chop the veggies, wipes his hands on a towel, and comes over to me. He shakes my hand and pulls me in for a one-armed embrace—not a hug, exactly, and I think maybe my arm will get crushed between us. "My boy," he says, then repeats it a couple of times. Looks like Nonna's the chatty one.

"We're almost ready for dinner, Patrick," Nonna says. "Why don't you sit, have something to drink? Regina, you get him something."

I feel better about my nickname having no impact when I realize Aunt Reggie's doesn't either. Nonna definitely does things her way. Aunt Reggie goes right to the fridge to get me water. Everyone else is drinking fancy Italian sodas, but she knows I wouldn't want one, even though we only talked about carbs, not sugar.

The kitchen isn't very big, but the dining room is, with an enormous table already covered with food—platters with slices of white cheese and salami and meats I don't recognize, along with piles of roasted vegetables. Aunt Reggie sits on one side of me, with Matt on the other; Mia and Uncle Mike sit across, leaving the head and foot of the table for Nonna and Poppa. We've just settled in when Nonna and Poppa start bringing in more food—lasagna, chicken cacciatore, meatballs, a bowl of pasta covered in sauce. There's way more stuff to eat than I expected, though Aunt Reggie whispers to me to avoid the meatballs—they've got bread crumbs in them. "Take some pasta and hide it under the sauce," she adds. "Nonna makes it by hand." I do as she says. I've never seen pasta like this before—each piece is like two long skinny tubes twisted together.

"*Strozzapreti*," Nonna says.

"Priest chokers," Poppa translates. "A little irreverence never killed anyone." He winks at me, and I'm relieved to know his reserved exterior hides a sense of humor.

I pile my plate with vegetables and chicken and am about to dig in when I see that everyone else has bowed their heads. Nonna clasps her hands together and begins to speak. "Bless us, Lord, for these gifts, which we are about to receive from your bounty. And thank you for bringing our Patrick home to us. Through Christ, our Lord. Amen."

"Amen," everyone replies.

I'm not used to saying grace, so I end up mumbling "Amen" a little late, but no one seems to notice. I'm all set to attack the food when the questions start.

Nonna's first. "So, Patrick, tell us about you. You've just graduated high school, yes? Are you going to college?"

I hate that all conversations post-graduation start here. "No college," I say. "I'm not sure what I'm going to do yet." I tell them about the gym and the police academy, but Nonna's not impressed.

"Business," Poppa says. "You should think about starting a business, like we did."

Nonna tells me about the specialty foods store in downtown New Haven they opened when they first moved here. She doesn't say it was after my mother went to prison, but I've gotten a sense of the time line from Aunt Reggie. "We had a slow start, but we always had things to eat."

Aunt Reggie laughs. "We'd come here for dinner back in those days and they'd serve candied fruit and Nutella on toast. I worked there for a while, before I started at the bank. You can only imagine how much fun it was to have your parents as your bosses."

"You could work at the store with us, if you wanted to," Nonna says. "You could stay here. There's a room in the back. We could make it a bedroom."

"Pack's already got a job," Aunt Reggie says. "And, I suspect, plenty of people pressuring him about his future." Thank god she's quicker than I am.

"We'll make it a bedroom anyway," Nonna says. "So you can visit. This won't be a one-time visit, now, will it?" The way she says it sounds more like instructions than a request, but in a good way.

"I'd love to come back." I don't want to sound awkward or anything, but it feels like I have to say more. "I'm just—I'm really glad I got to meet you all. I had no idea—" It's hard to put into words.

Aunt Reggie and Nonna exchange glances. They're having one of those silent conversations, but I don't know Nonna well enough to understand it. "Patrick," Nonna says, "I'm sure you have a lot of questions about your mother and why we've all been out of your life until now. I know Regina told you some of the story, but I want to emphasize that this was not our choice. Your mother told us to stay away, and when we didn't listen, your father took legal action. We've had a lot of time to think about why he did that, and while Regina says she understands, your grandfather and I are less convinced. But we respect the law, so we stayed away, and we respected Regina's decision to keep this secret from the children." She looks at Matt and Mia, then turns back to me. "You should know, though, that not a day has gone by that we haven't thought of you. We dreamed of this moment, and we're thankful to your mother for writing the letter that led you here."

No wonder she does most of the talking. She speaks in whole paragraphs, as if she's practiced. Her short version of the story is the same as Aunt Reggie's, too, so maybe that's all there is. Maybe my mother's just a bad person who deserved to be cut off from this family. Maybe the letter was just a way to get me here, to people who love me, even if they haven't seen me since I was a toddler.

Nonna doesn't wait for me to say anything else; she and Aunt Reggie get up and start clearing plates, and then they bring in dessert. There's a big plate of cookies, and pastries from a local bakery—I'm glad to know Nonna doesn't do everything by hand—but there's also a big bowl of fruit. Everyone talks about how full they are but takes handfuls of cookies and big pastries with lots of little ruffly layers. I take an orange and peel it slowly.

I offer to help wash dishes when we're done—I don't want Nonna and Poppa thinking Dad didn't raise me right, especially since they apparently hate him for keeping them away from me—but they say no. They won't even let Aunt Reggie help, though it's clear she's expected to ask. The night has gone by so fast I can barely believe it's over, though my phone says it's after ten and I'm getting really tired.

"Thank you so much for dinner," I say to Nonna.

She pulls me away from everyone else, back into the kitchen while they're all in the foyer. Her hands clasp my cheeks again, and she pulls me in close. "I can't talk about it in front of the others, but someday there will be things I can tell you. For now, try this address." She takes her hands away from my face, reaches into the pocket of her suit jacket, and removes a slip of paper. "I don't know for sure. But it's worth trying. It's not so far. Go as soon as you can, but tell me what you find, yes?"

I nod, too shocked to say anything in response.

Is this what I think it is? Does Nonna have my mother's address?

17

Nonna gave me more than an address, though there is one written there—it's in New York. Brooklyn, specifically, a place I've obviously never been, given that I've barely made it out of Brooksby. But there's also a name: Jennifer Shea. Unfortunately, there's no phone number. Nonna made it clear she intended me to go, so maybe that's why she left off the one piece of information that might make it easier for me to decide whether I should.

I'm tempted to start researching the minute I get back to the house, but dinner has wiped me out and I fall asleep on top of the covers. It's not until the next morning that I'm able to sit down and dig into some research; I wait until Matt's left to drive Mia to camp so I can be alone.

The first thing I do is plug the address into Google Maps, to see how long a trip it is. It looks like it's about an hour and a half without traffic, so I've probably already blown it in terms of going into the city today, but maybe if I leave early tomorrow morning it won't be too bad. It's better than trying to make the trip from Brooksby, and I have no intention of waiting, even if that means using up my last free weekend before work starts.

Next, I research Jennifer Shea. She has a Facebook page, but it's pretty locked down, and I can't see much except some of her basic history—she grew up in New York, and she went to Holy Cross for college. Maybe that's how she knows my mother.

I don't know whether Nonna's trying to tell me I'll find my mother there, or if she wants me to meet this Jennifer Shea person and get information, but it doesn't really matter. It's the only lead I have, so I have to make the trip.

I'm not sure how to explain what I'm doing to the family, though. I don't want to sell Nonna out and get Aunt Reggie all mad at her; I'm also kind of terrified at the thought of randomly driving to New York and showing up at yet another stranger's house. I decide it's time for me to trust someone, so after dinner I drag Matt into the guest room with me.

"I need a little help," I tell him. "I have to go to New York tomorrow. Brooklyn. I'll come back tomorrow night. I need you to cover for me, though."

"Brooklyn? Why? There's way more to do in Manhattan."

"You've been there before?" I feel stupid saying it, but it makes sense—New York isn't all that far from New Haven, and just because most people I know live twenty minutes from Boston but almost never go there (myself included) doesn't mean the same is true here.

"My friends and I go into the city whenever we can," he says. "They've got some underage clubs that are fun. And we go to the Bronx and watch the Yankees. Don't hate, Red Sox fan."

I laugh. "Sometimes I wonder how we can even be related, you supporting the evil empire and all."

"You sound like my mom. You Red Sox fans act like your team isn't second in line for that title. The days of the lovable losers are long over, cuz."

I like that he already has a nickname for me. Even if he's completely and totally wrong about baseball. "How long do you think it will take me to get there if I drive? I checked Google Maps today but it's so hard to know about traffic and all that."

"Depends what time you're leaving. Driving's not the best idea, though—you'll hit a ton of traffic. Better to take the train. It's way faster, even if you don't get the express. You can take the subway from the train station to get to Brooklyn. What's there, anyway?"

I take a deep breath. "I'm not sure," I admit. "Can you keep a secret?"

He holds up three fingers in a gesture I haven't seen before. "Scout's honor, yo." He must see the surprise on my face. "What? I was totally a Boy Scout. For about a minute. But seriously, you can tell me whatever. I know how to keep my mouth shut."

His face is so earnest I have no choice but to believe him. Or maybe I just want to so badly it doesn't matter. "I've got a lead on my mother. I need to try and find her."

Matt sits on the edge of the bed. "Whoa. That's a big deal."

"No kidding. You really think the train and subway are the way to go?" I hate to admit how intimidated I am, but there's no getting around it. I've been on the T a few times—like Matt, mostly to get to Fenway for some baseball games—but even that was kind of overwhelming, and I was always with Dad.

"Definitely. Driving in New York is madness. Even in Brooklyn. Isn't Boston kind of like that? I heard the drivers there are insane."

"I've never driven there," I say. "I haven't really gone into Boston all that much."

"New York will be a complete freak show for you, then." He tilts his head and looks up at the ceiling. "I could come with you. Help you navigate the trains and all that. Could be fun to watch you see it all for the first time. I mean, it's totally okay if you want to be alone, but, you know."

It never occurred to me to ask, but as soon as Matt offers, I jump. "That would be incredible. It might be a total waste, but . . ."

He gets up from the bed, all excited. "No, it will be great. We can take the whole day, do some fun stuff too, maybe." Then he sits back down. "But we need to tell Mom. Not what you're doing, but that we're going. They like to do family stuff on the weekend, and I'm sure they're planning something, with you here."

That makes me feel bad, but not bad enough to change my mind. "Can we say it was your idea?" I ask. "Like, you wanted to take me sightseeing or something?"

"Sure, that'll work. Come on, we'll do it together."

We head downstairs, where my aunt and uncle are drinking decaf coffee in the kitchen before bed. "Hey, Mom, me and Pack were thinking about heading into the city tomorrow. He's never been. I could show him around, tell him where the good pizza is. Kind of a cousin bonding trip."

"Pack doesn't eat pizza," Aunt Reggie says, but she's smiling.

"Fine, we'll just stay home and eat leftovers," Matt says. "God forbid I have a summer break before baseball starts."

I wish he hadn't moved right to being annoyed—can't he see Aunt Reggie's kidding? Besides, I have to make this trip. I just have to. "I've always wanted to see the Empire State Building. Or the Statue of Liberty. I'm nervous about going by myself."

"Of course you should go," Aunt Reggie says.

"It's a plan, then," Matt says, sounding relieved. "We're

going to take the train, so I'll leave the car at the station, okay?"

"It's your car," Uncle Mike says. "Don't leave anything valuable in it."

I almost laugh at the thought of thieves coming and stealing Matt's collection of dirty socks that lines the backseat.

"Be careful," Aunt Reggie adds. "The city is a dangerous place. You never know who's out there."

She's got that right.

I wake up at dawn again the next morning, though this time it's more out of anxiety than habit. Today there's a good chance I'll learn something real about my mother; I might even meet her. I have energy to burn, so I go to the park for what's become my usual makeshift workout, bringing my speed rope with me. Twenty minutes is enough to get a good sweat on, and it's still quiet when I get back to the house, so I take a shower and put on the clothes I borrowed from Matt yesterday. He won't mind, I figure, and I don't want to look like a gym rat if my mother turns out to really be in Brooklyn.

By the time I'm done, Matt is up and dressed, though everyone's still asleep. He's put on the same clothes as the day before, and we look at each other and laugh before we even say anything. "You ready to do this?" he asks.

"I have no idea," I say.

He nods, and we get in his car to go to the train station.

"Coffee first? There's a place right by the station."

"Definitely."

Matt parks the car at the station parking lot and we walk over to Dunkin' Donuts. I guess Connecticut is as orange-and-pink obsessed as Massachusetts—maybe it's a New England thing. I order a massive black coffee and grab a couple of bananas, too—thank goodness there's some fruit here, because otherwise Dunkin' Donuts doesn't have a single thing on the menu I can eat.

Matt checks out my order as he places his, which includes a whole-milk latte, a whole-wheat bagel, and a chocolate doughnut. Why bother with whole wheat if he's just going to eat a doughnut anyway? But he's in better shape than me, so who am I to judge?

"Is that all you're getting?" he asks.

"Yeah, fast food places aren't really my thing." We walk back over to the train station and go inside. I follow Matt, since I have no clue where I'm going or what I'm supposed to do when I get there. The station is big and spacious, with lots of windows to buy tickets. He leads me to the counter and we get two tickets to Grand Central Station. The tickets are super cheap, which means I can use cash without bankrupting myself; I don't want to have to use Dad's emergency card and clue him in that I'm not in Maine.

The train's waiting, though it's not scheduled to leave for fifteen minutes. We get on and look for two seats together—it's already pretty crowded, since it's Saturday and lots of people are going into the city for the weekend. We find two seats next to each other but facing in the opposite direction the train will travel, which Matt says will be more fun than sitting the regular way. "So I have a question," he says. "Do you not eat pizza at all, or was it just that the clams weirded you out? You didn't eat Nonna's pasta, either—do you not eat carbs at all?"

"Nope," I say. "I follow the Paleo diet." I explain to him what it is—basically meat, vegetables, fruits, nuts, plants, and seeds. No sugar.

"Wait, you don't eat sugar either?"

Just then the train starts with a lurch and begins chugging its way out of the station. It's strange sitting as if we're going backward, but Matt was right—it's easier to see what's behind us, and I discover I like that better than straining to see what's ahead.

"It's not that hard," I tell him. "Not once you get out of the habit. It just means almost no processed stuff—corn syrup is in everything. It's crazy."

He seems interested, so we spend at least the first half hour of the train ride talking about it—how it works, why I decided to do it in the first place.

"It's hard to picture you as a fat kid," Matt says.

Mia's not the only blunt Lombardi. "It's funny you say that—sometimes I dream that I'm still how I was in middle school and I wake up relieved. It wasn't even so much about being fat, even though that's what I thought it was back then; it was more that I was unhappy, like I was at war with my body. It's not like I'm a skinny guy now, but I feel like my body and I get along. I just worry sometimes that it would be easy to let it all go."

"So you're like one hundred percent strict? All the time?" I can't tell whether he doesn't believe me or whether he just finds the concept itself unbelievable.

"I am now. At first I made exceptions—cake on my birthday, chocolate at Easter, that sort of thing. But every time I ate something off plan I either felt sick or I wanted to keep doing it, especially when I ate sugar. The craving comes back so fast, and I'm just grateful to have it gone."

"Does it work that way with everything, though? Like if you drank a glass of milk you'd suddenly eat all the cheese?"

I think about it. "I've never reacted that way with anything but sugar. But it's also never seemed worth it to change what's working."

Matt doesn't say anything for a while. I look out the window as we whiz through the Connecticut suburbs. They look a lot like the Massachusetts suburbs, and the fact that they're similar makes it less scary that I'm getting farther and farther from home with every mile we travel.

I thought maybe Matt was done talking, but all of a sudden he starts up again. "I get what you're saying, and I know what you're doing is super healthy and all. But don't you find it kind of depressing? Missing out on so much?"

"Depressing?" That's surprising. Almost shocking. "I've never thought about it that way. It's been hard, sure, but I don't feel like I'm missing out." I'm proud of myself for what I've accomplished, the changes I've made to my body, the control I've exercised over my cravings, even if I hadn't thought about it in those terms before. "Going Paleo feels more like winning something than losing it, for me," I tell him.

"It's just so all or nothing. There's a whole world of food out there that's totally off your radar. I know I talked about getting pizza in New York, but honestly, it's overrated—the world's best pizza is in New Haven, I swear. And you missed out on Nonna's homemade pasta, and her cookies—she baked some of her best stuff for you, and you didn't try it. She usually only makes those lemon *dolci* at Christmas. It's like you brought Christmas with you in June and then slept through it while everyone else opened their presents."

"Wow," I say. "That's definitely not how I was looking at it."

"Sorry," he says. "That came out wrong. Food is such a big part of our family—Nonna has a recipe book that's been passed down forever. It's weird to think about living in a world where it doesn't matter the same way."

"It still matters. Me and Dad care about food a lot—we joined a farm-share program at the gym, and we eat only organic meat and produce, and I learned to think about food as fuel. It's like the gas in the engine of our bodies. But you're talking about something different, I think."

He nods, then shakes his head. "Different, but not different, too. Coach is always trying to get us to think of food as fuel too, and I never took him that seriously—you do a better job of explaining it than he does, and maybe it is time for me to quit doughnuts, at least. But there are other kinds of fuel than just the physical stuff. For us, maybe food is kind of an emotional fuel. We eat together, and we eat Italian food because Nonna and Poppa want us to remember where we came from. Isn't there a way to have both kinds of fuel?"

I'm glad what I said about food resonates with him, but what he's saying is new to me. "Let me think about it more," I say. "But now I have a question for you. How are you in such good shape, eating crap like that?" I point at the doughnut, which, despite his suggestion that it might be time to give them up, he's still munching on. "Is it really just baseball?"

"Just baseball?" He feigns horror. "Coach would shoot you for saying that. Actually, he'd make you run wind sprints until you were dead." He gets animated then, telling me about the training regimen his coach has him on, what they're going to do at baseball camp this summer. It's intense—the workouts are different than what I'm used to, but they make sense to me. They do heavy lifting to build specific muscle groups, especially in the shoulders; they do plyometric workouts to make the players move faster and more efficiently; they do all those wind sprints to work on endurance; they do body-weight exercises to build mobility. No wonder Matt's in such great shape.

I love that I can so clearly understand why the coach set up the workouts the way he did. It's like I learned a new language at home, and now I'm testing it out in another country. It makes me look forward to going back home and starting my new job. I really hope working at the gym this summer will help me make a plan for my future.

We talk the whole rest of the trip until we finally reach Grand Central Station and get off the train. I've only seen it in movies, but it's even huger and more overwhelming in person. There are people everywhere, more people than I've ever seen in one place in my life. I'm so glad Matt's here so I don't freak out; I follow him to the subway entrance, where he studies the map and his phone to find the best way to get to Brooklyn.

"I'm assuming you want to do this first, before any sightseeing-type stuff," he says. "But if you'd rather check out the Empire State Building first, it's just a couple of stops away."

I shake my head. "Later."

Matt figures out the train situation—on the map the trains all have colors but they also have names and letters and numbers and it's a confusing mess. He says we have to take the 4/5/6 to the R or the F, and I'm fine with just following him around like a lost puppy. I'm glad he knows what he's doing. We buy MetroCards and go through the turnstiles, which is kind of like what I remember about taking the T except there are like a thousand times more people everywhere—the subway's so crowded we have to stand up. It's filled with all kinds of people, many of whom don't seem like they should be occupying the same space. There's a guy with bright pink dreadlocks and a bull ring through his nose that looks really painful, right next to an old woman dreaming peacefully in the corner despite the chaos around her. Everyone seems completely at home here, on the subway, among the crowd but in their own little worlds.

We switch trains to one that's quieter, where we can sit down. "Next stop's us," Matt says.

I follow him off the train like a duckling. He has the street map up on his phone and tells me we have a few blocks to walk before we get there. We go up the stairs and into the street and it's like I've never seen the sun before—it's so bright after the dark of the subway, and it feels like my whole world is coming alive. If watching the Connecticut suburbs out the window of the train made me feel like the world outside Brooksby isn't so foreign, New York is having the exact opposite effect. The part of Brooklyn we're walking through is quiet and all neighborhoody, with brick buildings Matt calls brownstones and lots of little shops and coffee places. It's not so strange or unusual, but it feels different. There's an energy in the air I can't describe but that I definitely feel, and I like it. I didn't expect that. Maddie told me I needed to get out more, to see places beyond Brooksby. Is this feeling why? Had she known it was out there? Had she felt it? Or was that what she was hoping to find?

We walk until we come to one of those brownstone buildings with a little gate in front. The gate isn't locked, so we walk up the front steps. "This is fancy," Matt says, taking it in. "Your mom's friend is doing okay for herself."

I'm not sure what he means, but one of the mailboxes has Jennifer Shea's name on it, so we're in the right place. I find the doorbell and stare at it.

"So?" Matt asks. "We doing this?"

I blink twice and pull back my shoulders to steel myself. Then I ring the doorbell. Matt and I wait for a minute before the door opens. A woman answers, tall and blond, wearing jeans and a neatly pressed shirt. Definitely not someone related to me. "Are you Jennifer Shea?" I ask.

"Maybe," she says. "Who are you?"

"I'm Patrick Walsh," I say. "Natalie Russo's son."

She looks at me carefully, more of an evaluation than anything else, and then gives a little nod. "Come on in."

I don't know what's past the door, but I feel this sense of possibility. And with that, I step inside.

18

Matt lingers behind me. "Should I meet you somewhere?"

"Is it okay if he comes in too, Ms. Shea? This is my cousin Matt."

"Sure," she says. "But call me Jen."

Matt follows me in and closes the door behind him. I've never been in a house like this one before. The room we step into is long and narrow, kind of like a little library, with bookshelves all around and a leather chair and tall lamp in the corner. Jen quickly leads me through it into a living room with an angular gray couch, two square black chairs, and not much else, other than paintings on the wall that are just colorful squiggles. I don't see a TV at all.

"Have a seat," Jen says, and Matt and I each take a black chair. "Do you want something to drink? Some water?"

"We're good," I say. I want answers, not water. "Is my mother here?" Might as well get right to it.

Jen sits on the couch across from us. "No, she isn't. She was, but she left a few days ago."

I can't believe I was this close and missed her. The weight of it feels like a kettlebell dropped on my stomach. I have no words.

"How do you know my aunt?" Matt asks. Thank god he's here.

"We were roommates freshman year in college," Jen says. "We stayed in touch when she dropped out."

"Do you know where she is now?" I ask. "She sent me a letter, but she didn't give me a way to get in touch." No need to hide anything now, I suppose; Jen's the only lead I have left.

"She told me about that," Jen says, and smooths her hands over her jeans as if she were wearing a skirt.

"What did she say?" I'm starting to get impatient. Jen clearly knows things, but I don't know how to make her tell me what they are.

"You have to understand, this is all quite complicated," she says. "Natalie thought it was safe to write to you once you turned eighteen, when you were an adult. But she knew there were risks, especially if you told anyone. She got a call, and then she was gone. I don't know where she went."

Why can't she be straight with me? "I didn't tell anyone. Just my girlfriend. I didn't do anything wrong. Who called her? Why would she just leave like that?" I know I'm starting to sound angry, but I can't help it.

"Well, someone found out. I wish there was more I could tell you, Patrick, but she didn't tell me who it was. I can only assume it's the same person who's been keeping an eye on her for years, but she never told me who that was."

"What are you talking about?"

Jen sighs. "What do you know about her situation? Did she explain anything in the letter?"

How did she end up being the one asking the questions? "She didn't tell me anything. From what everyone else has told me, she kidnapped me, stole a bunch of drugs, got caught, went to jail. No one in my family's ever seen her again. That's what I know." By now I can sum it all up in two sentences, because those are the only two sentences that really matter.

"There's a lot more to it than that," Jen says. "She would never steal drugs. She had problems, yes, but drugs were well in her past. Someone set her up, and that person's been controlling her ever since. She said it wasn't safe to tell me who it was, but she has a phone that's just for calls from him. She thought it would be different now that you were grown up, that if she wrote to you directly and you kept it secret, then maybe someday she could find a way to meet you. That's why she didn't leave contact information; she had to know that you wouldn't tell your father. If you told, she'd get the call.

And she got it, so you must have told someone. Maybe she'll come back—she's done this before—but I don't know when that would be."

I've somehow unlocked the key to getting Jen to talk, but if I'm understanding her right, then she's saying this is all my fault. The letter was a test to see if I could keep my mouth shut, and I failed. But the only person I told was Maddie, and who would Maddie even tell who could possibly be the person on the other end of the calls?

"Pack didn't tell his dad," Matt says. "If he said he didn't, he didn't. He came all this way to find her, and now you're acting like his mom not being here is on him. Can you just, like, help him? Give him something. Anything."

I feel a crashing wave of love for my cousin.

Jen does the jeans-smoothing thing again. "It sounds like you already know the most important information. What do you want to know?"

I think about the gaps I have to fill in. Jen clearly can't help with the most important questions that affect me now, but maybe she knows more about the past. "Why did she leave in the first place? I don't get why she would go through all the trouble of stealing me from my dad, only to leave me with him when she got caught." That makes it sound like he's a bad guy, which isn't what I mean. "Not that she shouldn't have. I've had a good life. You can tell her that, if she comes back. But it doesn't make sense, you know?"

Jen nods. "I completely understand why that would be confusing for you. You have to know that she and I haven't talked about what happened for a long time. She told me some details way back when she first got out of jail and came to stay with me, but there's only so much I remember."

"Please," I say. "Just tell me what you do remember."

"It started when you were little," she says. "She'd gotten away from the people she used to do drugs with, but then one of them died. An overdose. He'd moved to a nearby town along with some of their other friends, and they told her they'd been getting their drugs from a cop in Brooksby. Your dad was working in the evidence room, and she became convinced it was him. She decided she had to get you as far away from him as possible."

I feel my mouth literally falling open. How could anyone ever think Dad would be involved in something like that? I get it together enough to say, "There's no way."

"You're right about that. But it wasn't until she got caught that she found that out for sure. I don't know how. She was wrecked by it, though—she'd ruined her relationship with your father, and she'd been wrong."

"Why didn't she ask him if he'd done it, before she decided to take me?" I ask. "And why didn't she explain everything to him afterward?"

"I'm not sure," Jen says. "I just know that somehow she learned who was really involved, and that person scared her so badly she decided she was safer in prison."

"And that's who calls her?" I can't imagine being that scared.

"As far as I know. Whoever it is, he's got her terrified, and she's been hiding from him ever since she got out. I don't know what he said to convince her to carry that awful phone around, but knowing her as I do, I'm sure it has something to do with keeping you safe. She took a big risk in reaching out to you. I know you say you didn't show that letter to anyone, but you might want to think about whether you did anything that would clue this guy in that she was trying to communicate with you."

She still doesn't believe me. There's nothing I can do about it, though.

"What about the rest of us?" Matt asks. "Why cut off my family?"

"That's not entirely on Natalie," Jen says. "At first she was embarrassed by what she'd done; she wanted to take some time to think about how to explain to everyone why she hadn't told them what was happening. Why she hadn't reached out for help. But because she didn't tell them the story herself, they all heard it from the police. They believed that she'd relapsed and stolen the drugs along with Pack, and it was too much for them to take. Natalie was devastated they would believe she'd do anything to hurt Pack or to let drugs back into her life, so instead of changing her mind and reaching out, she got stubborn."

"That does sound like someone who's related to us," Matt says.

"Does that mean no one ever found out the drugs were a setup?" I ask. "Did my dad ever find out?" Some of the pieces are starting to come together, but there's just so much it's hard to hold it all in my head. If everyone still thinks she really did run off with the drugs—not to mention me—then it's not totally shocking they still might not be inclined to forgive her.

Jen shakes her head. "As far as I'm aware, the only people who know are your mother, me, the person who set her up, and the person who told her it wasn't your dad. And those last two people might be the same person—she never would tell me. I've been trying to convince her to do something about it for years—I've got the resources to help her, but she's still too scared. Reaching out to you was her first big step, but getting that phone call sent her running. I don't know if she's protecting herself or you, but she's definitely convinced that something bad might happen."

So her staying away is a means of protecting me? Or protecting herself? "There has to be something we can do," I say. "Please. Is there anything else you can tell me?"

Jen sits quietly for a minute. "You really didn't tell your father about the letter?" she asks.

"I swear."

"And you want to find her?"

Those are tricky questions. I want the rest of the story. I'm still not sure how I feel about my mother. "Yes," I say. It's not technically a lie because I don't know whether the answer's really "no," either.

"Wait here." Jen gets up from the couch and leaves the room, returning after a short time with a purple duffel bag with HOLY CROSS stamped on it in white letters. She hands me the bag. "Natalie left some things here a long time ago. She said she wanted me to keep them safe, but if something happened to her, I could track you down and give them to you. I don't know that she'd want me to give them to you now, but you're here, so . . ."

I resist the urge to tear into the bag right in her living room. This alone makes the trip worth it. "Thank you," I say. "I really do want to help. I don't want to get her in trouble or anything." I'm not lying about this, at least.

"I believe you," she says. "You might want to think about who you did talk to, even if not about the letter, because someone knew she wrote to you. Maybe not everyone you know is as trustworthy as you think."

I get why she thinks that, but she has to be wrong. "Will you tell my mother I was here, if you speak to her?"

"I will," she says. "You take care of yourself."

* * *

As excited as I was to see New York for the first time, now I can't wait to leave. I like it here, I can already tell, and I definitely want to come back someday, but right now I want to get as far away as possible. That's why when Matt asks if I want to do something touristy before we go, like visit the 9/11 memorial, I tell him I just want to go to the train. He seems to know I'm not ready to talk, or to do anything else, and we walk in silence to the subway, ride in silence underground, battle our way through Grand Central Station in silence, and find seats on the train back to New Haven (facing the normal direction, this time) without saying a word.

After the train chugs its way out of the station, he turns to me. "Did you know," he asks, "that Grand Central Station is not actually called Grand Central Station?"

He's gotten my attention. "It's not?"

"Nope. It's really Grand Central Terminal, but no one calls it that. Know why?"

"Why it's Grand Central Terminal, or why people don't call it that?"

He rolls his eyes. "I see you got the family wiseass gene. Why it's called Grand Central Terminal, duh." We're traveling at a good clip now, and I'm looking forward to putting New York City in my rearview. Metaphorically speaking, of course, because I can only see what's coming, not what's behind me.

"No, of course I don't know why. But maybe you'd like to tell me?"

"Well, first, that's its name. Its real name. So that's what everyone should call it. But that's not the real answer."

"I would hope not," I say. "It's not a very satisfying answer."

"Be patient," he says. "The real answer is that it should be called a terminal because terminals and stations aren't the same thing. Terminals are the beginning and end points for trains, but stations are somewhere in the middle. Trains can stop and start there, but they can also go through. No trains go through Grand Central—they can only begin and end. Penn Station, on the other hand, is really a station—trains can go through there in all directions. But it's also a terminal, because it's the beginning and end point for certain trains."

"Then why wouldn't it be called a terminal, even though it also happens to be a station?"

"I guess because stations are more inclusive. Terminals only give you so many options, but at stations you can do just about anything."

"Huh." I think about it for a minute, what he's trying to tell me, though maybe it's just something to pass the time. "Where'd you learn all this, anyway?"

"From Dad," he says. "You haven't seen his trivia-buff side, but it's serious. 'Learning opportunities abound,' he likes to say."

It makes me think of my dad and his little life lessons. I

miss him, despite all the mixed feelings I'm having. I've been away for nearly a week without talking to him, the longest we've ever gone without speaking. I've sent the occasional text, and apparently that's enough, because after he tried calling a few times, he stopped and just texted back that he was glad I was having fun. I'll have to text that I'm coming home tomorrow, but I don't feel like doing that now. I'm way too focused on the bag I hold in my lap. I'm dying to know what's inside, but I'm not about to look with Matt here. I need to be by myself.

"How are you doing with all this?" he asks.

"I'm pretty lost," I say. "Jen helped put some of the pieces together, but I'm missing some of the really important stuff. I have to figure out who set my mother up, who's been calling her. And how they knew about the letter."

"Maybe that's the best place to start," Matt says. "You said Maddie's the only person you told, right?"

I nod. "There's no way she would tell anyone. She's the one who insisted I couldn't tell Dad."

"Then there are only a couple of other options. I know you're not going to like the first one, but is there any way your dad could have found out about the letter without you telling him?"

The image of going through the shoe box flashes in my head. If I was willing to snoop around his stuff, was I so sure he wasn't willing to do the same? "You're right that I don't like it, but it's possible," I say. "What's the other option, though?"

"Well, you said you asked your dad about your mom, even though you didn't tell him about the letter, right?"

"Right."

"Couldn't that be enough? If he told someone else about that conversation, they might suspect you were asking for a reason. They don't have to know about the letter to give your mom a warning."

I have to think about that one. It's possible that Dad could have told one of his friends at work that I was asking about my mother, when I never had before. Anyone at the station could have overheard him, and if what Jen told me is right, then this all started because there's a dirty cop in Brooksby. It does make a certain kind of sense.

I tell Matt my theory, expecting him to nod along. But he frowns. "I'm with you on the possibility that this person found out from your dad," he says. "And maybe it did happen at work, or somewhere else. But are you really so sure that it was some random cop overhearing him? For this person to have so much power over your mother, and so much power over your whole family as a result—don't you think it could be someone a little closer to you?"

For that to be true, we'd have to be talking about one of Dad's friends. That can't be right. "I know all my dad's friends. They'd never do anything like this." Even as I say it, though, I think about Manny and the odd things he said before I left, how he's always been kind of a dick. Could it be him?

"So you think it's just some random person who works with your dad?" Matt asks.

It's better than the alternative. "You don't think?"

Matt stretches his legs until they practically hit the empty seat across from him. The train is way less crowded going back to New Haven. "We had a thing on the baseball team last year. Someone was stealing from the locker room. There were only two guys who could have done it, given the timing and all. One of them was our best hitter, one of my best friends, one of everyone's best friends, really. The other guy was kind of an asshole, didn't really hang out with anyone, was always making snide comments and trying to get with other guys' girlfriends, that sort of thing. You see where this is going."

"It was your friend and not the asshole," I say.

"Yes, but we didn't figure it out for a really long time. Really, we didn't figure it out at all—we insisted it was the other guy until the real thief got caught in the act. We insisted on the reality we wanted, even though no matter what we did, we couldn't find any evidence against the guy we didn't like. And there's more."

"What else could there be?"

"We could have ended things a lot sooner if we'd actually looked at the facts. The asshole guy was rich—his parents totally spoiled him, and he threw cash around like it was his job. Like it would impress people. He didn't need money, though we spent ages talking about how even people who didn't need money sometimes used it as power, or to scare people—we came up with a lot of reasons why someone like him would want to steal from us, even when he didn't need to."

"And your friend?"

"His dad had just left and his mom had just gotten fired. We didn't know that right away; he kept it hidden from everyone, even those of us closest to him. He was embarrassed. He'd rather steal from us than ask if we could lend him a few bucks. Better to ask forgiveness than permission, I guess."

I've heard that expression before. I've always thought it was stupid.

"Anyway, if we'd done any research at all—asked questions, whatever—we could have solved the mystery quick. But we went with the outcome we wanted, and it took months until someone finally went into the locker room and found our star literally holding his wallet."

"It was you, wasn't it?" I ask. "You had to bust your own best friend."

"Wouldn't be a good story if it was anyone else, right?"

Matt's a good storyteller.

"I have to go figure it out," I say. "And I can't assume it's not someone just because I don't want it to be them."

"That's up to you, cuz. You decide what you want to do. Just remember that avoiding an answer because it's not one you want isn't the best way to get to the truth. If the truth is what you want."

"It is," I say. At least I think it is.

19

I'm anxious to get back to the Lombardis' so I can go through the bag, but by the time we reach Matt's car it's late afternoon, and when Matt points out that we haven't eaten anything all day, I realize I'm starving. "I have a suggestion, but you need to hear me out," he says as he drives out of the parking lot. "I think we should pick up food to bring home, for everyone."

"Works for me," I say.

"That's not all. I think you need to have a real New Haven experience, especially if you're leaving here tomorrow. You missed out on some of the best parts of Nonna's dinner."

"The stuff I had was amazing," I protest.

"You didn't even eat the meatballs. They're like ninety-eight percent protein and you still didn't try them."

"Bread crumbs." But it sounds pathetic even as I say it.

"That's what I mean. You let a teeny amount of bread

crumbs keep you from eating the best meatballs on the planet. Don't you think it's time to maybe relax a little?"

"What do you mean?"

"I mean, at this very moment I'm driving us back to Pepe's. It's the best pizza in the world, and you sat in front of it and ate a fucking salad. It wasn't even a good salad, because that's not what Pepe's is about. We love Pepe's for the pizza and only the pizza, and if I get takeout from there and bring it home it will make the whole family happy and it will blow your mind with how good it is. If you eat it."

"So I'm supposed to just give up everything I've worked for?"

"No, man, that's what I'm trying to tell you. You've got this idea in your head that you have to eat this way forever, that you can never slip for a second or you'll be immediately returned to where you were when you were what, twelve?"

"Fourteen," I say.

"Maybe fourteen-year-olds can't slip even once or everything goes to shit, though I doubt it. But you're not fourteen anymore. You've been this model of discipline for years, but you're also missing out on big stuff. You have to trust yourself a little, let go of some control. Sometimes you have to choose between what's good for you and what might not be good for you but could be really amazing for you."

Matt might think he's talking about pizza, but I'm hearing something completely different. He might as well be Maddie, talking about me leaving Brooksby someday. Much as I hate to admit it, she was right about that. Going to New Haven is probably the best decision I've ever made, and going to New York made me realize there are places I want to see. Possibly even places I want to live. If she was right, maybe Matt's right, too.

"Okay," I say. "But can we get a regular pizza too, not just that weird clam one?"

"We can get both, as long as you promise to try both. I have to get the clam one—if I come home with pizza from Pepe's and I don't get the clam one, Mom might not let me in the house." His voice sounds warm talking about Aunt Reggie; I hope that means he's ready to let her off the hook.

As soon as we walk in the door and Aunt Reggie sees the Pepe's boxes she raises her eyebrows at Matt and says, "One of those better be—"

"White clam," he says, winking at me. "I know, believe me, I know."

She frowns. "What's Pack going to eat?" She looks over at me. "I'm sorry my son is so inconsiderate. We've got some salad stuff in the fridge."

"It's all good," I say. "I'm going to try the pizza."

"You sure that's okay?"

Honestly, I'm not. I have no idea how my stomach will react to pizza and cheese after all this time. Hell, I've even been going easy on nightshades because Tom Brady's nutritionist says they're inflammatory, which means I've hardly eaten tomatoes. "I'll be fine," I say. "I used to love pizza. Too much, really."

Aunt Reggie tilts her head and looks at me carefully. "You having this pizza is something of an occasion, isn't it? Do you want to talk about it first?"

"Me and Matt covered it already. I just have to remind myself that eating pizza one time isn't going to automatically change everything." I know it on a rational level, anyway. The muscle I've spent years building won't disappear, and if everything I've read is correct, my taste buds aren't even the same as they used to be. Maybe I won't even like pizza anymore.

"You're an impressively disciplined young man," Aunt Reggie says. "But perhaps instead of using that discipline for absolutes, like never having pizza again, maybe you can use it to set some boundaries that are more flexible. So you can enjoy yourself without missing out on important experiences."

"You sound like Matt," I say, and he punches me on the arm.

"Matty's a pretty smart kid," Uncle Mike says. "Chip off the old block and all that."

We all sit down at the dining-room table and I take one slice of plain cheese pizza and one slice of the weird clam thing. I eat a bite of the cheese pizza first, so I can have my favorite food again and see if it's the same as I remember.

It turns out that it is, and also it isn't. I can tell right away that it's really good pizza—the crust is perfect, and it has exactly the right amount of cheese and sauce and all that. But my taste buds really have changed, because I'm super sensitive to how sweet the tomato sauce is. I haven't eaten sugar in so long that it's obvious to me the sauce has some in it. And that pizza sauce probably always has sugar in it, but I never could tell before. It's delicious, but not in a way that makes me think I'll be running back to eat pizza every day forever until I'm my fourteen-year-old self again.

The clam pizza is a whole other thing. I've never tried anything like it, and at first I'm almost afraid to put it in my mouth. Despite being a New England kid, I've never been much of a shellfish eater; I can handle shrimp and once in a while when I was a little we'd have lobster on special occasions, but once I was off butter lobster seemed pointless, and I've never gotten into things like mussels and oysters and clams. Aren't they basically marinating in their own piss? Gross.

But the clam pizza is the complete opposite of gross. It's perfect. There's no tomato sauce, so I don't have to think about sugar; there isn't even that much cheese. The clams are juicy and salty and the white sauce is some kind of magic I don't even understand.

Matt watches me wolf it down and laughs at whatever

expressions are passing over my face as I try to figure out why this pizza is so ridiculously good. "Told you," he says.

"Don't be smug," Mia says. "Want another piece, Pack?"

I do, but this is where the discipline needs to kick in. "I'm good. I need to get my stuff together before bed."

"You're not leaving before breakfast, are you?" Aunt Reggie asks.

"I probably should. I start work Monday, and I told Dad I'd only be gone a few days, so I bet he's freaking out. We've got some stuff to talk about, and I think he's off tomorrow, so I want to make sure we have some time."

"When we will see you again? This can't be just a one-time thing." She says it almost sternly, like she'll punish me if I say no. I kind of like it. It reminds me of how Nonna was too.

"Of course not," I say. "I'm so happy to have found you all. I just want—I hope—" How do I finish that sentence?

Aunt Reggie gets it. "You'll talk to your father, and then you'll be in touch. Okay? You're welcome anytime. I want you to know that."

"You have to come back," Mia says, all serious. "I don't like very many people, you know. I wasn't sure I'd like having a new cousin." She stops, then looks surprised when everyone starts laughing. "What?"

"You going to finish that thought?" Matt teases.

Her brows furrow, then she puts it together and rolls her eyes. "It's obvious."

"I knew what you meant," I say. "I wasn't sure I would like having cousins either. But I do. A lot." I'm trying to figure out what else I want to say when the doorbell rings.

"I'll get it!" Mia yells.

"Hold on, honey," Aunt Reggie says. "We aren't expecting anyone, so how about I come with you?" They get up from the table while I fight the urge to have one more piece of clam pizza. The sooner I go upstairs, though, the sooner I can start looking through the duffel bag Jen gave me. I know I should save it for when I get home, when I can truly explore it in private, but I don't think I can wait any longer.

When I hear the voice at the door, though, I know I will have to wait, and that waiting is the least of my problems.

Dad is here.

PART III

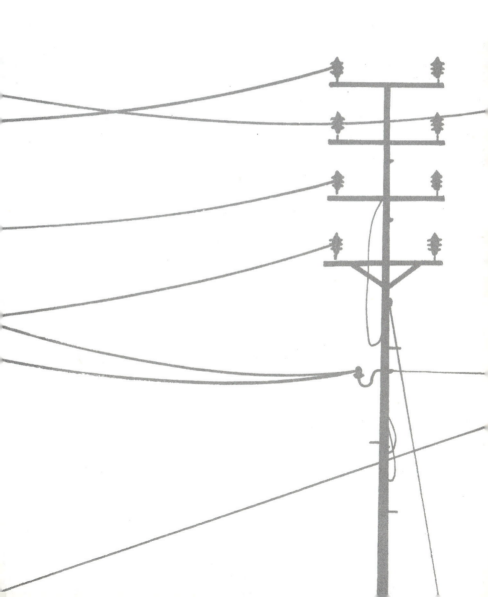

20

"Where's my son?" I hear Dad say.

Aunt Reggie starts to answer, but he's already barreled past her into the dining room, where the rest of us are still sitting. "What are you doing here?" I ask. I have no idea how he found me, but the fact that he's here makes it seem possible I have less privacy at home than I thought.

Dad looks down at the table, with the near-empty boxes of pizza and bottles of soda, clearly trying to process what he's seeing. "I'll be asking you the same question in the car. We're leaving now."

"Joe, sit down and we can talk about this," Aunt Reggie says. "Have a slice of pizza. We haven't seen you in a long time."

The expression on Dad's face is one I don't think I've ever seen before. I'm not sure if it's hatred or fury or some combination of the two, but his eyes look like they could shoot lasers and his teeth are gritted and he's turning so red I can feel the boil coming off him. When he opens his mouth I nearly wince, expecting him to explode, but his voice is creepily calm. "It's been a long time for a reason. I don't know what you did to get Pack here, but this little visit never should have happened, and it's never going to happen again."

Everyone falls silent, though tears start streaming from Mia's eyes, and it looks like I'm finally about to get to see Matt yelling. Uncle Mike stands up. "Joe, I understand why you're upset, and maybe you're not ready to hear from us. I hope you'll listen to Pack, though—he has a lot to tell you, and perhaps you'll be a little more forgiving when you hear what he has to say." I guess Aunt Reggie must have filled him in on our conversation.

"And we're not giving him up, either," Aunt Reggie says, putting her arm around me and squeezing my shoulders. "He's an adult now, so if he wants to come visit, he's welcome anytime. He knows that now. Don't you, Pack?"

What am I supposed to do? It would be easy to nod, to show these new family members how much they already mean to me. But the easy nod also feels like a betrayal. Less than a week of new-family bonding can't make up for eighteen years of Dad being there for me. But what about Dad and his lies? I don't know what to think. So I freeze.

"Come on, Pack. Let's go." Dad's never gotten physical with me before, and he doesn't now, but somehow I can tell he's fighting the urge to grab my arm, to pull me away from Aunt Reggie.

I don't like what's happening, but I can't see how to fix it. We have to leave. "My stuff's upstairs," I say, and Aunt Reggie's arm falls away from my shoulders. I run up to the guest room and throw my clothes into my backpack. I bring that and the duffel bag downstairs with me, trying to strategically hide the duffel bag behind my backpack so Dad doesn't see it. "Thanks for the visit. I'm so glad I got to meet all of you." I want to do more, to fall into one of Aunt Reggie's all-encompassing hugs, to hear Matt call me "cuz" one more time, to do something to stop Mia from crying.

But I also want to get Dad out of there. We're going to have a massive fight, and I don't want the Lombardis to hear it.

He's already at the front door, and he holds it open for me as I walk out. Not in the polite way, more like an implied threat, as if his body itself will keep me from running back in and saying a proper good-bye. This is not the Dad I know.

"Give me your keys," he says when we reach my car.

I look around, but I don't see Dad's Crown Vic anywhere. "How did you get here?" I try to sound calm; I don't want the Lombardis hearing me scream in their driveway. We can save the yelling for when we're alone.

"Took the train, then a cab. Thought we could use the ride home to talk. I'll do the driving, and you do the talking."

I'm not a huge fan of this arrangement, but I don't want to drive home in the dark, and it's after seven—there isn't much daylight left. I hand him the keys and throw my bags on the floor of the backseat before getting in the passenger side. The seat's pulled all the way up, just how Maddie likes it, and it reminds me of graduation day, the last time she was in my car. The last time anyone had been in it but me. I adjust the seat to stretch my legs and reach for the radio.

"Nope," Dad says. "No distractions. You're going to talk to me. Could've saved yourself the trouble by answering the damn phone."

I haven't looked at it all day, but now I turn it on to see fourteen missed calls. Oops. "I'm sorry about that," I say. I mean it, too. Dad catching me lying means I've lost the high ground. "How'd you find me, anyway?"

"You're not as good at hiding your tracks as you think you are. I might be working the desk now, but I've got a little experience finding bad guys. And right now, you fall in that category. So do your boys, by the way—Manny busted them drinking in the woods behind the school last night. Not hard to figure out you weren't in Maine with them after that. You've got some explaining to do."

This ride home's going to be fun.

Dad puts me in charge of the GPS, and I read the directions aloud to him until we hit I-91. That's when he launches in. "What were you thinking, Pack? What are you doing with these people? You have no idea who they are."

I'm tempted to hit back and accuse him of going through my stuff, but I'm struck by what he said. "I do too know them," I say. "I spent almost a week with them. They're good people, and they're my family. Why did you keep me away from them? And why have you spent my whole life lying to me? Even when I asked you to tell me the truth?"

"We talked about this already," he says. "I told you everything."

Is he really going to pretend he isn't busted? "My mother isn't dead," I say. "I can't find her, so I did the next best thing."

"What are you talking about?" He sounds genuinely confused. It didn't occur to me that he believed that part of his story, but now I wonder. Does he really think she's dead?

If I'm going to get him to tell me the truth, I have to be honest myself. "I didn't just ask you about her on my birthday out of nowhere. She sent me a letter, and I asked you to tell me the truth about her, and you told me she was dead. But she isn't. I needed to know what really happened, so I found her family. Because I couldn't count on you." I know it's harsh, but I need him to know how I really feel.

Dad pulls the truck over to the shoulder of the highway and puts it in park. He doesn't say anything for a long time, and I can feel the truck shaking as cars whiz by it, over the speed limit even in the far-right lane. Finally, he blows out a long, whistling breath, like the air coming out of a balloon, and when he speaks, his voice is quiet. "You can always count on me," he says. "I thought you knew that. And you have to believe that until just now, I really did think your mother was gone for good. There are reasons I kept you away from her family, reasons you know nothing about."

"I'm sure you think that," I say. "But I asked them to tell me the truth, and they did. Or at least they told me a story that sounded a lot more realistic than the bullshit you told me."

"What did Reggie say?" he asks.

"Nope." I'm the angry one now. "You don't get to hear that yet. Not until you say something I can believe."

He shakes his head and puts the truck back in drive. We get on the highway in silence, driving until we reach the Mass Pike, the sun setting behind us, the sky striped with orange and pink. I know I hurt Dad, but I don't care. "I loved your mother," he says, finally. "I loved her like you love Maddie. From the moment we got together, I wanted to be with her for the rest of my life. I wanted to marry her, and maybe if I'd insisted on it before you were born, or even after, things would be different now. I don't know."

He sounds unlike I've ever heard him sound before. Maybe he's being honest. At least it's something new.

"I assume Reggie told you she left, that she—" He pauses. "This part is hard, okay? Give me a minute."

I don't say a word. I want him to keep talking.

"I don't know why she took you, exactly. It might be that

I'd started working so much overtime—with you around I knew we'd need more money, and Brooksby needed help because of how bad the drug situation was in those days. This was before Tom took over; back then, we were on the team together, with Manny and some other guys. I was working too much, exhausted, not paying as much attention to everything as I should have. That's when I got shot."

"You what?" This is news to me. "How did I not know you got shot?"

"That's why I've been on the desk all these years. I got shot in the leg. That's where all the hip problems started. I know we didn't talk about it, but we didn't talk about a lot of things. You were never all that curious a kid. I wonder sometimes whether that's just how you were, or whether I made you that way, because of all the things I didn't want to tell you. Whether I failed you as a parent somehow."

I fight the urge to say something comforting, to tell him he hasn't failed me. But I'm not ready to let him off the hook yet. "You're getting off track," I say.

"Yeah, okay. Well, I didn't handle being on desk duty so great. I always thought of myself as a street guy—I just wanted to work cases. I wasn't much fun to be around, and your mom and I started fighting. I hated her being angry at me but I couldn't seem to stop being miserable. So I picked up more overtime. It was easier than being at home, and I could tell myself I was just making sure you were provided for. Wasn't like I was wearing myself out sitting in the evidence room, where they stuck me at first. I had to watch all my friends get promoted ahead of me—that's when Tom got put in charge of the drug beat, with Manny as his second-in-command.

"Anyway, I started working more and more hours, then the night shift, and we didn't see each other as much. We fought less, so I thought we were doing better. Then one day I came home from work and you were both gone. She left a note saying she had to keep you safe and I shouldn't try to find her. She'd make sure you had a good life." He rubs at his eye, and tears pool out when he pulls his hand away. I've never seen him cry before. "It was the worst day of my life. Losing either one of you would have been awful, but losing both of you at once?"

I'm tempted to tell him what I know, but I don't want him to stop talking. "Do you, like, want to pull over so I can drive?" Driving and crying seems like a bad combo.

He wipes his eye and shakes his head. "I'm fine." He clears his throat. "Anyway, I had to get you back. I told the chief you were gone, asked if he could put some good people on it but keep it under the radar. I had this idea that it was all a misunderstanding, that if your mom and I could just talk, we would work it out. I didn't want her getting arrested; I just wanted you both home."

"That's not exactly how it went," I mutter.

"No, it's not. The chief put a team together, and they kept it quiet, but she was arrested, and she refused to speak to me. She made some deal and went to prison, but she wouldn't put me on the visitor list. I got you back, but I lost her forever."

He sounds so sad, and I want to be a good son, or even just a good person, and say something nice. But I can't. Not when I'm so close to hearing everything. His story finally sounds enough like everything else I've learned to convince me he's being honest. "Aunt Reggie said you filed a restraining order against her and my grandparents. That you were the reason they couldn't see me."

Dad grips the steering wheel so tight his knuckles look like they've been drained of blood. "That family—they helped her steal you," he says. "She was going to Italy, and I'd never be able to find you. So yes, I wanted you as far away from them as possible."

"You're wrong that they helped," I say. "They didn't know anything about her leaving. And they cut her off when they found out what she did."

"They did what?" he asks, voice sharp.

"Cut her off," I say. "The trip was a bust—they don't know where she is. They haven't talked to her since she went to prison." I don't tell him about Nonna and the address she gave me in Brooklyn. I don't know whether she was just pointing out one of my mother's old friends, or if Nonna was in touch with my mother herself, in secret.

"That doesn't make sense," Dad says.

"None of this makes sense. Especially the drug stuff."

"Reggie told you that part too?"

"What, you thought it was a good idea to leave it out? Way to build trust, Dad." I was so sure he was finally coming clean. Looks like I got that one wrong.

Dad sighs. "Look, bud, I've been trying to keep you from knowing about all the terrible things your mother did to you, to us. She is the person I loved most in the world besides you, who did the worst thing to me anyone could even dream up. And it's wrecked me. I never wanted you to feel that way. Ever."

"But you were willing to let me think she basically sold me to you," I point out. "Like that wasn't going to make me hate her?"

"That was different," he says. "I knew it wasn't true. And it wouldn't send you running off to find her."

"Which wouldn't matter if she were dead," I say. "But are you saying you thought the drug stuff was true?"

"It made sense," he says. "She didn't take much money out of our joint account, and she didn't have much of her own. How was she going to take care of you without money? Without a job, in a foreign country? She'd been involved with drugs before."

Now is when I should tell him what I learned about the drugs, that my mother didn't really steal them. I should try and make him feel better.

But the sympathy I was starting to feel for him has quickly morphed back into anger. He might be telling me the truth now, but that doesn't change the fact that he lied before. And, I remind myself, he had to have gone through my stuff, or at least my browser history, to find out where I was. He embarrassed me in front of my family, a family he basically stole me from by getting restraining orders instead of talking to them. I'm not ready to make him feel better. Not yet.

"How much longer?" I ask.

"For what?"

Before I can trust you again, I think. Before things will start to feel normal. "Before we get home," I say.

"Soon," he says, and I want that to be the answer to all my questions, even though I know it isn't.

21

As soon as we get back to the apartment I run into my room and close the door. I have no interest in continuing the conversation with Dad, not until I've calmed down a little. Besides, I'm more desperate than ever to go through the duffel bag. Maybe it will have some of the answers I've been looking for.

Before I unzip it, though, there's one thing I want to do: I get out my phone and text Matt. **Sorry for the drama. Tell everyone else, okay?**

He must have been waiting to hear from me, because he texts back right away. **You okay, cuz? Your dad seemed kind of scary.**

He's not really, I write back, though I get why he would think so. **Long story.**

Okay. Keep in touch, will you?

I wrote that I would. **I promise.**

Texting him makes me feel better. I'll have to call Aunt Reggie at some point, too. But not now.

I probably should hold off on the bag until Dad either goes to bed or to work, though I'm pretty sure he's off tomorrow—that's why I'd wanted to make sure I got home in time for us to sit down together. That impulse to talk seems really far away now. After that drive, he'll probably leave me alone, and even if he doesn't, I'm not sure I care. I have to know what really happened. I have to know if what's in the bag will help me.

Inside the bag is a series of brownish envelopes of varying thickness, the kind with those metal butterfly clasps at the top, along with something lumpy in a paper bag. I dump everything out on my desk. The envelopes are unlabeled, no writing on them at all; there's no organized way to start, so I just pick one at random, pry the clasp open, and pull out the contents. It's a stack of photographs, bound together with a rubber band. I take it off and start going through them.

Every single picture is of me, as a baby. They seem to be in chronological order, starting from right when I was born—whoever says newborns are cute has never seen the slimy, dark-haired, purple-faced monstrosity I was when I came out of my mother. I flip through the stack, hoping for pictures of the two of us, but they're all literally just me. I'm relieved to see I got cuter with age—the big fluff of dark hair I was born with fell out and was replaced by a more manageable amount of dark fuzz, and I must have put on a lot of weight fast because I was super chubby even from this early age. Some of these pictures I've seen before, in Aunt Reggie's album; there I am in the christening gown, angry at having water flicked at my head.

But most are new to me. They tell the story of a happy, loved baby, in a stroller wearing little striped T-shirts, in a high chair spitting out mashed-up green peas. I could have been looking at some other kid's happy childhood. I've never seen baby pictures of me in this house, and certainly not in Dad's cardboard box.

My mother must have taken all of them.

This is what she kept, from her time with me. She must have really loved me. But she also must have been furious with Dad, not to leave anything behind for him. How could she go from that much rage to abandoning me? There are a lot of pieces of the puzzle missing, but right now, that feels like the most important one.

Most of the other envelopes have pictures too. One is a stack of photos of both of my parents—so strange, to think of them that way, together. Those are chronological, too—there are pictures of them looking impossibly young, back when they first met in high school. There's a duplicate of the prom photo I saw at Aunt Reggie's, and other pictures of the two of them with their friends. The most surprising one is of my mother and Manny, standing with their arms around each other as if they were close. The way Manny talked at the gym made me wonder if he and my mother even knew each other all that well; it's odd to see a photo of them together like this. The pictures move past high school, and I get to see Dad in his uniform back when he was in the police academy and just beyond, when he was in better shape and on active duty.

Why had she kept these? They're like a romance novel about someone she hated enough to leave, taking me with her in the process. What did she think Dad did to make her believe I was unsafe with him? There's no way to look at these pictures and not think about how desperately in love they'd been, at one time. If she hated him so much, why would she want to remember that? Or was it just that she didn't want him to have these pictures either?

It's the last stack of photos that kind of blows my mind, though. Another packet held together with an elastic band, this one worn from being used over and over; another packet arranged chronologically. Another packet of photos of me. But this one starts from when I was about two years old, after my mother went to prison, and they move through time until they reach my graduation. That's just over a week ago. How is that even possible? The only person who took pictures of me at graduation is Dad, and they're all on his phone camera. Is it possible he's the one who sent them to her? I'd actually believed him when he said he really thought she was dead. Was it just another lie?

The last envelope doesn't have photos in it. Instead, there's a notebook, one of those black-and-white composition books with the marbled cover. The sheets of paper inside have horizontal blue lines and a vertical pink margin stripe, just like the letter she sent me, but they're filled with barely legible scribbles. It's the same handwriting, but it's the writing of someone taking notes for herself, not being careful and writing for someone else to read. Some of it seems to be in some kind of code, too; I skim a few pages but the words don't make much sense. I'm going to want to go over everything more carefully, but first I need to see what's in the paper bag.

The bag is closed with a binder clip, so I take it off and reach inside. Once I see what's in it, I know my mother can't be as monstrous as Aunt Reggie made her seem. She may have done bad things, and maybe she isn't a great person overall, but I have no doubt that whatever she did, she did for me.

Inside the bag is Max, my Curious George stuffed animal. As soon as I see it I have the faintest memories of holding it, though maybe that's just my brain trying to fill in gaps, trying to give myself a history with my mother that isn't real. But the fact that she kept it, all this time—that's real.

I go back to the notebook, looking for some pages I can decipher as a way in. Once I've gotten used to my mother's messy handwriting when she thinks no one's reading but her, I make out a bunch of drafts of the letter she eventually sent me, with lots of crossed-out words as she figured out exactly what she wanted to say. The last one is a messy replica of the letter I have in my backpack; she must have copied it out on a clean piece of paper to make sure I could read her writing. Aunt Reggie said she must have spent a lot of time working on it, that she'd never cared so much about words before, and here's the evidence she was right. It's the letter of someone who would keep Max for all these years.

The other pages in the notebook are filled with scribbles that I eventually realize form a time line. There are dates written along the pink margin stripe, followed by brief snippets of text. The dates start from when I was really young, and at first some of the words are comprehensible. *J started working late. J shot. J in evidence. $$$ from where? XY everywhere but Brooksby. OD. No no no.*

J is obviously for Joe. Dad. She's tracked him on the job— first he started working late, then he got shot, then he got moved to the evidence room. This all lines up with what Jen and Dad told me. So far so good.

The dollar signs aren't hard to figure out either. Aunt Reggie said my mother was worried about Dad bringing home extra money; he said it was all from overtime, but apparently my mother didn't believe him.

XY takes me a little longer. I stare at the two letters for the longest time, but I don't get it until I say them out loud, over and over again, until they lose their meaning, until they sound less like "Ex" and "Why" and more like "Oxy."

OxyContin, everywhere but Brooksby. Followed by *OD*. She's telling herself the story of how she convinced herself Dad was selling drugs out of the evidence room. She's showing how she put the pieces together. The pieces that turned out to be wrong.

I keep reading. *Took P. 2 found me. H in suitcase.* I understand the first part, though seeing my own kidnapping described so casually feels a little anticlimactic. The last part isn't too hard, either—the drugs planted in her suitcase must have been heroin. What does *2 found me* mean, though? Is she referring to two cops? Did they put the heroin in her suitcase? How else could it have gotten there?

I put the notebook down so I can think this one through. The cops who found her must have been the ones to plant the heroin; they're the only ones who had access to her suitcase after she was arrested. She figured that out, but it wouldn't have been enough to convince her Dad didn't have a hand in it. He could have been working with those cops, giving them drugs that had been confiscated from dealers.

Then it gets weirder. *Bolo visited. Not J. J and P will be okay. Must keep P safe.* Who's Bolo? What did he tell her? It sounds like this is how she found out Dad hadn't done what she thought. This is the missing piece I've been trying so hard to find. If I can find out who Bolo is, I'll be that much closer to understanding everything.

But first, I have to keep reading. There's not much left.

The next line skips ahead five years. *Bolo tried to help me see P.*
2 found out. Tracking me.

One more line. I read it and feel a chill pass over me. I
look down to see goose bumps all over my arms.

This will never be over.

22

On Monday morning I go to the box in time for my regular class; I'll start my official workday immediately afterward. The workout—called "Fran"—is a quickie, and we race to complete three rounds of barbell thrusters and pull-ups as fast as we can. Thankfully Dad and his cop buddies aren't there; staying quiet with all the questions swirling around in my head would have been hard. The routine is quick but exhausting, harder than usual because I haven't been here in a week, and it takes up so much of my mental energy I almost forget I'm supposed to stay—I find myself heading out to the parking lot after my shower almost reflexively, until I remember I'm not going anywhere until four.

I spend most of the day learning how everything works: the cash register, the membership programs, the schedule sheets for trainers and nutritionists. I learn how to ring up sales of T-shirts and nutritional supplements and how to make smoothies at the juice bar. It's mostly routine stuff, though Lainie, one of the trainers, lets me help teach one of the afternoon classes. Not the noon class, though—everyone seems to know about the breakup, so I get sent to pick up lunch for people while Maddie is working out. I see her car pulling into the parking lot as I head for the salad place, but I turn away before I can catch a glimpse of her face. I can't handle seeing her right now, much as I want to; I've fucked things up so badly that I have some thinking to do before I can try and talk to her again.

The day goes by faster than I expected, partly because working with the trainers and the nutritionist is so interesting, and all the other parts of the job are easy. It's going to be a good summer. Before I know it four o'clock rolls around, and I can move on to phase two of my day. I decided after looking in the duffel bag that it's worth doing some research, to see if I can find out what cops were working the drug beat back when my mother left. It's a place to start, anyway. I'm pretty sure Dad found me by going through my internet search history, so using the home computer is no longer an option. I don't know whether I have access to the high-school computers anymore, so I figure my best bet is the public library downtown.

The computer lab is almost empty, so I get myself set up, wishing I'd brought a sweatshirt—the air conditioner seems to think it's August, not June, and I'm freezing. I get my mother's notebook out of my backpack, along with my own notebook; I'll use her time line to see if I can find some possible names, particularly those two cops and this Bolo person.

I begin my search with back issues of the *Brooksby Gazette* and start when my parents were in high school, to get a sense of history. I look for stories about drugs, and it's a bummer how easy they are to find. At first there's a lot of reporting on the prescription-drug epidemic, how more and more people are getting addicted to drugs like OxyContin and Percocet, leading to them shopping for doctors who are friendlier about giving prescriptions. The stories quickly shift to how people are turning to theft, then heroin, as their prescriptions run out. There are features on how this affected kids as well; I'm in the middle of a story about a hockey player who overdosed on heroin and died when I realize that's the boyfriend of my mom's that Aunt Reggie told me about. He can't be the OD in the notes, though—the time line doesn't work.

I keep reading, the stories escalating in their panicky tone as I move through my dad's first few years on the job, and my first couple of years in this world. I find the story about the heroin bust where my dad got shot—his name isn't in the paper, but given the description of the shooting I know I've found the event he was talking about. He and the rest of the team raided a run-down house in the old part of town that turned out to be where a major dealer stored massive quantities of heroin. The dealer was there, but he wasn't alone, and there was some sort of gunfight and Dad got hit. No one else was injured, and they never figured out which one of the dealer's men was the shooter; the gun was unregistered, and they did manage to bust the dealer, so finding Dad's shooter wasn't much of a priority, I guess.

I'm not surprised to find that Tom was the head of the team—that arrest was his big break, and after that he was promoted to lieutenant and put in charge of drug crimes. He was given broader authority, with more resources and people on his team. Some of the team members' names are in the paper, so I write them in my notebook; the only name I recognize is Manny's. There were op-eds both for and against the new strategy—some people were glad Brooksby was taking more aggressive action, but others pointed to how little progress the United States had made in the "war on drugs" since Reagan created the first federal drug czar position.

After a few months, it became clear that whatever Tom was doing was working, and the stories start taking a more positive tone. I read one front-page article about a major bust, and then the stories disappear. Well, not entirely, but they aren't big news anymore; they're buried in the metro section, along with the rest of the police blotter, which goes from multiple reports of drug arrests for both dealing and use to the occasional drunk-and-disorderly or neighborhood dispute. The next big story doesn't come for several years, in a weekend-edition update, with reference to a larger story in the *Boston Globe*.

I switch over to the *Globe* website. There's a profile of Tom for which he refused to be interviewed; he just issued a statement saying his team deserved all the credit and he was pleased Brooksby had turned itself around. He mentions some names; I check them against my earliest list and see that most are the same, though I note that Manny is no longer on it. The article mentions how impressive it is that Tom has basically ended Brooksby's drug problem, while neighboring communities, like Lynn and Revere, are still struggling. Perhaps, the reporter suggests, the police departments in those cities should start emulating Tom a little more.

Back to the *Brooksby Gazette*. But after that update, there's pretty much nothing. It's like drugs don't even matter in Brooksby anymore. I'm not going to find any more names, that's for sure. I look at the list I've written down and start working through each name online, to see if there's some obvious way to figure out who might have been responsible for my mother's arrest. I'm flying blind, though—I've got nothing to go on, and all I learn is that most of the guys on the list don't have much in terms of online presence—their Facebook pages are all set to private, and there's not much to find about them anywhere else.

I look back at my mother's time line. The point where she decided to leave comes after the OD; Jen had said the person who died was an old friend who'd moved away from Brooksby, along with some other people. I wonder whether learning the dead person's name will help me. I'm not sure where to start, since I know looking at the *Brooksby Gazette* won't help, so I go to the Lynn and Revere papers first, because those are the cities that came up in the article about Tom, but I don't find anything that looks right. Of course I don't—that would be too easy.

I move on to the archives of the Salem and Danvers papers, and that's when I find something that seems like it's worth digging into. There's a high-profile OD in Danvers, a man who would have been around my mother's age, maybe a couple of years older. I read his obituary and discover he used to live in Brooksby, used to play hockey with my mother's boyfriend who died. The date of the obituary doesn't match the date on the list, but it looks like the date of the actual overdose does. This is it.

But the man's name itself means nothing to me, and the article doesn't give me any other names to look into. I need help, but who should I ask? Usually when I have problems to work through I go to either Dad or Maddie, but neither of them is an option right now. I have to talk to someone who was on the force with my dad back then, someone who I can trust. The only person that comes to mind is Tom, but he's still in charge of drug crimes, and I'd basically be telling him two members of his team are crooked. What if he doesn't believe me? What if he starts asking around and I end up causing even more problems for my mother?

There's only one person who was around back then but isn't connected to the drug beat now, and that's Manny. Except he might be one of the people I'm looking for. It's hard to imagine, though—he might not be my favorite person, but he and Dad have been friends for years. I think back to all the time I've spent with him at the gym, or at barbecues at Tom's house every Fourth of July. It can't be him.

Can it?

23

Manny's at the morning class all by himself—no Tom, no Dad. I'm starting to think Dad's avoiding me as much as I'm avoiding him, but that's fine for now. I have to get answers on my own. It's just a question of how.

"Heard you got yourself in some trouble," Manny says while we're warming up. "Didn't mean to sell you out when I busted your boys, but man, your dad was pissed! Should've warned me you were sneaking off—I could have covered for you."

Would someone who ran my mother off be so interested in helping me keep out of trouble? I can't believe it. Maybe I just don't want to. "I went to visit my aunt," I say, and watch to see his reaction.

His face is stony. "That right?"

I nod, and wait.

"Regina, right? Nice girl. Knew her in high school."

"I bet you did," I say.

"You got something on your mind, little man?" Am I imagining it, or does his voice sound threatening? Maybe it's just because we went to get our weights for the workout, and he's picked up a thirty-six-kilogram kettlebell. It looks like a cartoon bomb, round and black. I grab my usual sixteen-kilogram bell and follow him back to the mat.

"Maybe. Some questions. You have time to talk to me?" I try to sound casual, but my voice shakes a little.

"Whatever you need," Manny says. "You want to stop by the station later on?"

Either he has no idea what I want to talk about, or he's testing me—there's no way I'm going to talk to him in front of my dad, let alone other cops. "Can we go somewhere more private?" I ask.

"You can swing by my place tonight, after my shift. Should be home by six. I'll pick us up some food. Beef subs from Vincenzo's sound good? Love that place." He sounds friendly now, which makes the prospect of going to his apartment alone more reasonable. I realize I've never been there, in all the years I've known him; every time we've socialized, it's been at Tom's place. It's not so strange; it's not like we have people over either.

"I'm more into salads these days," I say. "I'd take a Greek with no feta, if that's okay."

He looks like he wants to make a comment about the

salad, but I put on my best don't-even-try-it face, and he seems to figure it out. "Whatever you say, little man."

After the workout we go up to the main desk, and he writes down his address on the back of a membership flyer, and then he leaves. I've got the rest of the day to think about whether this is a good idea.

Work doesn't go by nearly as fast this time. I spend most of it cleaning—washing towels, wiping down mats, scraping built-up dirt and grime off the weights. I'm not quick enough getting out of the box at lunchtime to avoid Maddie—we pass each other as she's coming in and I'm heading out, and seeing her feels like getting punched in the neck. She has on the tank top I like with the little straps, her hair in a high ponytail, and I want so badly to talk to her, to tell her everything that's happened since we last spoke. But she just glances at me like she barely notices I'm there; only her lips tightening tells me she's even seen me, and that she's still mad. Of course she is.

The clock finally crawls its way to four o'clock and I kill time driving around before going to Manny's at six. He lives in an old factory that was converted into shitty apartments back in the seventies, the logo of the printing press painted on its brick wall. I walk up to the front entrance and press the buzzer, and when the door clicks open I go upstairs to an apartment on the third floor. The building is bare and almost institutional, with gray walls and linoleum floors so stained I'm not sure what color they are. I pass door after door, some of which have garbage bags sitting outside of them that have clearly been there for some time. This isn't exactly a high-class establishment. I feel a sudden surge of gratitude for home; it's not fancy, and sure, it could use some work, but it's in a nice development surrounded by green grass when the season allows it, rather than patches of dirt and the railway for the train to Boston. And everyone takes out their trash.

Manny's apartment is at the end of the hallway. I knock and he yells for me to come in. The place is pretty much what I expect. It's basically a studio, with a tiny kitchen on one side and a door that must lead to the bathroom right next to it. There's a mattress on the floor in one corner and a threadbare couch on the other, and on the back wall is a big TV. In between the bed and the couch is a small card table, the kind with vinyl covering an almost puffy surface. Someone cut through the vinyl at some point, so there's foam poking out. The apartment is making me very sad, and sorry for Manny, who's standing in front of the fridge.

"Something to drink, kid?"

"Water's good."

He pours me a glass from the tap, and I drop my backpack on a chair. There's a white Vincenzo's bag on the table, so I get out his sub and my salad and crumple up the bag. He comes over with my water and a beer and motions for me to sit in one of the rickety wooden chairs. Mine creaks when I sit down; I can't imagine how his doesn't break, given how big he is. He peels back the waxed paper around his sub and takes an enormous bite. I get out my salad and pick at it with a plastic spork, but I'm not hungry. I haven't decided exactly how to get Manny to tell me what I need to know. I should have planned this better.

"Pretty sad-looking dinner there," he says. "You're still on that Paleo shit, huh? Sure you don't want to ditch it and split this sub?"

He's gotten a Brooksby classic—an enormous long white roll with roast beef slathered in vinegary orange barbecue sauce. It looks amazing; I loved those subs when I was a kid. But I'm determined to make Pepe's a special occasion. "No thanks. So listen, I—"

"You want to ask me about your ma," Manny says.

I stare at him for what feels like a full minute, enough to see that he has a drop of barbecue sauce on the bottom of his lip, waiting to drip onto the table. He laughs at the expression on my face. "I'm not as dumb a lug as you think, kid," he says. "Besides, your pop talked about it at the station, you asking questions about her. Told him to be straight with you, but I could tell he wasn't going to listen. You're a smart kid, though. Knew you'd figure out he was full of shit. Dropped some hints to try and help you out, and you found Reggie, so it sounds like they worked."

My mind races back to that day in the gym, Manny singing that terrible song and razzing Dad about his high-school
girlfriend. He'd been the one to describe her in a way I could
easily recognize if I saw a picture. "You did that on purpose?"
If that's true, then I picked the right person to talk to. Manny
can't be one of the bad guys. I feel my shoulders relax—I'd
been so tense they were all scrunched up practically to my
ears. I hadn't realized how much I didn't want Manny to be
a bad guy.

"Least I could do," he says. "Had to be careful, though. If
you still got questions, you know why."

I don't know why, though. I don't know anything. Not
even what to ask next. "Why help me?" I ask. It's a place to
start, anyway.

"I loved your mom," he says simply. "She was my friend,
that's all—I'd never do anything to hurt your dad—but
there's no point in bullshitting you. I had a thing for her from
way back, and we were close. She got a bum deal. She made
some mistakes, sure, but who didn't? She's paid enough. And
so have you. So, did you find her?" His eyes are shiny and
hopeful, and I can see he still loves her.

And that he doesn't know where she is.

With that, the feeling of relief goes away. "No," I say. "I
got close, but she was gone already. I found some of her stuff,
though." I go into my backpack and pull out the picture I

brought with me, the one of Manny and my mother together. "She saved this."

He picks up the photo and stares at it for a long time. "She was a beautiful girl," he says. "Too bad I wasn't her type. Didn't think your dad was either, but hey, young love, am I right?" He closes his eyes for a minute, then opens them again, still fixated on the picture.

"You can keep that," I tell him. It obviously means a lot that she kept it with her for so long. I get out the notebook and open it to the page with the time line on it. "Can you help me understand this? Who these people are?" I tell him about my library research, going through the history of the drug problems in Brooksby. "I've got a bunch of names of people from Tom's team, but you would know way more about that than I would."

Manny reads carefully, and it's not long before he smiles. "Bolo," he says. "That's me. Your mom started calling me that after she came by the house one day and my grandma gave her all kinds of pastry. *Bolo* is Portuguese for cake. Natalie always said I was a sweetie."

Hearing him explain the nickname makes me see him completely differently. He always seemed like a big meathead to me, all gruff with the arm punching and the mean teasing. But maybe he hadn't always been that way, or maybe my mother saw past the rough parts into his actual heart.

But more than that—he's handed me the puzzle piece I've been looking for. He's the person who told my mother that Dad wasn't the one dealing drugs. That means he knows who was.

He's still reading the time line, though, and I don't want to interrupt him. I watch as the smile leaves his face, and I wait to speak until he gives the notebook back to me. "Does it make sense to you?" I ask.

"It does, but I'm not going to be able to help much," he says. "This goes way deeper than you think. It's not just your ma who could get hurt here."

There's no way I'm letting anything go, not after everything I've been through to get here, but I don't need to tell him that. "Please, tell me what you can. I've got a lot of it figured out already—I think my mother thought Dad was selling drugs out of the evidence room, and that's why she took me. From what it says here, though, you're the one who told her she was wrong."

He nods. "I wish she'd come to me before she split. I could have saved her the trouble."

I don't want to have to prod him, but he doesn't look like he's going to say anything else.

"How did you know?" I ask.

"That's the part you need to let go," he says.

"It's true, though, right? There were cops selling drugs.

Just not Dad." He looks puzzled for a second—something I've said confused him. But he doesn't say what.

"I'm telling you, kid, I can't give you any more about that side of things. All I can say is it's worse than you think, and there's nothing any of us can do about it."

That can't be true. It just can't. I open the notebook again. "Please, you have to tell me who the two cops are. I know she got set up—I know they planted those drugs on her. One of them has to be the person who sold heroin to her friend." I tell him about the phone she keeps, the person who tracks her. "Maybe they're the same person."

"Let's say I knew who it was. Even if I told you, what do you think would happen? You're going to go to the cops?"

"So you do know who it is," I say.

He shakes his head. "I'm not saying I do or don't. But don't you think I've tried to find a way out of this for her? You saw those notes—I tried to help her see you when she first got out of prison, and that turned out to be a real bad plan. If anyone ever found out I was the one who told her it wasn't your pops, or that I helped her out later on, I'd be in even worse trouble than she is. This goes way deeper than some crooked cops selling Gs out the back of a squad car, and you and me aren't going to be the ones to stop it. I know you want to find her, but she's got good reasons for staying away this long. If she wants to stay gone, you should respect that."

Does she want to stay gone, though? Isn't the letter an indication that she doesn't? But Manny's not going to change his mind. "All right," I say. "Thanks for talking to me."

"Anytime, kid," he says. "Anytime."

24

I leave Manny's apartment feeling a mixture of satisfaction and disappointment. It's becoming clear that no one person is going to be able to tell me everything that happened, but this patchwork approach of getting different pieces from different people is starting to yield some results. Manny helped me fill in some gaps, and it's surprising to find that the random conversation he had with Dad about Dad's high-school girlfriend wasn't so random after all. Manny has turned out to be a hero in my mom's story, not a villain, and I'm glad.

But this means that I was wrong about him. I spent years thinking he was a muscle-bound lug with a mean streak, and he's actually this big marshmallow. I'm starting to feel like I'm always going to be wrong. About everything. I was wrong about staying with Maddie forever, and I was wrong that me and Dad had this perfectly open and honest relationship, and I was wrong about not having a mother, or a family. Wrong about that not mattering. Wrong about the world outside Brooksby being something I didn't care about. Wrong that I'm not a curious person, because now I'm consumed by curiosity. I'm curiosity on legs.

Dad's been wrong about a lot too. He was wrong about why my mother left, and that her family helped, which means he was also wrong to keep us apart. He was wrong about her being dead, and I can't even imagine how he's dealing with that. I'm not sure he's ready to admit or accept any of it, though; that might be what's keeping me from going to him with all the things I've learned. I guess being a full-fledged grown-up doesn't stop you from being wrong sometimes, or even a lot; he's not the only one who screwed up here. My mother was wrong about my father, wrong to take me away; my aunt and grandparents were wrong to think my mother was back on drugs. It's a strange combination of comforting and disturbing—getting older doesn't keep you from fucking up, but maybe that means fucking up now isn't the catastrophe it feels like, sometimes.

The one person who hasn't been wrong about anything, at least not with respect to me, is Maddie. She was right that she was going to leave and that it was unrealistic for us to think nothing would change. She was right that there was something off about Dad lying to me about my mother. She was right that the world outside Brooksby was one I should have wanted to see. She was right that somewhere, deep inside, I really do want to know things. I really do want answers.

And what did I do, in my infinite wrongness? I hurt her. She tried to ease us into the new world we would enter in the fall, to find a way to keep our friendship even if we didn't stay together, and I had all but told her that if we weren't a couple, I didn't want to be friends. I made it sound like they couldn't be separated, but Maddie had been everything to me for so long—girlfriend, best friend, family—that I thought that was true. Another thing I was wrong about. Now that I have more family than just my dad, I can see how it might not be such a good idea for one person—or even two people—to be everything. And now that I don't have Maddie as my girlfriend, my friend, or my family, I've lost her in more than one way. I don't deserve to have any of those things back, but Maddie didn't deserve for our relationship to end the way it did.

I have to do something to apologize. Calling or showing up at her house isn't a good idea; based on her facial expression at the gym, she isn't going to want to talk to me in person for a long time, if ever. But we've had so few fights I don't know how to try and make up. I could buy her flowers, but that seems like something a boyfriend would do, and I want her to understand that I get it, that I would love to have her back in my life, as my friend more than anything else.

The mall is open for another hour or so after I leave Manny's, so I stop there on my way home and wander around, trying to think of a gesture that means something. It has to be more about her than me, but maybe I can still be in there? I end up at the sporting goods store and walk up and down the aisles for a while before I see the perfect thing: a pull-up bar she can put over her dorm room door. There's even a packet of bands I can buy to go with it, in case she needs more time to get her unassisted pull-up.

I run up to the register and buy it all before it occurs to me that this gift isn't enough. Not in terms of money—it costs almost all the money I have in my wallet, which is most of what I have right now—but in terms of the message. It says I'm thinking about her going away and I'm okay, but that's still too much about me. I want to show her that I've been listening, that I understand everything she's been trying to tell me.

So the next morning, before I go to the gym, I stop at Market Basket. I buy the fanciest, most beautiful cupcake I've ever seen—the frosting is silver and pink and looks like a rose—along with a bunch of bananas. I hope she'll see I'm trying to loosen up, that I don't want to deprive her of anything, whether it's a piece of cake at a party or her whole college experience. I put all the gifts in a bag, write her name on it, and leave the bag behind the main desk, instructing the receptionist to give it to her when the noon workout is over, after I've left for lunch.

I haven't figured out what my next step is in the quest to answer all my questions about my mother, but at least I've taken a step to deal with how I screwed up with Maddie. And that, for the moment, makes me feel a little bit better.

I don't expect her to respond to the gifts right away, but I have to admit I'm a little disappointed when she doesn't. All that week I keep the same schedule: I go to my morning class, work until lunch, take a break to avoid Maddie, work the rest of the day, and then go to the library to do more research for an hour or two, carrying some of the contents of the duffel bag around with me in my backpack. I stare at the photos my mother left, and the notebook, as if looking at them over and over again will suddenly give me a new idea. I obsessively Google the list of cops working drug cases to see if I can find anything I missed; I review the news articles to look for names I might have skipped.

I haven't found anything specifically helpful, but I notice that while Brooksby's drug problem is going away, the issues in other towns are getting worse. I guess the cops in those communities didn't take well to the *Boston Globe* reporter's suggestion that they all start working together. Or maybe Tom doesn't want to share the magic, though that doesn't seem like him. He's always been a good guy, a generous guy. There's a reason he and Dad have been friends for so many years, after all.

I only go home from the library after I know Dad's left for work. We've reached some sort of impasse. We're not avoiding each other, exactly; he comes to the morning class sometimes, and I make enough dinner for both of us, though including the library in my schedule means we're not home to eat together, which means he eats leftovers from the previous night before going to work. We've become cordial roommates, but when we see each other there's an undercurrent of tension. He might still be angry with me for leaving without telling him where I was going; I don't really care. I'm still angry with him for lying.

It's hard not to feel like our relationship has changed in some fundamental way. We've gone from him being both my father and my friend to this weird chilly situation, and I wonder how long it will last. I know there are lots of people who don't get along with their parents, and somehow they manage to forge these fragile relationships with them, as long as they don't run into any of the trip wires that start fights. Is this what that feels like? Will we be like this forever?

I hope not. But I also know the person getting in the way of fixing our problems is me. I don't want to go back to how we were, when I took everything he said at face value and didn't investigate for myself. I'm starting to consider whether living with him in Brooksby for the indefinite future is really the best idea. It's not that I all of a sudden want to leave, like Maddie; it's more that I'm open to the possibility that my world could be a little bigger than I imagined before. To the extent I imagined it at all.

Sunday is Rest Day at the gym, which means there's no set workout, just open gym—a couple of trainers hang around to help people work on areas they need to improve. It's also my day off, the first time I've had a whole day to myself since graduation, and it's not until the expanse of free time stretches out in front of me that I realize I don't know what to do with myself. I've exhausted my research, I'm still avoiding Dad, and it's still radio silence from Maddie. I text some of the guys to see if they want to go to the beach or hang out, but everyone's busy, whether with summer jobs or family stuff. I'm alone, with no plan and nothing to look forward to. I try watching TV but I'm too restless, so I decide to go to the box and use the open gym time to work on some PRs.

As soon as I pull into the parking lot I see Maddie's car, and I look at the clock to see that it's noon. I thought my deal with her was for actual classes, but we didn't actually sit down and negotiate. Should I go in, or should I respect the arrangement and go back to the empty apartment, to a depressing afternoon of convincing myself watching cold-case shows without Dad is still fun?

I'm going in, I decide. The gym is my happy place, and I'm not giving up the possibility of salvaging the day. We can avoid each other just fine. I steel myself and head inside.

Maddie's over by the pull-up bar, her foot in an orange band, straining to lift her head above the bar. She's done what she set out to do, it seems—she's gotten comfortable with the red band and moved on. I feel this surge of pride, as if her accomplishment is also mine, but the surge fades as I think about what it means for her to have moved to the next phase. By July she'll be doing pull-ups on her own. By the end of August she'll be gone.

She's so focused she can't see me, which is helpful. The weights are in a separate room, so avoiding her isn't hard. My favorite trainer, Jeff, has come in to spot people, so I go tell him what I want to work on and we get set up.

Lifting usually makes me feel better. I get so intense about what I'm doing, my brain has no space to think about anything else, and it's such an adrenaline rush to accomplish something I've never managed before. A lot of people talk about the endorphin high of running, but I've never pulled that off—running is distracting, sure, but it never gives me the same sense of satisfaction lifting does.

Until today, that is. I warm up until I'm ready, then Jeff and I plan a sequence of lifts that will get me to my record. The clean and jerk is a lift I've always found difficult; I can do the clean part no problem, where you squat, lift the bar, and then squat again, with the bar balanced almost on the fingertips of your lifting gloves, elbows bent and up as high as you can get them, racking the bar on your shoulders. But the jerk part—where you throw the bar above your head, jumping into a split stance for balance—that's always really hard for me. The heavier the weight, the more likely I am to tip over as I push the weight overhead, and then I lose my balance and have to drop the bar. Today's no better—I'm fine for the warm-up lifts, but every time the weight gets heavy I only get the bar to about eye-level before I have to let it go. The clanging noise of weights hitting the floor is starting to bug me.

"It's a trust thing," Jeff says. "You're leaning forward because you don't believe you can get the weight where it needs to be, and it's a self-fulfilling prophecy. If you don't make yourself believe it, it won't happen." He tells me to try leaning further back than I think is correct, to trust that I won't overextend and hurt my back. "Your body will be there for you, I promise."

It's one thing for him to say it; it's a whole other thing to believe it myself, and then to convince my body to go with it. After I take a break and give my tired muscles a chance to simmer down, I take another shot, focusing as hard as I can on not just powering the weight up and over my head, but backward, almost behind me.

I'm shocked to find that it works. The weight's pulling me backward a little, but the split stance helps me stay upright, and then it's easy to walk my legs together and keep the bar in the air. Jeff's right, as usual.

But the satisfaction I usually get from achieving a PR is nowhere to be found. It feels good to pull it off, but that elation, that sense of accomplishment, is dulled somehow. Maybe it's because this isn't the goal I really want to achieve.

Or maybe it's that there isn't anyone I can tell about it.

Then I hear the sound of clapping coming from behind me, by the door to the weight room. Jeff's standing where I can see him, so it has to be someone else. I turn around to see Maddie. She's been watching the whole time, apparently.

"Great job, Pack," she says.

Jeff looks at me, then at her, then me again. He knows what's up. Everyone here does. "Right on, Pack. Take a rest and we can work on your dead lift in a while, if you want. I've got some stuff in the office I have to take care of."

Sure he does. Not subtle at all, Jeff. Now Maddie and I are alone, for the first time since that night at the graduation party, when it all went to shit. What am I supposed to do now? "Thanks," I say.

Maddie walks all the way into the room and sits on one of the benches in front of me. "You've been working on that lift a long time," she says. "It must feel good."

"I guess." If anyone would understand why it doesn't feel as good as I expected, it would be Maddie, but it doesn't feel like it's okay to tell her. "I saw you on the orange band," I say, instead. "How long have you been off the red?"

"Not that long. I've been working hard on it. And waitressing is definitely helping with the upper-arm strength. You wouldn't believe how many plates of food you can fit on one tray."

Right, her job. "You enjoying it?"

She shrugs. "It's nice to be on the water." The restaurant where she works is a tourist joint in Salem, a couple of towns over, specializing in lobster and clam chowder. It gets really busy at night in the summer, so she's probably making good money. More than I get here, anyway. I'm about to say that, but then I think it makes me sound like an asshole. Making small talk with Maddie is hard. Nothing sounds right, so I don't say anything. The silence gets a little awkward, but I don't know how to break it.

"Practicing at home is really making a difference too," she says finally.

I'm confused. "Practicing carrying trays?"

She laughs. I forgot how much I love the sound. "No, practicing pull-ups. I set up the bar you gave me in the doorway to my bedroom."

My heart beats a little faster. So I'm more excited about this than the PR? Funny. "Your mom must hate that."

"She is not a fan," Maddie agrees. "It doesn't work with the design aesthetic, as she puts it. But I told her it's just a couple of months, and then I'll take it with me to school."

We're already right up against the hard topic. "That's why I bought it. I didn't know what kind of gyms they had out there."

"There's one not too far from campus, but I'm still deciding whether I want to keep doing CrossFit when I get out there. It might be time for me to try something different."

Does she have to rub it in? I'm glad we're talking, but we've gone from small talk to a coded path back to what we last fought about, and that's not what I want. "You don't have to take it with you," I say. "I just thought since you were practicing—But I know you want change. That's what the cupcake was for. The bananas were for balance."

She smiles, then frowns, then smiles again. "I didn't mean to sound like I don't appreciate it. The whole thing—the bar, the cupcake, the bananas, all of it. It was very thoughtful."

"I was trying to apologize," I say. "I wasn't sure how to explain." It's still hard, really, but now I feel like I didn't do as good a job as I wanted. "I didn't mean to be so awful. At graduation. You tried to clue me in for ages, but I didn't want to hear it. And when I did, I freaked out. I really am sorry for that."

"I know you are," she says, and reaches back to adjust her ponytail, like she always does when she's nervous. I hate that I'm making her feel that way. "And I was really mad at you for that, and it took me a while to calm down so I could understand why you acted that way. I mean, I know you well enough to figure it out, but I needed to wallow in how furious I was at first."

That I understand.

"But I should have thanked you sooner," she continues. "I could tell how much thought you put into it. I wanted to wait until I was ready for us to really talk."

Is that what we're doing now? "I get it. You don't have to thank me. You're not the one who screwed everything up." It's getting awkward standing in front of her, especially when I'm trying to say something real. "Do you mind if I sit? With you? Or somewhere else?"

She stands, and I worry I've messed up again. The connection between us is so fragile, like the shell of a raw egg, and I hope I haven't cracked it. "Actually, I have to go. I'm working tonight and I start at three. But I'm off tomorrow night. Maybe we could hang out and talk?"

"I would love that," I say. "I can come get you, if you want."

She pauses, and I can tell she's trying to decide whether that would make it feel too much like a date. But it's stupid to take two cars, and Maddie's rational. "Okay," she says.

"I get off work at four, so after that? We can get coffee, or early dinner—" I already sound too eager. "Or we could just chill somewhere. Low key." Not a date, I try to signal.

"Low key sounds good," she says.

But my heart does that little bounce again. Not a date, I remind myself. Not a date.

25

I have to find a place to take Maddie that makes it clear it's not a date, even if in my secret heart I kind of wish it were. I don't want to mess up the delicate eggshell of our potential friendship by making the same mistakes I made before. The right place will say what I so awkwardly tried to tell her in the weight room: she's going to leave, and I accept that. I want her to find everything she's looking for, even if what she's looking for doesn't include Brooksby, or me.

I think back on everywhere we've gone together, but our regular spots come with too many memories. Our favorite Thai place, the movies, Good Harbor, even the parks we went late at night, to be alone. Nothing is right.

Then I remember this one time Maddie took me to Winter Island, in Salem, near where she works. It's not that far from Brooksby, just a few minutes away from Salem Willows, where we'd play Skee-Ball. There are lighthouses there, and a little bit of beach, and paths where you can walk around the island. Maddie wanted to spend the day there, but all I did was complain about how the sand was brown and gritty and parking was as expensive as Good Harbor. Maddie wanted to look at the boats, to dream about where they might be headed; I just wanted to leave. At the time, I didn't understand why someone would want to go someplace close to home only to think about people going far away.

On the way to Maddie's house that afternoon I stop at Vincenzo's, in case we're there long enough to get hungry. I'm about to order my usual salad when I remember Manny's sub, how much he enjoyed it while I moved salad greens around with my spork. Maddie and I bonded over sharing food restrictions; maybe it's time to show her what I'm learning about flexibility. I get us both small subs, rather than the foot-long monstrosity Manny downed so quickly. Baby steps.

I text Maddie from outside her house so I don't have to knock on the door and deal with her parents or her sister; I have no idea what she told them about our breakup, but I'm sure I didn't come off looking like a particularly good guy. She comes out right away, wearing loose-fitting jeans and a striped T-shirt, hair down, not much makeup. I wonder whether she's put as much effort into making clear this isn't a date as I have, though she can't know how cute she looks even when she isn't trying.

"Thanks for coming to get me," she says. "Where are we going?"

"It's a surprise." She looks worried, like she thinks I've planned some big statement. "Low-key surprise. Just someplace different."

This seems to be enough. We spend the drive talking about innocuous stuff, mostly work—she's enjoying the job and the tips she's making, and she met some girls who just graduated from Salem High who are also going to UMass, so the job's an even bigger win than she hoped.

I tell her about working at the gym, how fun it is to help teach classes and to learn more about how everything works. I don't tell her that I'm starting to second-guess my plan to stay in Brooksby and keep working there; we're in the keeping-it-casual part of the conversation, and it's not the right time to change gears.

We reach the Winter Island parking lot, and I hand over my ten dollars, park the car, and get my backpack out of the backseat. "This is where we're going?" Maddie asks. "You hate it here. Dirty beach sand and all that, remember?"

"I didn't really give it a chance," I say. "I thought it might be a quiet place to take a walk."

She nods. "I know the paths pretty well. I come here by myself a lot."

I hadn't realized that. I never gave a lot of thought to what Maddie did when she was alone, I realize. If I'm going to be a better friend than I was a boyfriend, that will have to change.

Maddie leads me to a path around the island, lined with bright green grass and tall trees. The air smells clean and salty, and we walk for a while without talking. It doesn't feel awkward like it did at the gym; being with her seems natural, even if I know it isn't the same. We leave the path and Maddie shows me some of her favorite spots: an old ammunition bunker that looks like some sort of low-slung fortress; the different lighthouses, squat and white, one of which we have to climb on rocks to get close to. We walk for long enough that the sun starts to get lower in the sky, and Maddie takes me to a park bench that looks out over the water. "I've always loved watching these boats," she says.

"I remember. You wanted to imagine where they were going, and I couldn't understand why you cared so much. I'm starting to see it now."

She turns to me. "You sound different. I know we've only been apart a few weeks, but I've felt different too. I thought I was making it up. But it's you, too. It's not just me."

I want to tell her everything that's happened since I last saw her, but that's not what a good friend would do now. "How do you feel different?" I ask.

She considers the question. "When I was in middle school, feeling so awful about myself, I didn't think I would ever be with anyone. Then I saw you starting to change, and you were so great about helping me change too, and I fell in love with you and couldn't imagine being alone—it was like I did a complete one-eighty."

I like hearing her talk about falling in love with me, even if it hurts.

"Now that I'm alone again, I'm starting to see it as not such a bad thing. Not that I have any regrets about being with you, because I don't. I think we were really good for each other for a long time. I spent so many years feeling bad about myself, and to have spent most of high school feeling so good—that's a big deal. And I wouldn't have wanted to spend that time with anyone else. But now I'm starting to separate the things *I* want from the things *we* wanted, to find out what I'm like without you, and it's actually been okay starting that process before I leave for this whole new life. Even if that's not what I planned."

Wow—she's given me way more of an answer than I expected. I never thought about our relationship that way before, about how the things we wanted together might not be the same as what we want separately. But I'm glad she told me. I'm glad I asked.

I don't know how to respond, though, so I reach into my backpack and pull out the Vincenzo's bag. "Is Paleo one of the things you're reconsidering? Because if so . . ." I hand her a sub.

Maddie's mouth falls open in surprise. "Pack, you're the last person I'd expect to bring me a sub. Even after that cupcake. Please tell me this is what I think it is."

"Roast beef with sauce," I say. "Does anyone order anything else from Vincenzo's?"

"You and your salads," she points out. "Is that what you got?"

"Nope." I take out a sub. "I'm branching out. Not often, but on special occasions. I'm trying to see if there's a way I can give myself room to enjoy things like this once in a while."

"I'm guessing you didn't come up with that on your own."

"You know me well," I say. "I'll tell you all about it, if you want."

"Definitely." She unwraps her sub and takes an enormous bite, and with her mouth full, says, "You talk, I'll eat."

"Classy, Maddie. Real classy."

She grins and takes another big bite. "Get cracking."

I decide it's best to go in order. I tell her how I hit a dead end looking for my mom but found my aunt instead, how I went to New Haven and met my family. I tell her about Nonna slipping me the address and going to New York to find I missed my mother but getting her bag of stuff instead. How Dad came to find me, how I went to find Manny, how I've now gotten so many different versions of the story it's hard to believe there's one true one in there somewhere, but that I feel like I'm getting close to figuring it out. I talk and talk until Maddie finishes her sandwich and I've run out of words.

Maddie's eyes are open so wide they've practically doubled in size. "Holy shit, Pack, that's a lot."

"I haven't even told you about the pizza," I say. "But we can save that for another day. Right now, all I can think about is how stuck I am. I think I understand everything up to the whole thing about the two cops planting drugs on my mom. Who are they, and why would they do that? I've run out of places to look."

"Have you talked to your dad?" Maddie asks. "He's kind of conspicuously absent from this narrative of yours, now that you're back from New Haven."

"I haven't," I admit. "I'm still pissed at him. We aren't really speaking."

"Oh, Pack," she says. "That must be awful. I know how close you guys are."

She can't imagine how awful it is; I'm not about to tell her it's worse because I don't have her, either. "I should talk to him, I know. He has no idea why any of this happened. He didn't even know she was still alive."

"He must be so confused right now," she says. "But if you tell him, he's going to want to find out who did it more than you do. And if Manny's right about how dangerous it is, maybe that's not such a good idea. Maybe you were right not to say anything. You're the kid here—it's not your job to make him feel better."

I get what she's saying, but we've always been more than

just father and son, even as I'm starting to realize the ways in which that might not be a good thing. "I should tell him something, at some point," I say. "But it would be nice if I could tell him something more. Like where she is. I think he still loves her."

"I don't know if that's incredibly romantic or incredibly depressing. But maybe that's why he never got together with anyone else."

I think about the parade of gym ladies and how he never invited any of them over for dinner. The idea of him meeting the love of his life in high school seemed romantic when I thought Maddie was the only person for me, but now his refusal to move on makes me sad. "I just wish I knew what to do next."

"Do you want help?" she asks. "Not to overstep or anything, but . . ."

"Are you kidding? I want help desperately."

"Do you want to show me the stuff your mom left? A fresh pair of eyes might be useful."

I've got the photos and the notebook with me; I keep them in my backpack all the time now that I'm afraid Dad might go through my stuff. I get everything out and hand it to Maddie in a stack.

"Is there any particular order?" She's opened one of the envelopes of pictures first, the one with photos of my parents.

"Doesn't really matter," I say as she scans through them.

"God, they were so young. Your dad was actually kind of handsome. And your mom—she's beautiful. You look just like her."

"You think?" I kind of think so too, but maybe I just want it to be true.

She's already moved on to the baby photos. Maybe I should have filtered. "So adorable! Look at all that hair, and that squishy face—"

I grab the pictures away. "Okay, enough. Look at the notebook." I flip it open to the time line page and tell her about Manny being Bolo, what it means.

"Yeah, he's always been a big softie," Maddie says.

"That's not how I saw him."

"He's one of the most supportive people at that gym. Early on, if it wasn't for him, I'd have quit."

"I had no idea," I tell her.

"Bolo's a perfect nickname for him. Now you're trying to figure out the 2?"

"Yup." I walk her through all the research, the days and days of looking up the internet histories of every cop who's ever worked drug crimes in Brooksby. "I've got nothing. Complete dead end."

She peers closely at the notebook. "Maybe we're looking at this wrong." I like how she says "we," as if it isn't obvious that if anyone's looking at it wrong, it's me. "Maybe the 2 doesn't stand for the number two, as in two people. Maybe it's more of a nickname, like Bolo." She goes back to the stack of high-school photos. "You said a lot of these guys were buddies back then, played sports. Any of them wear the number two?"

"I think there are some pictures of Dad with the football team," I say, and peer over her shoulder. "Let's take a look." She finds the picture, but no one on the team wears that number. "It could be the baseball team. There aren't any photos of them here, but maybe I can find one somewhere else." Even as I say it, though, I remember Manny looking confused when I talked about two cops. "What if it isn't the number two at all? What's if it's something that sounds like two?"

"You mean like too, as in also? Or to, as in a place you'd go to? That's a pretty strange nickname," Maddie says.

But I know I've figured it out. I don't want to be right, because if I am, that means the one person I never considered is not who I thought he was. "It could be initials," I say.

"T.O.," Maddie says.

"Exactly," I say. "Tom O'Connor."

26

I've stunned Maddie into silence. Hell, I've stunned myself into silence. Tom is the closest thing to an uncle I had until I found my New Haven family. He's my dad's best friend. He's the last person I would ever think might be involved in something that would hurt Dad and me. Yet all that research I've done, all those articles I've read about the drug problems in Brooksby, the near-magical cleanup—they're all about Tom. I kept looking past him, but he's been right here the whole time.

"That can't be right," Maddie says.

"I know. Except I think it has to be." So many of the pieces fit—Tom would have access to drugs from the raids; he knew my mother from way back in high school, so he probably knows how to manipulate her; he's got access to my dad's Facebook page, so he could have sent her pictures of me from there. But why would he do this? What's the connection to the

OD that had my mother convinced my dad was dirty? Is Tom the crooked one? Has he been all along? Maybe Brooksby's magical solution to the drug problem isn't so magical after all.

Maddie goes back to the pile of pictures from high school, carefully examining each one. "You know, there's not a single picture of your mother and Tom together," she says. "There aren't any pictures of him at all, except for the football team. Maybe they have a history. Like, not a good one."

"I guess if he's the one doing this to her, she wouldn't want to see his face if she could avoid it. It's not proof, but it's something. It might help me explain all this to Dad—I have to talk to him now. I can't wait anymore." I don't know if there's anything he can do, but he needs to know. I may have solved the biggest piece of the mystery, but I still don't know what it means. Maybe he will.

"You know, it's pretty amazing what you've been able to put together, without a whole lot to go on," she says. "I'm sure it doesn't feel like enough, but I'm really impressed."

"You'd have figured all this out soon," I say, but I'm proud.

"It's a talent, really," she says. "And it seems like maybe you've enjoyed it? I mean, not the circumstances, but the investigation itself."

"I have," I admit. "I never would have thought so."

"Really?" She arches an eyebrow at me. "All those years of solving TV crimes didn't clue you in that a real-life mystery might be something you'd want to solve?"

I shrug.

Maddie balls up the waxed paper from her sub and puts it back in the Vincenzo's bag. The sun is just hitting the horizon, which is prime time for gnats—they swarm all around, alternately visible and invisible depending on what your eyes are focused on. "It's getting kind of gross out here," I say. "We should probably go."

"This was nice," Maddie says. "Hanging out with you here, as friends."

"It was," I say. "I know you talked about how being alone is a good thing, and I don't want to mess with that. But do you think we could spend some time together this summer, as friends? Not all the time—you'll still have lots of time to be alone."

"I'd like that," she says.

I take her home and then go back to my house, unsure of whether I want Dad to be there or not. We need to talk, but I could use some time to decide exactly what I'm supposed to tell him. That his best friend is responsible for ruining his life? I wanted to go to him with good news, that I'd found my mother, that I'd come up with some plan for everyone to forgive everyone else so I could have a real family. Instead, I'm going to go trash one of the only relationships he can count on.

I'm relieved to find he's left for work already, which means he'll either be sleeping or just waking up when I get off work tomorrow. That gives me some time to get my head together, and I need it.

The next morning, I leave him a note before I go to work, telling him I want us to have dinner tonight and talk. The gym's pretty quiet, so in between helping with workouts and making smoothies, I have time to sort through everything I've learned, all the questions I still have. There are the obvious questions, like what Tom's done, and how, and why. But those are logistical questions, and now that I have the outline of the facts, I'm finding I don't care about getting those answers as much as I thought. I want to know about motivations: Why did my mother think leaving was the right answer, and then change her mind and leave us both? Why would Tom, Dad's best friend, behave in a way designed to hurt him so badly?

Then there are the questions I have to ask myself. Is finding my mother so important, or do I just want to put the final pieces of the mystery together? Am I hoping for some sort of fantasy reconciliation between her and Dad? And if I am, is it really because I want Dad to be happy? It's not hard to see that a happy ending for him gives me hope of a happy ending for me, but after one day of talking to Maddie, I'm not sure that would be a happy ending for her.

The workday ends before I've answered a single question, before I've decided how to tell Dad the whole story. It doesn't worry me too much, though; it seems like maybe just knowing these questions are out there is the point. That, and realizing Dad is the person I most want to help me answer them.

I go home and get dinner started while Dad's still asleep, going with something simple: a roasted chicken with some root veggies, onions, and garlic cloves. All I have to do is chop everything up, season the chicken, and throw it in the oven. He left a note saying he's looking forward to dinner and has the night off, so we can talk as long as we need to. I hope he's ready to stay up late.

I expect him to stagger out of his room all bleary, but he's taken the time to get himself together, almost like he wants to make a good impression on me. I didn't think about what a toll us not getting along might be taking on him. "Hey, kiddo, smells great in here," he says. "Need me to do anything?"

Yeah, he's definitely trying. "No, it's all ready. I've got the table set up."

Dad raises his eyebrows. "No couch tonight?"

"We're going to be grown-ups," I say. "I know I haven't been acting like one, but I'm going to try."

He nods. "Okay. I'll get us some water."

I get the plates together and bring the food out to the table, and we sit and eat quietly for a while, save for Dad telling me how good everything is. He's not lying, either—it's probably the best meal I've ever made, or maybe it's just nice for us to be sitting together, not fighting, like adults.

When we're done, I try to think of where to start, but Dad

beats me to it. "Look, bud, I know you've got things you want to say, but let me go first, okay?"

Easier than figuring it out myself. "Sure."

"I'm sorry I busted in on you in New Haven. I was worried, but I didn't handle it so good. You have every right to want to know your family. When I realized you were with them it just brought me back to when all the bad stuff happened with your mom, but that's on me, not you. I won't keep you from seeing them, if that's what you want."

Guess he took the time we weren't talking to do some thinking of his own. "Thanks, Dad. That means a lot."

"So what's on your mind? I've missed talking to you. Seemed like you needed some space."

"I did," I say. Now for the hard part. "That letter from my mother raised a lot of questions for me. Not just the obvious stuff, like where she's been all this time, but bigger things, too. Like what it means to have a family, what it means to be able to trust people. I've been looking for answers, and I haven't found all of them yet, but I think I'm starting to find some, and they're not all good."

"Son—"

"I'm not talking about you." I can't let him interrupt, not now that I've begun. "I was really mad that you lied to me, and not just once. It took me a while to get past that, but I know you were trying to help. I wish you'd trusted me earlier, but there's nothing we can do about that now. Besides, I know I have to trust you in return, so that's what I'm going to do now." I take a breath, and continue. "I've talked to a lot of people and did a lot of research, and I've got a lot of the story worked out, but I need your help with the rest. I learned some hard stuff, though. Do you want the good stuff first, or the bad?"

Dad's mouth has fallen open a little. I've totally thrown him. "You pick, kid. It's your story to tell now."

"Good, then." Why make this harder than it has to be? "My mother didn't leave for the reasons you think. I'll tell you all about that in a little bit, but you should know that she's been carrying around pictures of you with her all these years. She has pictures of me, too, but these are the ones that really matter." I've got everything set up on the chair next to me, where he can't see it, and I pick up a stack of photos of the two of them together and happy and hand them over.

Dad goes through them slowly. He starts blinking fast.

"She took me because she thought you were doing something wrong, but she found out it wasn't true," I say. "I don't know why she never told you that, or why she left us both, but I think she still loves you."

He doesn't say a word. Maybe I should have told him the bad news first.

"Do you want to know the rest?"

He slumps in his chair, nods.

"I think she took me because she thought you were

stealing drugs from the evidence room and selling them," I tell him. "After she got busted, Manny told her she was wrong. He wouldn't tell me how he knew, or anything else, but I'm trying to figure it out. From what I can tell, she was right about someone selling drugs the Brooksby police confiscated from raids, and whoever that was planted drugs in her suitcase when she took me. She wasn't using, and she wasn't going to sell them. She was set up. I don't know why. But I'm pretty sure I know who." I'm not trying to be dramatic, but it takes me a second to get the words out. "I think it's Tom, Dad."

Dad looks like I've punched him in the gut. He starts shaking his head fast, then slow, like it's sinking in. Then he gets up and brings our dirty plates into the kitchen. He's gone for longer than it takes to put them in the sink, but I don't hear the water running, so it's not like he's washing them. I'm tempted to go in and see how he's doing, but maybe he needs a minute to himself.

When he comes back, his eyes are red, but he seems calm. He sits down, takes a long gulp of water, and looks directly at me. "The sentence for kidnapping is only a few years," he says. "The sentence for intent to distribute the amount of drugs your mother had on her is much, much longer. If she'd been convicted, she'd still be in jail. There would have been no keeping the story out of the papers. You'd have been the kid with a mother in prison for dealing heroin. She would never have let that happen."

I must look as confused as I feel.

"You said you didn't know why someone would set her up," he says. "Someone who knew her would know that she'd make a deal before she'd do anything to hurt you like that. Someone who knew her would know they could hold the threat of hurting you over her forever."

I get it now. I'm right about Tom. "I think he's still threatening her," I say. "I found her friend, where she'd been staying. Someone called her on a phone she's supposed to always keep, and she left. Her friend thought it was because of the letter. Maybe it was enough that he knew I was asking questions. Did he know, Dad? Did you tell him?"

Dad squeezes his eyes shut, then opens them. "I asked him for advice. I asked him how to talk to you about her. He's who I ask about these things. I didn't know—I had no idea—"

"Of course you didn't," I say, and I reach out to touch his arm. We don't usually do that, but it was so comforting to me when Aunt Reggie hugged me. If I can give Dad even a little of that comfort, I have to try. "But do you have any idea why Tom would do something like this to you? To us?"

"I wouldn't have thought so," he says. "But there's a lot that's gone on at the station over the years that I've had questions about, and you may have just given me some answers. You need to leave that part to me, though. Your job is to decide what's next for you. If you want to find your mother, I'll help you, but I can't make that decision for you. Not if we're going to be adults together."

"I sort of want to find her, but honestly, I don't know if that's more for me or for you. I have this vision of you guys getting back together and we're all a family. Or something." It sounds stupid even as I say it out loud.

Dad sighs. "Bud, I get it, but it's not going to happen. I know we're talking like adults here, but on this one you've got to let me be a father and say this: you don't know what it means for someone to break you. I know things are tough with Maddie, and it hurts to know she's leaving and not coming back, but trust me, it's not the same."

It's not hard to see the disconnect between a high-school breakup and what my mother did. "So you can never forgive her?"

"That's not the issue," he says. "Some things are beyond forgiveness." Funny, that's what Aunt Reggie told Mia. "Sure, might help for us to sit down and hash things out, someday. But if you want to meet her, it has to be for you. Not for me."

"I guess I have some thinking to do, then."

"You can handle it," Dad says. "I've got your back."

27

Dad tells me it's going to take time for him to unravel the Tom situation and that I should enjoy the summer, but even though I told him I'd let him handle it, I'm having a lot of trouble keeping my promise. He's playing private detective at his own job, and though he grumbles about it, I can tell he's having fun. He's been stuck behind that desk way too long.

The first thing he does is to try and get Manny to tell him what he knows, but Manny's just as close-mouthed with Dad as he was with me, so that gets him nowhere. That means there's no one at work he can talk to until he's sure. "Let me help," I beg him. "I've gotten really good at research, I swear."

Dad looks skeptical, and he's right to—he of all people knows how much I used to complain about writing term papers. But I keep pestering and pestering him until he gives me something to do. "I need crime statistics for all the towns around Brooksby," he says. "Drug crimes, especially. Whatever you can find."

"Sure thing." I've already got some information from when I'd looked at old papers before, and it turns out I'm pretty good at finding what he's asked for and putting it all together so he can make comparisons. Based on what I'm seeing, I have a feeling I know what Dad thinks is happening, but it's not until he starts meeting with cops in nearby towns and interviewing them about the drug trade over the past fifteen-plus years that it all comes together. Between the two of us, we come up with an explanation of what's been going on that pretty much covers everything.

Basically, Tom's success in ridding Brooksby of drugs is bullshit.

I help Dad get it all down on paper, with charts and graphs and transcripts from interviews, and Dad goes to the police chief to explain how Tom got drugs out of Brooksby by moving them to nearby towns, working with local dealers and taking a cut of their sales. Half the department is in on it. Thankfully, the police chief is in the other half, and he's quickly convinced Dad's right. The story blows up quick, and the Drug Enforcement Agency steps in to take over the investigation. Dad gets to be the one to arrest Tom, though, so that's pretty satisfying.

"Did you question him about my mother?" I ask. "Did he tell you where she is?"

Dad shakes his head. "Wouldn't say a word. Wouldn't have expected him to, though."

That means I'm no closer to finding her than I was before.

In the meantime, there's still a lot of summer left, and I have lots of things to figure out. Like what's going on with me and Maddie. We've been hanging out as friends pretty regularly since that Winter Island trip, and it's been really confusing for me. My rational self knows it's best for us to stay platonic, to accept that we're over even if I want to hold out hope there's still a chance for us someday. My irrational self isn't having it, though, and my physical self isn't too into it either. The more time we spend together, the more I want to touch her. Not even so much the sex part; it's more the casual closeness we had, where we'd sit on the same side of the table at a restaurant, our legs touching. Now it's like there's this one-inch barrier between us, and I want to cross it and see what happens.

Doing it comes with a lot of risk, though, and it all comes down to whether I'm willing to sacrifice the friendship we're building on the off chance I can get the relationship back. When I think about it that way, the decision isn't hard. While more things have changed for me than I can count, there's no reason for me to think anything has affected Maddie's desire to go to college free to be whoever it is she decides she wants to be once she gets there. So the barrier stays up.

For now.

There's also the matter of how I'm going to get my new family to act like a family. Matt and I text regularly, and from what he tells me, things have gotten kind of ugly in New Haven— he's gotten over being mad at Aunt Reggie for keeping me a secret, but after Dad's surprise visit, he ended up telling his parents about our trip to Brooklyn. I can't blame him, really; I'd never have been able to keep that secret if it were me. Now Aunt Reggie knows Nonna had information about my mother, so the two of them aren't speaking. It makes me feel awful, like I've broken the family apart.

I end up calling Nonna. I'd told her I would fill her in on what I found in Brooklyn and I never did, and I've been feeling bad about it ever since. I tell her about showing up and having just missed my mother, and how helpful the visit was despite her absence, between talking to Jen and getting the duffel bag. "How did you know to send me there?" I ask her.

"I wrote her letters every week while she was in prison," Nonna says. "I asked her to let me visit, but she didn't respond until she was out on parole. She didn't want to meet, but she gave me an address where I could keep writing. I've kept writing all these years, though she rarely writes back. She hasn't yet forgiven me for believing the worst of her. But if she still wants my letters, there's hope. That's the most important thing."

"What about Aunt Reggie?"

Nonna tells me Aunt Reggie needs time. "She hasn't imagined herself in my place yet. When she does, she'll come around."

"I can't wait that long," I tell her. "If I promise to get her there on a Sunday, will you make dinner?"

"I make dinner every week," she says. "I want to be ready whenever she changes her mind."

We agree on the Fourth of July—it's not like Tom's going to be having a barbecue this year—and I convince Dad to drive up to New Haven with me. Matt promises he'll strong-arm Aunt Reggie, and by some miracle, he's able to pull it off.

All my family, together in one room.

It's super awkward at first, no shock there. I'd had to explain to Dad a million times that no one had helped my mother, that they weren't upset with him about the restraining order anymore (which was only sort of true, but whatever), that they really did want him to come. By the time we get there I think he believes it all; he definitely hides it well if he doesn't, and everyone manages to be polite. Even Nonna and Aunt Reggie. They don't have a big heart-to-heart while we're there or anything, but they're civil, and Poppa looks thrilled to see them together.

The Fourth of July is a holiday, and I have this amazing

family now, so I decide to celebrate properly. "Mia, can you pass the meatballs?"

"Only if you take pasta too," Matt says.

"No pressure," Aunt Reggie says.

I roll my eyes. "I was planning on it."

Dad winks at Mia. "You've all had quite an influence on Pack," he says. "I've been trying to get him to ease up on the whole Neanderthal thing for years."

I want to remind him that he knows it's Paleo, but he's just teasing. And he's right that easing up is appropriate now. If I've learned anything by working with the nutritionist this summer, it's that my relationship with food has been kind of messed up for a long time. I've been using food as a means of control, but I've also been using it as a way of avoiding making my own decisions, letting other people tell me what it was okay to eat so I could just go along. I didn't believe I had the power to make good choices myself, or even to make the occasional bad choice and not have it be a catastrophe. That's what Matt was trying to tell me that day on the train, I think, and I'm only just starting to get it. "Whatever," I say. "Nonna, did you make any *dolci*?"

One cookie won't kill me.

I'm not sharing my cookie revelation with the people at work. If there's one thing I've figured out this summer, it's that I like working out at my gym a whole lot more than I enjoy actually working there. I don't love training people all that much—I lack Jeff's knack for finding the best way to talk people through the difficulties they're having, not to mention his patience, and I had no idea how much science there is in understanding how different muscle groups work and what that means in terms of planning effective workouts. Not to mention nutrition science. I thought I could learn to become a trainer or a nutritionist on the job, but there's no way to do it without more education, and I'm not sure that's the kind of education I want.

To be honest, I'm starting to think about going in a whole other direction. It's ironic that the only person who ever suggested I go to the police academy was Tom, but I'm starting to think maybe he was right. Investigating a real crime turned out to be way more fun than just watching someone else doing it on TV, or even playing along. Dad will be shocked, but I might surprise him by enrolling. Classes start in the fall, right around the time Maddie leaves for college. I have just enough time to redesign my workouts to get ready for the physical entrance exam, and I start doing them instead of the regular classes at the gym. I'll have to do a bunch of obstacle courses, so I need to work on speed and stamina, which means more running. Yuck. There's a trigger-pull test to show I can fire a gun quickly with either hand, so I add in some special hand exercises and start going to the firing range to learn how to shoot. Then there are sled push and pull exercises, to get me ready for these other drills meant to mimic saving people. Working out with a purpose in mind is way more fun than trying to beat my time or max weight in a regular WOD.

I'm even contemplating signing up for a program that would take me away from Brooksby. There are lots of police academies in Massachusetts; I don't have to choose the one closest to home, in Reading. I could go to Boston, or Worcester, or somewhere out on the Cape. Or Springfield, way out in the western part of the state. Two hours away from home, an hour away from New Haven. And only about forty-five minutes away from UMass. Just in case.

There's still one last thing.

One day, near the end of August, Dad takes a rare Sunday off and tells me to get in the car. We drive for over an hour until we get to the federal prison where Tom's being held pending trial—his wife refused to post bail for him when she learned what he'd done, and most of their money's been seized by the government anyway.

"I don't understand," I say. "What are we doing here?"

"I thought you might want to talk to Tom. See if he can give you some answers." He leads me through security until we reach a room that looks like a smaller version of a high school cafeteria, with tables where a few prisoners are meeting with their families. Tom is sitting at one of them, alone. He looks thinner than I remember; apparently he's not one of those guys who spends all his time in prison working out. His hands are clenched into fists, and I wonder whether he's angry. He hasn't seen us yet, and I'm tempted to turn around and leave before he does.

"How do you know he'll talk to me?" I ask.

"I've been here a couple of times already," Dad replies. "He won't tell me much, but it's been a long summer for him, and his kids won't come visit. He asked for you."

We walk over to the table and sit down across from him. I have no idea what to say, but he talks before I have a chance to come up with something.

"Heard you helped out with all this, kiddo." Tom motions at the room. "Nice work."

How am I supposed to respond to that? Dad looks like he's about to jump in, but I knee him under the table.

"Ah, I'm just kidding," Tom says. "Joe, can you leave us alone for a minute?"

"Not on your life," Dad says, but I kick him this time.

"Come on, Dad." It's the first words I've managed to get out of my mouth.

He gives Tom a death glare, but then he turns to me. "I'll be just a few feet away." He walks over to an unoccupied table and sits down, watching us.

"He's a good guy, your dad," Tom says.

"Then why would you do this to him?" I ask.

"It wasn't about him. It wasn't about any of you. And I'm

not about to get into it here. I'm working on a deal, and it will all come out then. But Joe's done a good job making me feel like shit for keeping you away from your mom. So maybe there's something I can do for you."

I stare at him for a long time. "Why would you?" I ask again.

"He really was my friend, you know. That's why I kept him away from everything. I had my guy shoot him in the leg just to get him out."

Holy shit. "Does Dad know that?"

"He does now." Tom makes a face that on someone else might have been a smile. "Things would have gotten ugly if he'd figured everything out, and if your mom had come back, he would have. He was a good cop, you know. Better than he ever gave himself credit for."

I know that now, that's for sure.

"He says the only way I can fix this is to set your mom free. To let her know it's over. Like she hasn't already figured it out from the papers."

She hasn't, I'm sure. Otherwise she would have gotten in touch with me. I think. I hope.

"Anyway," he continues, "it's not like it matters anymore. So here." He unclenches one of his fists and I see a scrunched-up slip of paper. It's part of a piece of notebook paper, with ten digits written on it. As soon as I see them, I know what they are.

"I made her carry a burner," Tom says. "So she'd know I could get hold of her at any time. If she doesn't know about me getting busted, then she still has it. You might want to call her soon, though—if she hears I'm out of the picture, she might get rid of it."

My stomach drops. The thought of losing the one link I have to my mother when I've only just gotten it makes me feel a little sick. I snatch the paper out of his hand, stand up, and start to walk away.

"Aren't you going to say thanks?" Tom calls out after me.

After all you've done? I want to say, but I don't bother. I just keep walking, trusting that Dad is right behind me.

We don't talk on the drive home, either. It's not until we get in the house that I manage to ask Dad what I should do. "Are we even sure it's the right number? Will she answer?"

"Won't know unless you try, kid," he says.

You'd think after months of agonizing over a decision like this I'd have come up with an answer by now. "Maybe you should call her first."

Dad shakes his head. "It's you she reached out to, not me. You don't have to use this, you know. But look, I'm wiped. Going to take a quick nap now. Wake me up for dinner, okay?"

I nod, still staring at the slip of paper. Am I ready? Am I really going to do this?

I am.

I get out my phone and punch in the number, then wait

for it to ring. It rings several times before I hear the click of someone picking up, and then a voice I don't recognize. A woman's voice. "Hello?"

I'm so surprised she picked up I forget the words I've rehearsed in my head.

"Hello? Are you there?"

"Hi, Mom, it's Patrick. Your son." I pause. I wish I'd written a script; there are a million things I want to say. But in the end, I keep it simple. "I have some questions I want to ask you."

ACKNOWLEDGMENTS

Thanks to Richard Abate and everyone at 3 Arts Entertainment. I can't believe how many years it's been since I first submitted stories back in grad school, but I'm so glad we stayed in touch!

Thanks to Jocelyn Davies (who is as wonderful in person as she has been online and over the phone) and everyone at HarperCollins. Special thanks to Ellen Leach and Bethany Reis—I am embarrassed and grateful to learn about all the writing tics I never realized I had. If we are ever in New England at the same time, the grilled bagels are on me.

Thanks to the Virginia Center for the Creative Arts for providing time and space to write and a fantastic group of people with whom to share that time. Thanks also to the Writers' Police Academy (and to Sisters in Crime for funding assistance) for helping me learn about what it means to be a police officer; all inaccuracies are mine and mine alone.

Thanks to all the organizations that have provided community, both in Chicago and elsewhere, especially SCBWI, the Mystery Writers of America Midwest Chapter, the Chicago salon, and certain unnamed Facebook groups. I'm so grateful to be included in your ranks, even if I'm not always the most vocal (especially online).

Thanks to Katherine Bell and Rebecca Johns Trissler, the two people who have to read everything I write before I'm willing to let anyone else see it. There is no substitute for friends who can look past the flaws of early drafts to help unlock the potential of what lies within.

Thanks to my writing group, especially Brandon Trissler, Jessica Chiarella, and Dan Stolar. Your feedback was invaluable.

Thanks to the people whose life details I borrowed for this book and others (although perhaps I should say "stole" rather than "borrowed"—I felt like a magpie going after shiny objects). In particular, thanks to Cristina Prochilo, whose family has been so dear to me for so long; I thought of all the Prochilos often as I wrote, and I hope I didn't do a disservice to anything I've learned from the family over the years.

Thanks to all the friends who've provided love and support, but especially Nami Mun, Gus Rose, Vu Tran, Elisa Lee, and Justin Kramon.

Finally, thanks, as always, to my family. During the time I was working on this book some very sad things happened (we miss you terribly, Jeff and Lou), along with some wonderful things (I'm talking to you, Ryan), and I was reminded (as if I needed reminding) how important you all are to me.